NICE GIRLS DON'T DATE DEAD MEN

"Fast-paced, mysterious, passionate, and hilarious. . . . Sure to please fans and keep them laughing as they navigate their way through one awesome story."

—*Romantic Times* (4½ stars)

"With its quirky characters and the funny situations they get into, whether they be normal or paranormal, *Nice Girls Don't Date Dead Men* is an amazing novel, deserving of *Romance Reviews Today*'s coveted Perfect 10."

—Romance Reviews Today

"Molly Harper is a premier writer of paranormal romance with an abundance of sharp-edged humor. . . . Magically believable, imaginative, and brilliantly witty, *Nice Girls Don't Date Dead Men* is an enchanting story of the paranormal."

—Single Titles

"One of the funniest books of the year."

—Bitten By Books

NICE GIRLS DON'T HAVE FANGS

"Hysterical laughs are the hallmark of this enchanting paranormal debut. . . . Harper's take on vampire lore will intrigue and entertain. . . . Jane's snarky first-person narrative is as charming as it is hilarious. . . . Harper keeps the quips coming without overdoing the sarcasm."

—*Publishers Weekly* (starred review)

"Quirky characters, human and vampire alike."

—*Booklist*

"Jane is an everygirl with a wonderful sense of humor and quick sarcasm. Add in the mystery and romance and you have your next must-read novel!"

—*Romantic Times* (4½ stars)

"Charming, sexy, and hilarious. . . . I laughed until I cried."

—Michele Bardsley, bestselling author of *Over My Dead Body*

"Wicked fun that had me laughing out loud . . . Molly Harper has a winner. . . . I read it all in one delicious sitting!"

—Candace Havens, bestselling author of *Dragons Prefer Blondes*

"A brilliantly written adventure chock full of clever prose, hilarity, and hunky vampires!"

—Stephanie Rowe, national bestselling author of *Ice*

"Molly Harper's debut novel is the first in a hopefully long line of books featuring Jane and her entertaining crew. *Nice Girls Don't Have Fangs* is a wonderful treat."

—Romance Reviews Today

"If you are a fan of humorous vampire stories, please pick up *Nice Girls Don't Have Fangs.* Jane is such a great character, and there are so many funny lines and scenes that I dog-eared my copy just to go back and re-read them."

—All About Romance

"The word that just keeps popping into my head is . . . incredible. That about sums it up."

—Books, Books and More Books

The Art
of
Seducing
A Naked
Werewolf

molly harper

POCKET BOOKS
New York London Toronto Sydney

Pocket Books
A Division of Simon & Schuster, Inc.
1230 Avenue of the Americas
New York, NY 10020

This book is a work of fiction. Names, characters, places, and incidents either are products of the author's imagination or are used fictitiously. Any resemblance to actual events or locales or persons, living or dead, is entirely coincidental.

First Pocket Books paperback edition April 2011

POCKET and colophon are registered trademarks of Simon & Schuster, Inc.

For information about special discounts for bulk purchases, please contact Simon & Schuster Special Sales at 1-866-506-1949 or business@simonandschuster.com.

The Simon & Schuster Speakers Bureau can bring authors to your live event. For more information or to book an event, contact the Simon & Schuster Speakers Bureau at 1-866-248-3049 or visit our website at www.simonspeakers.com.

Cover design by John Vairo Jr.
Cover illustration by Robyn Nield

Manufactured in the United States of America

10 9 8 7 6 5 4 3 2 1

ISBN 978-1-4391-9587-1
ISBN 978-1-4391-9589-5 (ebook)

*For Dad, who put up with an awful lot of strangeness
from the author*

Acknowledgments

IN JANUARY 2009, WE had a huge ice storm in Kentucky. I spent a week camping out in my in-laws' living room, in front of their fireplace, with two children under the age of five.

It was a looooong week.

Fortunately, I used being trapped by frigid, icy weather, in the dark, to get in the right frame of mind to write twenty (longhand) pages of a werewolf romance set in Alaska. That eventually became *How to Flirt with a Naked Werewolf*. And one year later, just as I started writing this manuscript, it started snowing heavily.

My first thought: if I have to sleep in someone else's living room again, one of us isn't getting out alive. Although it snowed for two days the power stayed on, giving me time to get back to that cold, claustrophobic place. So thank you to my husband,

David, for keeping me supplied with hot cocoa, mini-marshmallows, and sanity.

I feel the need to thank some of the important gals in my life, including agent extraordinaire Stephany Evans; the ever-patient Jennifer Heddle; and super-publicist Ayelet Gruensphect. Thanks go to my niece Carrington, whose unprecedented hair inspired Baby Eva. And to her mother, Manda, who lovingly accepts my inability to operate voice mail. To my sister-in-law, Cassie, the level-headed Mo to my loud, occasionally vulgar Maggie: It's not easy being the nice one. And to Brandi and Caroline, who might as well be my sisters, for all that they've seen, heard, and dutifully ignored. To Darcy, the best miniature publicist a mom could ask for. And to my mom—yes, I ended up with a little girl just like me. Please, stop laughing.

The Art
of
Seducing
A Naked
Werewolf

1

Dante Hosts a Baby Shower
in the Seventh Circle

THE BEST THING ABOUT being a werewolf was that you never needed a sports bra.

It's hard to explain to humans the absolute free-dom of running on all fours. The feeling of my feet hitting the ground without anything between the pads of my skin and the earth, the undeniable pull of the moving forward, the spring of the leap, the scent of the cold north wind.

It's all of the awesome Nike commercials com-bined, without having to fork over a hundred bucks for shoes. Because you don't need any shoes. Or boob binders.

I dashed through the underbrush, following the fresh scent trail left by a panicked rabbit. I yipped in my excitement, barreling between trees and under low fingers of pine. The foliage grew thinner,

golden-green light filtering through the pine needles as we approached a clearing. Silly rabbit, heading for open ground. My canine brain was rolling
over the potential hilarity of a silly rabbit as a sitting
duck, distracting me from a less familiar scent on the
breeze.

Man.

A strange man was not supposed to be wandering
this close to the Crescent Valley, a fingernail-moon-
shaped dent in the Alaskan interior that was a lush,
game-filled heaven on earth for werewolves. Alone,
there was nothing I could do but hide and hope he
wasn't armed. Without breaking my stride, I turned,
ducking under the branches of a pine tree the width
of a minivan, and waited. I didn't recognize any part
of this human's scent. It was smoky, mossy, but sort of
fresh, like new leaves and my mom's homemade bread.
My mouth started to water a little.

That was weird.

My ears perked up at the sound of footsteps
trudging through the soft, dry grass. I hunched close
to the ground and waited for his boots to appear in
my line of vision. I held my breath, knowing that I
would growl and give myself away. The delicious
greenery-and-home-cooking smell invaded my head
as two feet stepped precariously close to my hiding
spot. Old boots, worn and well cared for, stopped
just outside the tree line, as if the wearer was waiting
for something.

I heard him uncap a canteen, take several swal-
lows of water, and then step away. I crept farther
from the branches, getting a better look at the tall,

broad-shouldered form. From the back, I could see wavy blond hair sticking out from under an old navy blue baseball cap on his head. All he had on him was an old backpack and the canteen. So, not a hunter. Probably just a hiker, wandering too far away from the nature preserve.

Still, the fewer humans who saw wolves near the valley, the better. He stopped again and turned. I ducked back under the brush. Branches obscured my view of his face, but his scent grew stronger, and my brain sort of, well . . . stilled. Everything seemed calm and clear, and the usual organic alarms that shouted "Stranger danger!" quieted.

I huffed, trying to shake away the strange, numbed feeling. I liked my alarms blaring, thank you very much.

The man tramped into the woods, away from my little village. Some magnetic pull drew my paws in the same direction, to follow. I managed to break the spell and sprang out from under the pine needles, running toward home. The pounding of paws on dirt had almost cleared my head when I picked up a more familiar scent.

I skidded to a stop, my paws dragging into the cool, packed dirt and sending clods spraying onto my mother's candy-pink wool dress.

Mom had a full, round, happy face, with twinkling brown eyes and a mouth made for smiling. That didn't mean she couldn't be downright scary with maternal wrath when she wanted to be.

"Margaret Faith Graham, you get on two legs right now," she commanded sternly, tapping her slippered foot against the ground. From my oddly fish-eyed, waist-height perspective, it should have been intimidating. But I'd been getting that same look since I was old enough to turn wolf. My sister-in-law, Mo, stood behind my mother, giving me her best "I tried to stop her" expression.

I sat on my haunches and huffed. Mom cocked her fists on her hips. "Don't you sass me, young lady. Alpha or no, I'll phase and bite a chunk out of your hide."

Rolling my eyes, I concentrated on my human form. Arms, legs, fingers, and toes. I felt a warm, tugging sensation, a thread being pulled through my chest, as my body stretched and pulled. I rolled my neck, enjoying the release of tension as my vertebrae snapped into place. My vision blurred into a golden haze, then focused. Finally, I was standing on bare human feet.

I smirked at Mo, who still wasn't completely comfortable hanging around with the frequently nude. She covered her eyes with one hand while making warning gestures with the other.

"How could you just not bother to show up?" Mom demanded.

I stared at her, my face blank, as I tried to figure out what exactly I'd missed. Honestly, there were a couple of options. Behind Mom, Mo held her hand over her head, making wiggling motions with her fingers. I arched my brow at her. She wiggled her fingers even harder, which really was so much clearer.

"I was . . . attacked by a squid?" I guessed.

Mo's hand dropped to her side, and she glared at

me as Mom turned to her. Mom rolled her eyes at both of us. "How is this," Mo demanded, waving her hand over head, "attacked by a squid?"

I shrugged.

"Shower," Mo said, wiggling her fingers again. "Baby shower."

"Well, don't blame me because you suck at Charades."

"You skipped out on Katie's baby shower," Mo told me. Suddenly, Mom wearing her good church dress in the middle of the woods made a lot more sense.

"Oh, well, I wasn't going to that anyway," I said, shrugging.

Mom spluttered. "You told me you'd meet us at the community center this afternoon!"

"To help you clean up!" I exclaimed. "There was no way I was going to spend my Sunday measuring Katie's belly with toilet paper and eating little mints that taste like toothpaste."

"Well, you're about two hours late to help with cleanup."

I looked up at the sky, gauging the height of the late-afternoon sun. "Oops. I must have lost track of time."

"How could you skip your own cousin's shower?" Mom demanded.

"Because I have eighteen cousins, not counting second cousins, and at any given time, at least one of them is pregnant?"

Mom gave me a sharp look and stalked toward the village. Mo gave me a sympathetic grimace.

"Oh, don't you stand there all pious and pretend you had a good time at the shower," I told her as we followed Mom's trail through the trees.

She made a face and whispered fiercely, "You know I didn't. Hell, I didn't have a good time at *my* baby shower. Baby showers should be reserved as punishment for betrayers in the Seventh Circle of Hell. But I went. Why? Because that's what being part of a family is all about, spending a Sunday afternoon doing stuff you really don't want to do."

"Says the woman who moved three thousand miles to be away from her parents," I said, shrugging into the Carhartt jacket Mo shoved at me. My brother's light autumn coat practically hung to my knees and could wrap around me twice.

"Yeah, because my parents would have the mother-to-be naked in a drum circle, drawing down the moon goddess. By comparison, your werewolf stuff is downright Rockwellian."

I snorted. Mo's parents were unapologetic hippies. Two years before, Mo had moved to Grundy all the way from Mississippi just to get away from them, only relenting and allowing them to visit for Eva's birth. Now that I'd met them, I couldn't blame Mo for picking werewolf pack drama over constant hovering and deep discussions of colonics.

I picked up my pace to catch up with Mom. "Wasn't I sweet as freaking pie to Mo the whole time she was pregnant?" Mom and Mo both raised their eyebrows. I added, "For at least the last trimester. Didn't I show up when Mo had her pup and present my new niece to the pack like Simba in the damned *Lion King*?"

"Please stop calling Eva a pup," Mo muttered. "You know I hate that."

"My point is that I'm plenty supportive of the women in the pack when they have babies. I just don't want to be there for the frilly free-for-all," I said.

Mom, who'd given up on correcting my colorful vocabulary years ago, simply stared at me.

"Mom, please don't make me pull the alpha card on you."

"Being the alpha doesn't mean you get to do whatever you want to do without regard for the feelings of others," Mom intoned in her "important pronouncement" voice, turning away and walking out of the tree line.

"Kind of does," I countered, but softly, under my breath.

"I can't wait until you get pregnant," Mo said. "And you're forced to sit through your own shower. We'll probably have to duct-tape you to your pink-bedecked mother-to-be throne."

The very idea of being pregnant made me stop in my tracks and burst out laughing.

"Oh, haha, laugh as much as you want, Scrappy," Mo told me as I braced myself against my knees for support. "You're planning on marrying a male wolf—"

"I didn't say 'plan,'" I clarified. "I said, when I get around to mating, I'm going to marry another wolf."

"Well, you'll be pregnant before you leave the

altar. You know you have superabsorbent eggs. It's hereditary. Your brother's ninja swimmers scoffed at modern prophylactics."

"Damn it, Mo, I did not need that picture in my head." I scowled at her. She preened a little and loped after my mother.

My brother and his mate were nearly sickening to watch. They were a combination of every nauseating chick flick ever made and the complete catalogue of Barry Manilow's love songs. But in its own twisted way, their Disney-movie love affair helped me reconcile with said brother after years of not speaking and/or knock-down, drag-out fights. (The knocking and the dragging were mostly done by me.) So I was the tiniest bit fond of her, as fond as I could be of a human outsider.

Mo and I were a study of contrasts. I was small and what I prefer to think of compact and sporty—like one of those Porsche coupes. Mo was one of those "shouldn't be hot but somehow through the combination of interesting features is" girls. She was willowy and tall, with a curly black halo of hair that had grown out to her shoulders while she was pregnant with Eva. I had stick-straight, aggressively brown hair that I never cut. She tried to be nice to everybody, where I never really bothered with that kind of crap. I charged into situations; she actually thought them through . . . which usually meant I got the first swing in.

Thanks to Mo, my mom was finally able to do all the froufrou girlie bonding shit she wanted to do when I was growing up. You'd think I'd be jealous, but honestly, I was happy for my mom. She's a smart cookie. She knew that stuff made me miserable and that I would only be suffering through it for her. While Mo actually enjoyed getting her nails done and going shopping for something besides hiking boots.

Mo cleared her throat and pitched her voice into an intentionally cheerful tone. "Speaking of your brother—"

"If the next words out of your mouth have anything to do with sex, I can and will hurt you."

"Fine," she said, frowning. "Then the next words out of my mouth will be 'fire extinguisher.'"

I scowled at her, self-consciously rubbing at the crown of my head, where she'd actually once beaned me with a fire extinguisher to break up a tiny altercation between Cooper and me. Total overreaction on her part.

"Speaking of my brother," I prompted her, while sending her a mildly threatening glare as Mom opened the front door of our snug house on the outskirts of the village.

Mo and I stepped through the door as Mom strode into the kitchen to make tea. That was what she did when she was angry . . . or upset . . . or happy. Really, she was an all-occasion tea drinker.

I pulled on a pair of sweats and a T-shirt, wondering how long I would be apologizing for this latest misstep.

"Cooper wanted to know if you could drop by the Glacier in the morning."

"Why not the house?" I asked, quirking an eyebrow at her.

"Well, there's someone he wants you to meet, or at least see."

I groaned at Mo. "Mo, please tell me he isn't going to try to set me up on some lame blind date."

"Not quite. There's a guy who's been coming around the saloon asking questions about the attacks last year. Cooper thinks he's some sort of investigator. Nicholas Thatcher, PhDs. As in, he has more than one. He's not your typical *Paranormal State* wacko. There's not a dowsing crystal in sight. He seems to be doing actual scientific research. Since you're alpha, Cooper wants you to come by and get a look at him, see what you think."

I quirked my lips at her. "That was low."

She grinned at me. I was the youngest leader in our pack's history and eager to prove my mettle. I'd inherited the job under less than ideal circumstances from our previous alpha, creepy-ass—and by no coincidence thoroughly dead—Eli, who took over the job for my self-exiled brother.

It's a long story.

I took my job as pack leader seriously, and Mo knew the best way to get to me was to appeal to my position. She could be a conniving, sneaky wench, our Mo . . . hence my being the tiniest bit fond of her.

"Why the big discussion? Let's just get rid of him. Run him back to the lower forty-eight. Or we could go with a slightly less pleasant, but bloody and satisfying, second option."

"Cooper and I think you should meet him before you jump to any conclusions."

"Fine, I'll meet him, and then maybe his tires develop problems while he's in the saloon, and he ends up careening into a ditch, never to be heard from again."

"You're a werewolf, not a hit man."

"It'll look like an accident."

My mother shot me a sharp look, snatching the kettle from the stove with a clatter. "How many family conversations are going to be interrupted by me telling you, no, you can't kill someone and make it look like an accident? Now, would you two please sit down and drink this tea before it gets cold?"

"Yes, ma'am," we chorused sheepishly, taking seats at the table.

"Way to go, you got us into trouble," I grumbled.

"I wasn't the one planning the cold-blooded murder of a complete stranger," Mo stage-whispered.

"No, you only plan cold-blooded murders when someone takes the last chocolate chess square without asking."

"A girl's got to have her priorities," Mo insisted.

2

I'm a Loser, Baby . . .

By the time I arrived at the Glacier, I'd worked up a pretty good head of steam.

I'd done a little bit of research on Dr. Nicholas J. Thatcher, and my Google results were disturbing. Mo was right. Thatcher wasn't your typical lonely tech geek who fancied himself a paranormal investigator. He was calling himself a "zoological anthropologist." He'd already decided that werewolves existed; now he just wanted to know how we came to be, how we lived. This was just the type of guy who would blindly stumble into proof of our existence, sell it to *National Geographic*, and send my whole family running away from scientists bearing tranq guns and skull saws.

Here's the thing. I loved being a werewolf. I couldn't imagine living in just one skin. And I was lucky to be able to turn into such a cool animal. I could have been stuck as a were-skunk or something equally lame. (They do exist. Poor bastards.) Were-wolves changed day or night and had the most complete, dependable changes. And we had the stable pack structure, led by an alpha male mated to the female of his choice, who becomes the alpha female. Unless the alpha male handed his office over to, say, his much cooler and wiser younger sister.

And don't believe all that crap Hollywood tries to peddle about being bitten and cursed by the full moon. You had to be born into our little club. No matter how many times we bit someone, that person would not go furry. They'd probably bleed a lot, though, and maybe get an infection.

Humans had no idea that we existed. Sure, we were the subject of lame movies, and every Halloween, we put up with little kids running around with fur glued to their faces, yelling "Grr!" But humans would freak out if they realized that they saw us every day at the grocery store, in their schools, in the woods. Hell, some wildlife experts could see us in wolf form and would never know they were looking at anything but a large, but otherwise normal, wolf. A picture of my cousin Samson made it into *National Geographic* the year before with a caption calling him a "magnificent specimen." He'd been carrying the damn article around in his wallet for months, using it to impress werewolf chicks.

Basically, we'd gotten by undocumented with cunning and a lot of dumb-ass luck.

If people knew, really knew, that the things that go bump in the night existed, we'd be hunted. Simple as that. Our children would be taken from us and put in special detention centers. We'd be studied, dissected, chased.

Nick Thatcher would be lucky to leave Grundy with all his parts intact.

I took a deep breath and let myself wallow in the delicious, happy noise of the Blue Glacier before I had to get down to business. My cousin Evie owned the saloon, which was part diner, part bar, part dry goods store. The dining room was lit by picture windows and obnoxious neon beer signs. The scent of smoke from the black iron woodstove and potatoes fried in peanut oil had pictures of double cheeseburgers and apple-raisin pie dancing behind my eyelids.

Evie's husband, Buzz, had churned out plain old burgers and fries from the saloon's kitchen until Mo came along with her magical spatula. She overhauled the menu, started baking desserts from scratch, and turned out to be a bit of a marketing genius to boot. For instance, she figured out that while her new neighbors found "shepherd's pie" to be pretentious and British, if she called it "mashed potato pot pie," we'd lap it up. She even developed a signature moose meat loaf sandwich that got the place mentioned in some outsider foodie magazine.

Evie had even given Mo a stake in the place to keep her from quitting when she had the baby. I chose to believe that was why Mo and Cooper named the baby after Evie, instead of, say, a favorite sibling.

Trust my brother to mate with the best cook on

this end of the state. Most werewolves are masters
of the kitchen. If you can kill it or cover it in gravy,
we'll serve it and serve it well. It is a biological ne-
cessity. Our metabolism is so high that we have to
scarf down calories all day just to sleep all night, like
a mini-hibernation. If you were a member of PETA,
you would not be happy at a werewolf Thanksgiving, because in terms of menu, we take "all of column A and half of column B" from the available
woodland creatures. Still, none of us could compete
with Mo in the kitchen. And trust me, several of my
aunties tried.

I stopped to steal Alan Dahling's cap from the bar
and plopped it on my head. "Hey there, Ranger, you
ever catch up to that bear with all the pickanic bas-
kets?"

"Haha, mock the public servant," Alan said,
scowling at me and snatching the cap back. Alan had
been one of the most eligible bachelors in our end
of the woods until he'd hooked up with Kara Reynolds, who just happened to be one of Mo's childhood
friends. Kara had come up for Mo and Cooper's
wedding, jumped Alan, and never bothered leaving.
Can't say I blamed her, really. Despite their recent
engagement and the fact that he regularly solved
problems with bear traps, Alan was still a headliner
in my personal fantasy rotation.

What? I like uniforms.

"Kara won't like it much if she sees you eyeing
Mo that way," I said, nodding toward the kitchen,
where Alan was watching Mo flit from counter to
stove.

Not for the first time, I envied the way Mo moved. I was stealthy and quick. I knew how to land on my feet. But Mo moved with the kind of fluid grace that made you think of swans and toe shoes. Then again, every once in a while, she had a fantastically spazzy moment and ended up falling on her ass, covered in brownie batter. I felt that balanced the scales.

"I'm not eyeing the girl," Alan told me. "I'm eyeing the sandwich."

He grinned as Mo delivered a steak melt, piled high with her special beer-battered onion rings.

Kara appeared at Alan's elbow, stealing one of his rings. She grinned and winked one of her china-doll green eyes at me. "It's true. Since high school, I've never been able to compete with her lunch plates," she said in that honey-and-whiskey accent that kept the local guys circling Mo and Kara like confused, horny bees.

I snickered and snatched one of the onion rings for myself while Alan was distracted with nauseating prelunch smoochies. They were perfectly matched, Alan and Kara. Blond, blue-eyed and tanned, although Alan was about three heads taller. It was as if Alan had ordered her out of a happy couples catalogue or something. Sometimes I looked at all the smug, settled couples around me . . . and I wanted to yark a little bit.

"There's a joke in there somewhere, but I don't have time to find it," I said, rolling my eyes when Cooper started waving at me from across the bar.

Oh, right, I came here with an agenda.

"Where is he?" I demanded, taking the stool next to Cooper.

"Watch yourself. Here, you can't make a bloody public scene while holding the niblet," he said, holding out my niece like a tiny human shield.

"Darn your powers of cuteness," I grumbled at the baby, who babbled and grabbed at my nose. I smiled despite myself. Little Eva was a sight to behold. I had never seen hair like this kid's, a shock of blue-black that stood out as if she'd licked a light socket. She was born looking as if she was wearing a doll's wig. Between that and the marshmallow cheeks, she was basically a living Cabbage Patch Doll.

As beautiful and adorable as she was, Eva's birth was a blow for the pack. Cooper was born to be the alpha, our pack leader. He was the fastest, the strongest of us all. Being alpha wasn't exactly a hereditary monarchy, but it tends to stay in families with strong wolf genes. You can't get much stronger than Graham DNA. Despite the fact that he'd turned the alpha position down and mated with the thoroughly human Mo, it had been expected that his baby would be a wolf. The early signs were promising. As in any pregnancy involving werewolf DNA, Mo had the typical shortened gestation. Eva had been a sturdy nine-pound newborn with a ridiculous amount of hair. But here she was, four months old, and not a tooth in sight. She was completely and utterly human.

The pack loved her, as much as we loved any of our "dead-liners," family members who had all the same genetic opportunities we did but none of the wolf magic. Eva was cuddled constantly at family dinners, to the point where she fussed if she was put in a high chair or anyplace but a warm werewolf auntie's lap. Still, it was a bit of a disappointment that she wouldn't continue the line. Which put that much more pressure on me to produce the next Graham werewolf . . . which sometimes brought up old resentments against Cooper . . . which made me feel no guilt whatsoever for stealing half of his sandwich.

"You know it's extremely fucked up to keep your baby in a bar, right?" I asked, stroking her hair, making a game of trying to find her scalp.

"Easy, that's my pup you're holding," Cooper warned me, cupping his hands over Eva's ears.

"We're in a bar," I pointed out again.

"She's a smart kid. She's going to start repeating everything she hears any day now," Cooper said. "If her first word is 'goddamn,' her mom *will* blame one of us. And I'm not above letting you take the fall."

"You are so whipped."

"Baby sister, when your wife looks like that"—he pointed toward Mo's kitchen ballet—"and cooks like this"—he scooped up some homemade chips and popped them into his mouth—"being whipped isn't so bad."

"Ew."

"I take it Mo told you about Dr. Thatcher?"

My fragile good mood dissipated like the steam from Mo's buttermilk biscuits. "This guy is trouble, Coop. He's already come to the conclusion that we exist. Now he's just trying to confirm his theories on 'pack structure' and 'mating rituals' for some 'groundbreaking' book he's working on. Just the fact that he actually used the words 'mating rituals' makes me want to punch him in the mouth."

"That's your solution to just about everything," Cooper noted dryly.

"And so far, it's worked out for me." I snorted, snatching a few of the chips off Cooper's plate. I chewed them while I surveyed the room. "He's probably some forty-something virgin who lives in his mother's basement and touches himself while watching *The Howling*."

"Look, Mags, I'm not any happier about him being here than you are. But I think we should take a more subtle approach than your usual 'bite first, bite again, keep biting until they're too busy bleeding to death to explain themselves' method."

"If it ain't broke, don't fix it," I shot back. "So, where is this loser?"

I scanned the dining room, stopping on a plaid-clad form hunched over a notebook at his table. My mouth stopped mid-chew. *Helloooo, yummy goodness.* He looked like those old pictures of Vikings you'd see in history textbooks. Wheat-colored hair that was just a little too long. A white-blond goatee dusted around a mouth that was curved into a smile. Blue eyes so bright I could spot the little lapis-colored ring around the iris from across the room. I could practically hear the freaking ocean when I looked at them. Strong chin, lantern jaw, high cheekbones. Lips that were currently being gnawed on as he scribbled in his notebook.

And when he slid those little wire-rim glasses on

his nose, I started drooling. Saliva was literally leaking out of the side of my mouth.

"Mama likes," I whimpered as Mo approached behind the bar. I growled softly as the resident bar wench, Lynette, sidled up to his table and started flirting. She giggled and tossed her hair. She was practically scrawling "Do me" on her boobs in maple syrup. "Who is that, and how much will I have to threaten Lynette to keep her skanky ass the hell away from him?"

Mo grinned at me. A series of little mental tumblers clicked into place in my head.

"That's the loser, isn't it?" I groaned, to Mo's delight.

"Pay up!" she crowed at my brother, who begrudgingly handed her a dollar bill. She smiled winsomely at me as she stuffed the bill into her stained blue apron. "I bet Cooper a buck that you'd pick him out of the crowd as soon as you saw him. You Grahams have a thing for outsiders. We are the forbidden fruit you just can't wait to get a bite of. Face it, accept the outsider hotness, and move on."

A couple of locals watched with bemused interest as Mo did a little victory shimmy behind the bar. Cooper's hands rushed to cup Eva's ears again as I narrowed my eyes at his wife. "That was low, Mo. I thought this guy made you nervous."

"Doesn't mean I can't find the entertainment value in all this," she said, shrugging. "What? We don't have HBO."

Cooper grumpily shoved a fry into his mouth.

"You owe me a buck, Mags. He's not the type of guy I thought you'd be interested in. Too pretty."

I snorted as Mo slid a cheeseburger plate in front of me, extra pickles, no tomato, double onion rings. These were the moments that made up for my sister-in-law being an occasional pain in my ass. "So, who exactly do you think is my type?"

Cooper pursed his lips for a moment as I devoured the burger. "What do they call those guys who fight in the octagon?"

I slapped at his arm, choking a little on Mo's ambrosial half-pounder with cheese. Cooper was about to protest when Lynette streaked past us in a huff, pulling the shoulders of her artfully shredded Bon Jovi T-shirt back up over her sparkly purple bra straps. I shot a look back over to Dr. Thatcher's booth, where he was casually thumbing through some battle-scarred book, blatantly ignoring the tray-tossing hissy fit Lynette was throwing in the kitchen. Dr. Thatcher was apparently immune to her cleavage-y charms.

For a brief, horrible moment, I wondered whether he was gay and mourned the potential loss. Not just for me but for all womankind. This led to thoughts of Dr. Thatcher naked and sweaty, and I started feeling uncomfortably warm in certain places.

"Still want to murder the good doctor *Goodfellas*-style?" Mo asked, smirking at me.

"What's that supposed to mean?" I growled.

"Just that you're not looking at Dr. Thatcher with *blood*lust right now . . ."

"Oh, I'm supposed to just overlook that he's trying to expose my entire species because he's got a pretty face?" I said quietly. "That's sexist. As a matter of fact, the idea that he's trying to exploit innocent furred people instead of modeling for underwear ads—the way God obviously intended—is reason enough to kill him. "

"OK, calm down, crazy eyes," Mo told me. "Here's the deal. He's been asking questions about Jacob Bennett and Craig Ryan. About Susie Q and Abner, anyone who suffered mysterious bite wounds last year. I think he's trying to play it off as just general interest, like every yahoo who's seen the news reports about the attacks. I don't know what to make of him, Maggie. It's not that I think he has bad intentions. In fact, I find myself sort of liking him and feeling sorry for him because I know what it's like to be the new guy around here. But he seems to be the type who's smart enough to bring this whole 'fur issue' crashing down on our heads. Frankly, I'm surprised you guys have pulled it off for this long."

"So, what do you want me to do now that I've seen him?" I asked. "Since I'm not allowed to run him out of town on a rail, I feel as if my hands are tied."

"You had an actual rail ready, didn't you?" Mo asked.

I didn't respond.

"I'm checking your truck later," Mo muttered under her breath.

Cooper shrugged. "I thought it would be helpful for you to talk to him. To get an idea of what he's looking for. And maybe feed him a little misinformation."

"You could do all that," I pointed out.

He grinned. "I'm not the alpha, oh great leader. We both know if I started doing your job for you, I'd wake up missing parts."

"Parts that I hold in high esteem," Mo added, wandering down the bar to take an order.

"Is that where she holds them?" I asked, snickering. Cooper growled at me. "Fine, I'll play nice, for now."

I turned to hop off my bar stool, and there he was, standing in front of me in all his plaid-clad glory.

This close, I could appreciate Dr. Thatcher all the better. He *was* pretty. The beard almost camouflaged the generous curve of his lips. It drew the eye away from the fine, straight nose. Maybe that was the point. You could catch a lot of crap in this kind of place, being a pretty boy. And from what my cousin Caleb told me, you could get some unwanted attention from truckers at rest stops.

Still, he was tall and broad-shouldered and moved with a sort of competence. And Geek Squad was hiding some serious muscles under that Simpsons T-shirt and flannel. I started having some weird waking-dream hallucination in which I pictured him busting into the saloon like Aragorn entering the royal halls of Rohan in *Lord of the Rings*. As the Dr. Thatcher-Aragorn hybrid made his away across the floor in full armor, I stared up at him with saucer eyes and a mouth full of drool but no words. All

I could manage in the scope of this guy's little grin was an incredibly un-wolf-like squeak.

This was a first for me. I didn't have trouble talking to guys. Hell, Samson and Cooper named me an "honorary dude" when we were kids, to save their pride after losing so many foot races to their baby sister. But I was used to relating to guys on that familiar, buddy-buddy level. The Grahams are related to almost every family in our little valley. It's difficult to find a potential date who doesn't cross some creepy genetic boundaries.

And this was the point where I realized that I was having my own personal mental vacation, staring blankly at a complete stranger.

"Dr. Thatcher, this is my sister-in-law, Maggie," Mo said, filling the awkward silence.

"I'm Nick Thatcher," he said, stretching out his hand.

I froze. Cooper watched me, his brow furrowed. Normally, he would be afraid that I would punch Nick. At the moment, I think he was afraid I was going to throw up on Nick.

Nick reached forward, grabbed my motionless hand, and shook it. As he moved closer, his scent hit me full force, and I had to put a hand on the bar to steady myself. New leaves. Thanksgiving dinner. A smoky note of moss. I narrowed my eyes at him. I recognized that smell.

The hiker. Dr. The Truth Is Out There had been wandering in my backyard.

"I know who you are," I said, looking up to find those seawater eyes of his pinning me to the floor.

He was staring me down. Nobody stared me down! Eye contact is a serious no-no with predators. In the animal kingdom, it basically says, "I'm not afraid of you. I plan on taking your food and your dignity, and there's not a damn thing you can do about it."

I found it was a lot easier to be annoyed by that than hypnotized by his evil baby blues. I ratcheted my chin up a few degrees. "What brings you to our neck of the woods, Dr. Thatcher?"

He smiled. "Just a little research trip. I think I disappointed some of the locals, though. They heard 'doctor' and thought a new MD had come to town."

I entertained myself with the image of the locals showing up at Dr. Thatcher's door, requesting help for hemorrhoids and plantar warts.

"Well, we don't get a lot of academics up here." I tilted my head and smiled back, a hundred percent guile-free. "In fact, how did you hear about Grundy? Was there an ad or a brochure that caught your attention?"

The doctor was an equally skilled bullshitter, which earned him a little bit of my grudging respect. There was no trace of hesitation as he said, "Something like that."

He smirked. And I wanted to lick his chin. I actually had to keep my jaw tense to fight the urge. Sensing the weird energy that seemed to be swirling around my body, Cooper's eyebrow winged up to his hairline. Mo leaned against the counter, her head whipping back and forth as if she was watching some sort of dirty tennis game.

"So, Maggie, do you live nearby?" The question

seemed loaded, just by the tone Nick was using.
I stared at him, trying to decipher the slight tilt to
his head. A good hunter excels at interpreting body
language, whether it's an elk preparing to bolt or a
guy sneaking peeks at your ass. Dr. Thatcher already
knew where I lived. I could only assume he had
asked me that because he wanted to talk about the
valley.

"Not too far," I said blithely.

"I was thinking Maggie might be able to show
you around the area, Nick."

My facade dropped for a second, and I shot my
brother a meaningful look, the meaning being "shut
the hell up."

Cooper didn't even blink, as if butter wouldn't
melt in his mouth. "Well, Nick heard I was a field
guide, asked me to take him on some of the tougher
trails around here. But I really don't have time in my
schedule. And since you're the only one who knows
the area almost as well I do . . ."

"That won't be possible," I said, my voice flat.
"I've gotta work."

"Oh, you can move your schedule around," Mo
said, grinning at me. "Your hours are pretty flex-
ible."

OK, that was going too far. Being an unofficial
official for the pack meant settling disputes between
pack members, monitoring the wildlife (i.e., food
sources) available around the valley, controlling the
pack when we ran together. And it's hard to find a
day job that will accept "got kicked in the ribs by an
agitated moose" as a reason to call in sick. The vil-

lage paid me a salary for maintaining records and appearances at the town hall. And I was the closest thing there was to law enforcement in my valley. I didn't have time to escort the yummy doctor around by the nose.

OK, that wasn't true. I spent a good portion of my "work day" bored out of my ever-loving mind. But no one, particularly the yummy doctor, had to know that.

"Mo, my hours are none of your business," I said through a clenched, fake smile.

Nick shrugged, and the motion brought his arm brushing across my shoulder. It felt as if a warm electric current had passed through my skin. I held my breath, willing away the tremor that skittered up my spine.

"Well, if you find a way to fit me into your schedule, let me know. I'll probably just wander around the eastern butte for a few days, take in the sights," he said. "I'm a climber, and I'm eager to see what sort of trouble I can get into around here."

"Why would you do that?" I asked. The eastern side of the Wheeler Mountains range was where Buzz had uncovered the bones of hikers who disappeared the previous year. "That's not exactly a beginner's slope."

"I'm not exactly a beginner," he said, smiling.

"So says every goofball who manages to hike across the parking lot to a sporting-goods store and buy a North Face jacket," I muttered.

"You're saying I need a guide."

"Yes."

"So, you'll go with me," he said, as if the matter were obvious and settled.

"Ye—wait, no. Wait, what?" I spluttered.

"I'll give you a call to settle the details," he said, nodding at Cooper and Mo. "It was nice to meet you all."

He turned and walked out of the saloon, leaving me gaping after him.

What just happened?

"Are you high?" I asked Mo, slapping her arm. "Why did you guys tell him that I would show him around?" Evie shot me a sharp look, and I lowered my voice. "This is the man who wants to reveal our existence to the world, and you want to set me up with him? Are you and Cooper *that* desperate to double date?"

"No, I figured this was the best way to keep him out of our hair. He's your problem now. What better way to keep an eye on him than to accompany him on his investigation? He gets nothing but goes home happy. You . . . get a little something and go home a lot less cranky," Mo suggested, giggling unrepentantly when my brother winced. "What? After watching you talk to him, I think we should change our approach. Keep our enemies close, so to speak. Hell, maybe you could convince him that a Sasquatch did it or something."

"Nah, we couldn't do that," Cooper said. "Sasquatch is a pretty nice guy."

"Sasquatch is real, too?" Mo whispered. "Why do I have to find things out like this? I'm in the family, too."

"Look, we don't speak to Thatcher," I told Cooper as Mo dashed back to the kitchen to check on some pies in the oven. "We don't take him into the woods. Nothing. As far as we're concerned, Dr. Thatcher doesn't exist."

"Is that a decree from the alpha?" Cooper asked, lowering his tone to a whisper.

"Do I need to make it a decree, or do you have the sense to admit that we need to stay away from him?" I asked.

"What's the verdict?" Mo asked, coming back to refill Cooper's coffee mug and top off my Coke.

"Maggie said she doesn't want us talking to him," Cooper said, sipping his coffee. "No visits, no tours, no spilling of ancient family secrets."

Mo frowned. "I don't think you're giving us a whole lot of credit. I think I'm clever enough to maintain a friendly conversation without vomiting up forbidden information. I have just as much to lose as you two. And if he tries to interview me, I'll just tell him I'm afraid his pocket recorder will capture my soul or something. Come on. Maggie finally has a crush on somebody. This is going to be better than one of those Japanese game shows."

I glared at her.

She shrugged. "For the rest of us."

"One of these days, I'm going to catch you without your trusty fire extinguisher. And then your ass is mine."

"Bring it on, Scrappy Doo."

3

Chuck Norris and the Calendar of Death

I SAT AT MY DESK in the community center/town hall, writing out the whopping four paychecks the village issued each week. One to myself; one to our village physician, Anna Moder; one to my cousin Teresa, who taught twenty-six kids in all twelve grades at the village school; and another to my gargantuan cousin-but-might-as-well-be-my-brother, Samson, who was the closest thing we had to a civil engineer. He delivered the mail, ran our modest recycling program, and maintained our handful of public buildings. He also occasionally fell asleep while driving a snowplow, but he was such a cheerful guy it was hard to stay pissed at him. Besides, every village needed an idiot.

I didn't live in a normal little town. Every single household in my valley was either were or descended from were. And I was related to each and every person there on one side or the other, and I'm very aware of how wrong that sounds.

Dating as a werewolf is complicated, particularly for packs in the Great North. Every pack has to maintain close relationships with other packs and "import" mates at every opportunity, to prevent inbreeding. You practically have to review your extended genealogical history before you can agree to a movie and dinner.

This might sound isolated and sort of claustrophobic, but wolves don't know any other way. A pack generally lives in close quarters, filling an apartment complex, a subdivision, or a gated community in the case of more urban, affluent clans. In southern packs, it usually means parking a number of double-wide trailers on a farm. For us, it was a self-contained, nearly self-sustaining, community surrounded by some of the richest hunting lands known in the Great Northwest.

Not that I like to brag or anything.

I munched on a handful of red Swedish Fish I kept in a huge apothecary jar on my desk. I had to refill the damn thing about once a week, depending on how often Samson stopped by. The rest of my morning would consist of checking on a pothole in the parking lot of the village clinic and writing up a schedule for the community center that might finally settle the ongoing feud between the local quilting group and the bridge club.

It was good to be the queen.

OK, so I had the most boring job in the village. I considered it a trade-off because the rest of my responsibilities—running, hunting, protecting the borders of the valley, and so on—were pretty awesome. And busting my ass for a few hours that morning meant I could get a few precious moments of quiet and read the copy of the new J. D. Robb paperback I had hidden in my filing cabinet. I wasn't a classics girl, despite Mo's best efforts. The woman actually bought me a subscription to the English Writer of the Month Club. I was shameless in my supermarket-shelf mass-market taste. I loved King, Evanovich, Grisham, and Brown. I won't lie; the official-looking filing cabinet in the corner is actually stuffed full of my paperbacks.

I might have been reading at that very moment, if I could manage to concentrate long enough to write a damn check correctly. I'd slept about three hours each night since my humiliating meeting with Nick Thatcher. I kept waking up all sweaty and tangled up in the sheets, with visions of his cheeky little grin still dancing behind my eyelids.

Jumpy and irritated, I spent hours trying to get back to sleep, only to end up stomping out of the house to run through the woods on all fours. It was the only thing that could clear my head. By the time I got back to the house, everybody was bustling around town. And it hardly served as a good example for me to flop back into bed. Lazy never works for wolves. Read a few fables. So, for the last four days, I'd basically been skimming by on caffeine and luck.

Beyond day-to-day operations, I also served as a sort of figurehead for the pack. I was "the face" for the valley and its inhabitants. And that face had some pretty serious undereye luggage. Now that I was alpha, the pressure for me to settle down and birth a litter went from good-natured rumbling at holidays to an all-out roar. I couldn't walk from my office to my house without one of my relatives accosting me with some promise of the man of my dreams.

While a lot of girls—particularly girls living in one of the most remote, eligible-werewolf-bachelor-starved regions in the world—would be thrilled to have such a devoted network of matchmakers, I thought about following in the shoes of Jan Brady and making up my own "George Glass" to get them off my back. Most of their recommendations were either far more interested in becoming the alpha for my pack than in me as a person. Or they were more interested in Samson than they were in me—which was disappointing. Then there were Cro-Magnon wolves who hadn't quite grasped the whole "females are my equal" concept.

Fun times.

I was not counting on a love match. Not everybody had a marriage like my parents'. My mother had come from a pack in Oregon. She moved to Alaska after meeting my dad on one of his rare trips to the mainland. He came into her uncle's garage to get a part for some motorcycle Samson's dad wanted. My mom was doing the books in the office. She looked up and smiled at him, and he was so distracted by that smile that he walked into a wall. Dad died when I was a baby, but Cooper told me a lot of stories about what I'd missed growing up. The silly jokes, the googly eyes, Dad bringing bunches of wildflowers to her when he came home from a run. He once told Cooper that the trick to a happy life was to find the person you can't breathe without and marry her.

How was any guy I chose going to compete with that sort of romantic goo?

So, given my candidate pool, marriage and kids weren't exactly things I was looking forward to. I loved Eva. I loved cuddling her, the sweet apple and baby-shampoo smell that radiated from that crazy hair. But the best part was that I could give her back. When the cuteness was over and she had a smelly diaper or a tantrum, I could just claim ignorance and hand her over to Mo, who somehow had the patience needed to deal with stuff like that.

I was basically a selfish creature. I liked sleeping and being able to leave the house without making sure I had a half-dozen toys and a Baggie full of Cheerios. But not having kids wasn't an option. For one thing, I wasn't planning on dying a virgin. And in my family, if you have sex, you're going to have kids. And second, I sort of owed it to my bloodline to pass the werewolf magic along.

It seemed blatantly unfair that I seemed to be suffering from some hormone surge when Nick Thatcher came into the picture. Clearly, some wire labeled "Don't mess around with men who could ruin your life" had short-circuited in my brain. I'd known plenty of guys with big blue eyes, guys with pouty, kissable lips, guys who smelled like Sunday lunch. I'd just never met one who had all three qualities.

That was the problem. It was all looks. It was my primal brain at work. It wasn't that he was smart or funny or that he actually managed to thwart me in conversation, which until now, no one but Mo could do. And it definitely wasn't because I'd developed some weird, creepy, stalker-at-first-fascination thing with him . . .

Moving on.

As hard as I tried to shrug off his thrall, Nick just kept popping up, like one of those damn plastic whack-a-moles. First, I found out my cousin, Evie's husband, Buzz, unaware of his wolfy in-laws' involvement in the debacle, had given Nick an extensive interview about his search for the killer wolf. Alan Dahling had taken Nick up the mountain to the area where Walt and Hank had shot the huge male timber wolf we were letting the public believe was responsible for the attacks. I had to hand it to Nick, he was good at his job. If you considered being a giant pain in my supernatural ass a job.

And the final blow? Mo was delivering Tupperwared meals to his house like some cross between a Welcome Wagon and Marie Callender. He tried to pay for it, and she refused to take his money. She considered it some sort of outreach program. I think the point was reaching out to drive me crazy.

"Let me get this straight," I'd hissed at her over the phone. "I say don't have anything to do with the nosy outsider, and you start delivering care packages to his door? I can't get your meat loaf in my freezer, but you're dropping them on Thatcher's doorstep with reheating instructions?"

"I saw him at the market the other day, and the poor guy had twenty Banquet dinners in his cart," Mo said, her voice rising to a disturbing, defensive octave. "Do you have any idea how expensive those things are up here? Plus, they're all fat and sodium, and he's too pretty to be allowed to get all bloated."

"But I told you—"

"Look, with all the questions Nick is not so subtly trying to work into conversations, it would look weird and suspicious if I went all silent religious-compound wife whenever he walked into a room. Doesn't it make more sense that we would remain neighborly?"

There was silence on my end of the line . . . unless you counted the sound of my teeth grinding.

"Maggie?"

"I'm trying to find a hole in your argument that doesn't involve me threatening you," I grumbled. "I got nothing."

She snorted.

"What sort of questions is he asking?"

"Oh, little things, about how Cooper and I got to know each other. He heard from a few of our neighbors that we weren't exactly an instant love connection. Some of my better insults are fondly remembered. So he's using 'getting to know you' conversations to ask what turned the tide, what couples around here do to date, that sort of thing."

"And what are you telling him?" I asked.

Mo huffed. "Oh, I told him that Cooper showed up on my doorstep with a bear trap clamped around his leg, told me he was a werewolf, and we decided to go steady."

"Ha freaking ha."

My sister-in-law was not to be trusted.

My embarrassment was replaced by annoyance, frustration, a desire to be rid of Nick that bordered on religious. It was obvious that he had been sent to torment me for some horrible wrong I'd committed in a past life.

I failed to see how turning me into a blithering, sleep-deprived idiot was going to make me a better person. As a concept, karma was ass-backward.

"Oh, good gravy, snap out of it, you loser!" I groaned, thunking my head against the desk.

"Well, that seems harsh. I just walked in the door," a voice boomed over me. I looked up to see Samson towering over my desk.

I snickered, leaning back in my chair.

"Now, what kind of werewolf doesn't even notice when her office has been invaded?" Samson smirked, ruffling my hair. "What's up, Midget?"

My cousin Samson, ladies and gentlemen, the five-year-old trapped in a pro wrestler's body, the man who gave me the Chuck Norris Fact of the Day calendar on my desk, which was why I tolerated abuse from him more than I would from most people. I loved him just as much as I loved Cooper. His mother had died before I was born, and his dad was a screwup of the first order, abandoning him to live with us when we were just kids. He'd been the one who helped keep me somewhat in line when Cooper left, and as my unofficial second in command, he was the first member of the pack to call me out when I was being a jerk.

Well, the first to call me a jerk to my face and walk away without a limp . . . ok, without a permanent limp.

He walked it off.

I scowled up at him, but there was no real heat in it. "Everyone's a midget compared to you."

"Doesn't make the nickname any less fun."

"You know, the ink isn't even dry on this yet," I retorted, pointing to his paycheck.

"It's not signed, either," he noted. "You only *think* I don't pick up on stuff like that."

"Go on, you've claimed your thirty pieces of silver, go do something crazy like put gas in that penis replacement you call transportation."

"First of all, don't mock the truck or my junk," he said sternly, pointing out the window toward the mammoth F-250 required to haul his ass around. "And it's not compensating for anything if it's to scale."

"Ew." I shuddered but was grateful for something to think about that did not involve hot outsider eggheads. I was still shuddering in revulsion when a sandy-haired werewolf stuck his head in the door, toting a jam-packed postal box.

Clay Renard was one of a handful of people in the valley not related to me by blood or marriage. In fact, that handful was pretty much limited to Clay, his widowed sister, Alicia, and her two boys. Clay was a few years younger than me. He was a likable, easygoing sort of guy, friendly and helpful, without being a pain in the ass about it. He was as close to the all-American type as werewolves got, with a strong, square jaw, high, sharp cheekbones, and light blue eyes. Even though his hair was brownish-gold, he had dark eyebrows that served as exclamation points on his open, expressive face. I liked the way they tilted when he smiled. And he had a cute little overbite that caught his bottom lip when he tucked the smile away.

"Hey, Clay, what are you doing with the mail?" I asked, grinning at him.

Clay shrugged. "Samson was pressed for time, so I stopped by the Grundy post office to pick up the mail for him."

I frowned. Clay worked in a garage on the outskirts of Grundy. But the errand still meant he had to drive twenty minutes out of his way to do something Samson was supposed to do three times a week.

"Oh, you did, did you?" I narrowed my eyes at my cousin. "You were pressed for time? Would that be nap time?" Samson shrugged. "I'm giving Clay half of your paycheck."

"I knew I should have made you sign it," Samson muttered.

Clay chuckled. "I don't mind. I got to stop by the saloon for one of Mo's burgers."

"Aw, why'd you have to go and mention Mo's burgers?" Samson moaned.

"Oh, cheer up, buttercup, Mom made chicken and dumplings," I told him.

"Meh," Samson said in a disinterested tone.

"You're going to be in soooo much trouble when I tell Mom you said that." I laughed. Samson cringed. "Clay, are you too full to join us?"

"I am never too full for anything," Clay said solemnly.

"I'll call Mom, let her know you're coming," I told him. I turned to my cousin. "You, on the other hand, have some mail to deliver. Jackass."

"I'll give you a hand," Clay said, following a grumbling Samson out the door.

"Suck-up," Samson shot back.

I was in a much brighter mood as I finished up a few housekeeping tasks and closed down my computer. I called my mom to warn her we'd be having a guest for dinner, but she didn't pick up, which was weird. But Mom always cooked enough to feed an army with Samson around, so I figured we were covered.

I left my office without bothering to lock it. I mean, seriously, there were sixty people in the village, and they had just as much business going into the building as I did. That was the benefit of being related to nearly everyone you lived with. There was a certain level of trust that was expected. As I walked the whopping half-block to my house, I congratulated myself on finding a pleasant evening's distraction from plotting the violent demise of one Nicholas Thatcher.

Clay and I had been on a few friendly outings that didn't quite qualify as dates. I'd taken him hiking up the north pass, near the elk hunting grounds. We'd

gone to see a movie, some date-appropriate Will
Ferrell comedy we'd abandoned halfway through
in favor of the action flick two theaters down. As
a candidate, he was far less complicated than . . .
other people, but he was a cautious soul, which I re-
spected.

Besides Clay, I'd gone on a fix-up or two with
boys from other packs in Olympia and Anchorage.
It always had this weird game-show feel to it. The
grand prize being "lifelong mated bliss and a half-
dozen purebred werewolf pups." And then I realized
that the reason these guys needed to be fixed up by
the interpack dating service wasn't the scarcity of female candidates but the fact that they were obnoxious, stupid, or creepy—or all of the above.

Every once in a while, I thought an entrepreneur-
ial were should set up some sort of online supernatural dating service. But, you know, that is the sort
of thing that attracts attention. Some smartass little
hacker would get into it, and next thing you know,
there'd be a complete list of supernatural creatures
in America, and some nut job might take it seriously
and go Van Helsing on our asses.

I spotted Clay's truck in my great-aunt Billie's
driveway and decided to duck in to tell Alicia that
her brother would be at our place for dinner. I took
a few deep breaths before I knocked. Visiting Billie
was always sort of awkward. Besides being a murder-
ous, back-stabbing traitor, her son, my alpha pre-
decessor, Eli, had also been the primary caretaker
for Billie. Between setting us up for a takeover with
another pack, attacking humans at random to drive

Cooper away, and trying to kill Mo, I honestly don't know how he found time for it all.

Billie had dementia, a rare affliction among were-wolves, and it had wiped her once-sharp mind like a slate. She needed almost constant care to keep her from phasing and running away. The last time she did this, she was found wandering naked in human form at the grocery store in Grundy.

The pack didn't hold a grudge against Billie for her son's actions. As the mate of my grandfather's late brother, James, she would always be considered one of us. And while the rest of the pack was more than willing to take over her care, it seemed right when Clay and Alicia, Billie's niece and nephew, left their pack in Ontario a few months before to move in with her. They were a welcome addition to the group; they were smart and hardworking, and they could hunt like nobody's business.

Still, considering that it was Cooper who brought Eli down, with my help, I always felt little twinges of guilt when talking to Billie, even though she probably had no idea that Eli was gone.

I knocked a little harder on the front door, but there was no answer. Nudging it open, I could hear a cartoon blaring from the living room. Someone was moving around in the kitchen. "Hello?" I called.

Paul, Alicia's youngest, toddled up to me. His four-year-old brother, Ronnie, sat mesmerized by dancing animated bears. The boys didn't resemble Alicia or Clay with their white-blond hair and huge brown eyes. But they were adorable. Sort of sticky and always had runny noses, but adorable. "Up!"

Paul commanded, tugging on my jeans. I slid my hands under his arms and hoisted him onto my hip as I walked into the kitchen.

"Nana?" he said, his tone hopeful as he eyed the fruit bowl on the counter.

Billie was in a rumpled blue and green plaid housedress, her thick white hair tumbling around her face. She was shuffling back and forth between the cabinet and her counter, spreading peanut butter on six slices of bread. I peeled a banana for Paul, which he promptly devoured.

"Aunt Billie?" I murmured quietly.

She turned, her deep brown eyes focused and alert but vacant. Whatever she was seeing, it wasn't what I was seeing. She smiled, her still-smooth cheeks dimpling prettily.

"Oh, Maggie, honey, have you seen Eli?" Billie asked, topping each of her half-dozen sandwiches. "You need to tell him it's time for lunch. He can go out and play with Samson and Cooper later."

I swallowed the little lump in my throat and nodded. "OK, Aunt Billie, I'll tell him."

"I'm cutting the crusts off for him," she said, adding the sandwiches to a massive pile on the counter. I found myself blinking back against hot, wet pressure in my eyes. Sure, Eli had turned out kind of evil, but he was still my cousin. I'd grown up with him. I could remember the afternoons that had trapped Billie's mind. I could remember him as a little boy, arguing with Cooper and Samson over who had to be Aquaman when they played Justice League. And I'd taken a part in killing that little boy. It was a weight on my heart that wouldn't go away.

"Oh!" Alicia said, nearly dropping her laundry basket as she came through the kitchen door. Alicia was a compact little female, with short-cropped dark blond hair. She smiled, seeming relieved that the surprise guest in her kitchen was me.

"Sorry, Alicia, I just stopped by to see how Billie's doing. I knocked, but . . ."

"I was in the laundry room," she said, putting the laundry basket on the table and surveying the gummy mess on her counter. "I didn't hear you. Did Maggie give you a 'nana, little man?"

Paul grinned at her, his cheeks puffed out with fruit. "Nana!"

"Clay's going to be at our place for dinner," I told her. "Did you want to join us?"

Alicia smiled, ruffling Paul's hair. "Thanks, but we've got a pretty good routine going. And any interruption to that routine kind of sets Billie off."

"Does this sort of thing happen often?" I asked, setting Paul down as he strained toward the living room. I'd served my purpose as the 'nana provider, and the theme music for *Barney* was starting up. It's hard to compete with that chipper purple bastard.

Alicia shrugged, giving me a tired smile. "She has good days and bad. Today hasn't been a good day."

"Do you guys need anything?"

The village kept an account to pay for most of the pack's seniors' groceries and medicine, including Billie's. Alicia moved to a little Filofax by the phone and handed me a short stack of receipts for reimbursement. She watched as Billie continued to make sandwiches. "Well, it looks like we need more bread and peanut butter."

Billie turned, as if she was just now registering Alicia's presence. "Who are you?" she asked, suspicion creeping into her voice. "What are you doing in my kitchen?"

Alicia sighed, and smiled at her. "I'm Alicia. I'm your sister Judy's daughter."

"I don't know you!" Billie cried, throwing the butter knife across the room at her. Alicia plucked it out of the air, looking tired and worn.

"She does this at least once a day," Alicia told me. "I'm your niece, Aunt Billie. We're here to help take care of you."

"I don't know you! I don't know you!" Billie yelled, throwing herself toward me. "Maggie, make her go away. Tell Eli. Tell him I don't want her in my house! I don't want strangers in my house!"

I looked to Alicia for guidance. She was more accustomed to Billie's episodes than I was. Looking sort of tired and resigned, Alicia reached up into one of the cabinets and pulled out a pill bottle. She put a little white tablet in my hand with a juice box. "Nap," she mouthed.

"Billie, we'll get this all straightened out, OK?" I said, putting my arm around her and leading her to her room. The dresser was dusty. And the sheets looked as if they hadn't been changed in a while. Alicia wasn't much of a housekeeper. Then again, I couldn't imagine trying to keep up with two toddlers and a senile werewolf who occasionally played knife thrower.

THE ART OF SEDUCING A NAKED WEREWOLF   47

"I don't know her," Billie whispered. "Tell Eli I don't want her in the house, please?"

"I will," I promised. "But why don't you just stay here in your room for a while, get some rest? Eli and I will work this out."

I handed her the pill, which she took without a fuss, and she drank the juice. I lifted her legs onto the bed and pulled the blankets up to her chin. "You're a good girl, Maggie," Billie said, her voice slurring slightly from the pill's effects. "I don't care what Eli says."

I smiled. "Thanks, Aunt Billie."

I walked home, feeling a bit deflated. Alicia's intentions were good, but she was stretched so thin. Billie wasn't exactly cooperative. And Clay didn't seem to know what to do with the kids. I started composing a schedule in my head, arranging for the aunties to come by and give Alicia a break—give her some help with Billie and maybe even watch the boys, so Alicia could do some errands or just go for a run.

I stomped the mud off my boots and shucked them near the front door, knowing better than to track dirt into Grace Graham's house. I might be the baddest, toughest wolf in my pack, but there are still times when my mother can make me cower like a newborn pup.

Mom never had much money while we were growing up, but her home was a showplace. The living room was meticulously clean, decorated with scattered photos of Cooper, Samson, and me in various stages of childhood. The walls were a warm, creamy

color. A bright blue throw rug was settled comfort-
ably in front of a large brick fireplace. On the mantle
were three carved wooden wolves that Cooper made
with his own hands. The house pulled you in, made
you feel instantly at ease and at home. While other
wolves might disarm you with fangs or claws, my
mother did it with kind words and good meals.

"Something smells good!" I called, inhaling the
scent of my mother's chicken and dumplings. She
served huge vats of it with fresh, crusty sourdough
and as much of her homemade applesauce as you
could eat. "I hope it's OK, we're going to have some
company for dinner."

"Yes, I know!" she called back. "I'm in the
kitchen."

I rounded the corner and heard Nick Thatcher
in mid-sentence, "There are a lot of theories about
where exactly the line between man and animal
is drawn. Psychologically, spiritually, physically.
Where do the two lines split on the evolutionary
scale? Is the missing link some step along the way?
Or could legends that link man and animal be signs
of a step forward? A mix of the best of both worlds."

Nick freaking Thatcher was sitting at my kitchen
table while my mother served him chamomile tea
and a piece of her special apple cake. My favorite
apple cake.

"Oh, my God! Is nothing sacred?" I howled.

Faced with my mental tormentor, the interrupter
of sleep, and his head-clouding scent, I'd expected
to feel awkward and bashful again. But mostly, I felt
anger. Sweet, clarifying anger. Who the hell did he

think he was, waltzing into my valley, with his stupid feet under my table, eating my freaking cake?

His feet did look awfully big, I noticed, biting my lip. And from what I could gather from a lifetime spent around men who were comfortable in the nude, the old wives' tales about foot size tended to be accurate.

Gah!

Focus, Maggie, I commanded my wandering brain. My eyelid actually twitched when he looked up at me.

"Hi, Maggie, it's nice to see you again," he said, smiling so sweetly I thought I might need insulin.

"Your work sounds so interesting, Nick," Mom said, ignoring my outburst and turning back to the stove to stir the contents of a huge iron pot. "But how do you even study something like that?"

Nick smiled. "Eyewitness accounts. As many police reports as I can get my hands on. Local legends. Scientists tend to downplay the importance of oral history."

While he ticked down the list with his long, strong fingers, my mouth went dry. My worst fears were confirmed. He was just smart enough to be dangerous.

"What are you doing here?" I demanded, tired of being ignored.

"Well, I thought we got off on the wrong foot the other day, so I wanted to come by and try to make a better second impression. Your mom was nice enough to keep me company while I waited and serve me some of this delicious cake."

I scowled. I had to stop thinking about the cake. And Nick. And Nick smeared in cake icing. I glared at my mother. Clearly, this conspiracy was wider spread than I thought. I gritted my teeth and reached for my mother's cake plate.

"No cake for you," Mom said, smacking my hand away. "You'll spoil your dinner."

"He has some!" I pointed out, shaking my smarting fingers.

"He's a guest."

I narrowed my eyes at Nick while he smarmily chewed on a big bite of cake.

He would pay for this. Dearly.

"And I wanted to ask about your brother's suggestion that you'd show me around. I'd be more than happy to pay you whatever you'd charge for guiding me around the trails. I've hiked around a little bit myself. But I haven't seen much in the way of wildlife. Your brother has such a solid reputation in the field guide community, I was hoping you might show me the best places to look."

"I just don't have the time," I lied.

"Nick, you're going to stay for dinner, yes?" Mom asked, stirring the huge vat of chicken and dumplings on the stove. She had a knack for relieving the tension in a room by pretending my rudeness away with cooking. Many, many chickens had given up their lives to cover my conversational shortcomings.

"No, he's not."

"Maggie, I know you have better manners than that."

Damn it. Mom was right. Werewolves have this whole thing about hospitality and making sure that guests are safe and well served. Guests never left werewolf land hungry or unhappy. I was behaving very badly, and I should have been ashamed, even if I wanted to make him swallow that stupid Yankees cap along with *my* cake.

I cleared my throat, recognizing when my mother had been pushed too far. "I'm sorry. What I meant to say was that Samson already invited Clay for dinner," I said. "I wouldn't want Nick to be uncomfortable."

"Oh, I don't mind," Nick said, his cheek dimpling.

"Shut it," I hissed under my breath.

He smirked at me and pushed back from the table, pausing to scrape one last bite from the plate. Just to irritate me. "I'd love to stay, Gracie. And as much as I appreciate the invitation, I've got to head back to Grundy before it gets dark," he said, packing his little notebook into his messenger bag. "I'm moving out of the motel into a rental place in town."

"Rental place?"

"Yes, Mr. Gogan set it up for me," he said, hitching his bag onto his shoulder. "I think the owner's name is Quinn?"

My lip rippled back from my teeth just a tiny bit. Susie Q had been the first person Eli attacked the year before. She'd had to move in with her daughter in Texas because of her injuries. I wondered if he'd chosen the house on purpose or if it was a coincidence. More important, renting a house meant Nick was planning to stay in Grundy for more than just a "little research trip." And despite the fact that I knew this was a bad thing, I couldn't help but be a little happy about it.

Damn it.

"Could I have a rain check?" he asked my mother.

"Absolutely. Anytime you're close by, come on over," she said, shaking his hand. "It was lovely to meet you."

"He's a nice boy," Mom told me as Nick shrugged into his jacket and moved toward the front door. "He has good manners."

"You cannot invite a man into your home just because he calls you ma'am," I reminded her.

"What if he has eyes the color of the morning sky and a butt that won't quit?" she whispered.

"Ew, Mom!"

She lowered her voice to a range only she and I could hear. "I'm middle-aged, sweetheart. I'm not dead."

My mother had been widowed young, and she hadn't been on so much as a movie date since. It was starting to show. Filing that under "problems I have to solve before they become psychologically traumatic," I followed Nick onto the porch.

"I don't know what you're trying to pull," I told him as he took the steps. "But I want you to stay away from the valley. You'll scare the locals . . . or annoy them into kicking your ass."

He seemed honestly insulted, frowning up at me and pouting those soft-looking, pouty, full, pouty lips . . . and there went my train of thought . . .

"Why don't you like me?" he asked. "I'm a fairly likable person. I could get you testimonials from a half-dozen or so people."

"My mom doesn't count," I spat.

He objected, "Your mom should count twice. *She* loves me."

"No shit," I deadpanned. "Why are you here, Dr. Thatcher? Why are you so hell-bent on spending time around me?"

"I like you," he said, shrugging. "You're funny and prickly, which works for me. You know you're beautiful, but you don't seem to care about it all that much. And your bullshit tolerance is low—"

"Then you should realize that I'm not buying your answer."

"Fine." He lowered his voice and leaned ever so slightly toward me. We were at eye level and so close I could feel his warm, frosting-scented breath fanning over my cheek, making my mouth water. I could almost feel the burnt-gold strands of his hair brushing against my skin. "Besides hoping to charm you into a date, which is obviously not working, you know exactly why I'm here, Maggie. Your family can't expect to protect Mo forever."

Insert awkward pause in which I stare at Nick as if he's whistling "O Canada" out of his left nostril.

"Wait . . . what?"

"Your sister-in-law has been sweet, polite, downright hospitable. But she has an uncanny way of wiggling out of answering questions."

Hmm. Mo *was* way smarter than I gave her credit

for. But I would never, ever tell her that to her face. I scoffed. "Why would you even talk to Mo?"

"Because I studied the reports for the wolf attacks last year. Do you realize that besides the occasional bar fight, there's nothing in the state police reports even mentioning Grundy for the last two years until Mo reported being attacked by a trucker named John Teague?" he asked. I gave a noncommittal nod, so he just barreled on. "And then, all of a sudden, there's a rash of wolf attacks around town. And wolf attacks are pretty rare. Wolves don't normally come close enough to humans to attack them."

"Unless they're sick, which was Alan Dahling's theory about the timber wolf Walt and Hank shot last year," I told him.

"That wolf wasn't nearly big enough to leave the bite marks left on Abner Golightly. And it certainly wasn't big enough to kill two fully grown hikers," he said. "Look, everything seemed to start with Mo. And she was connected to each of the attacks thereafter. She took in Susan Quinn's dog. The missing hikers ate at the saloon just before they disappeared. She found Abner in the woods. Everything comes back to her. I think that Mo could be something more than human. And I think you and your family are helping her cover it up."

If he was trying to imply that Mo was a werewolf, I was going to pee myself laughing. Wait, I think I was going to do that anyway. I had propped myself against the siding and was trying to contain the loud, hiccupping guffaws. "So, you think my sister-in-law, the shorthand cook, loving wife, and mother, is a *werewolf*?"

Somehow he managed to say with a straight face, "I think it's possible that John Teague was a werewolf and that somehow, when he attacked Mo, he changed her."

And now I was back to laughing. "That is the dumbest thing I have ever heard!"

"Why? There are shape-shifting legends found in almost every civilization. The Central Asian stories about snakes that could assume human form and the Japanese *kitsune*, fox spirits that were able to become beautiful women. When you go westward, you find the Wendigo, the Deer Woman, skinwalkers—"

"What does this have to do my with my sister-in-law supposedly wolfing out and terrorizing the townsfolk?"

"Why won't Mo talk to me about the attack, Maggie?"

My laughter died as if he'd flipped a switch. From what I understood, Mo had been closing up the saloon last year, alone, and John Teague decided she was a prime target for robbery and possibly way more disturbing activities. He'd knocked her around when she wouldn't cooperate, leaving her with bruises and scrapes across her face. She'd managed to get a few good licks in before my brother swooped in on four paws and saved the day. Mo didn't connect human-shaped Cooper to the wolf at the time and thought maybe her furry savior had eaten Teague. However, Teague had managed to make it to his truck, then passed out from his injuries and died in a fiery crash outside town.

"She won't talk to you about it because she won't talk to *anyone* about it," I growled. "Do you realize that most people in Grundy don't even know about that night? Mo didn't want a big fuss, the questions, the pitying looks. She just wanted to go on with her life. And then you come along with your questions, stirring everything up again. You're surprised she's not just hopping up and down to give you the full Barbara Walters treatment?"

For a moment, a flash of shame flickered across Nick's face. "I didn't realize. She seems so sturdy, you know? No-nonsense. I just . . . That doesn't change what happened after the Teague incident. It doesn't explain why she was so close to every wolf attack that followed."

"Shit happens!" I exclaimed. "We live in the middle of one of the biggest untamed wildernesses left on earth. We're bound to run into animals every once in a while. Sometimes there are no explanations! No matter how hard you try to force it to fit one of your bullshit theories, there's just no explanation."

"There's always an explanation," he countered, color rising into his cheeks as he stepped closer. I could hear his heart beat in his chest, practically hear the blood humming through his veins as we stood nose-to-nose. "Sometimes you have to sift through a couple of 'bullshit theories' before you find the right one, but eventually something clicks. If you would just explain to Mo that I don't mean any harm. If anything, I want to help her."

"Who says she needs help?"

"Well, then, why are you being so difficult?"

"Because it's fun!" I shot back.

Nick tilted his head back and groaned in frustration.

"Maggie, are you driving another guy over the edge?" Samson asked from behind me.

I looked over to find Samson and Clay smirking at us. Well, Samson was smirking. Clay seemed to be glaring a little bit. Nick turned and made a motion to introduce himself to Samson, but I cut him off.

"Dr. Thatcher was just leaving," I told them.

Samson's face hardened at the mention of his name, and Nick, wisely, drew his hand back. Samson muttered, "Good."

Apparently, Cooper had filled Samson in.

"Clay, why don't you go inside?" I said. "Mom's just setting the table. You, too, Samson."

Clay moved past me, his hand squeezing mine, and warm little tingles sizzled up my arm. He shot Nick a curious look before walking through the door. Moving after Clay, Samson didn't break eye contact with Nick, who couldn't seem to understand the sudden shift in demeanor. It would have been far more impressive if Samson hadn't nearly walked into the doorjamb headlong.

"So, that guy in there, Clay," he said, jerking his head toward the door. "Are you dating him?"

"Yes, he is my possessive, recently paroled fiancé."

His lips quirked. "So . . . no?"

"None of your business!" I yelled. "How did we

go from 'Your sister-in-law's a werewolf' to 'Are you seeing anyone?' Can't you just have one conversation at a time, like a normal person?"

He shook his head and gave me another beautiful, irritating smile. "I'll call you in a few days, to see if you change your mind about the guide thing."

"I won't change my mind, because you are clearly insane."

"I'll call you then," he said, shrugging as he hopped into his truck. "And ask you out on a proper date. Your mom gave me your number."

"Well, I won't answer!" I called as he turned the ignition and waved before speeding off. I huffed out a breath. "How did that happen?"

4

Of Mistaken Identities and Wounded Ass Cheeks

Cooper didn't look happy when he answered his door—probably because I was beating on it. A lot.

"If you wake up the baby, I will smack you down like the hand of God," he growled as I moved past him, deliberately shoulder-checking him.

I was in a foul mood. Despite his easy promise that he would, Nick had not called. It had been two days, and not a peep. I can't say I was sitting by the phone staring it down, but there were a few times I ran across the room to grab for it when it did ring. I also might have unplugged and replugged it a few times to make sure it was working, but I will never admit that to a living soul.

This was unacceptable. I was Maggie Fucking Graham. I did not get wound up over some man. Yet here I was, twitching and pacing across my brother's living room, with no idea what stupid excuse I would make for coming over beyond "I'm confused, and I want to hit something."

Fortunately, the tension breaker I needed came in the form of Mo stumbling into the room wearing what looked like a sports bra, one of Cooper's flannel shirts, and some basketball shorts. Her hair was pulled into one of those weird shih tzu puffs on top of her head. She blinked at me blearily. "What's going on?"

I recoiled. "Gah! Is that outfit what you're doing for birth control now?"

"Shut up," she grumbled, pulling the ponytail out and fluffing her hair.

"Yes, because the ponytail was the problem." I snorted. She punched my arm and yawned. I chuffed and shoved her back.

"So, what brings you to our door at this time of night, besides insulting me?" she asked, handing me one of the many bathrobes she kept on hand for when I dropped over on a run. She had this thing about not wanting naked people on her upholstery. Prude.

Clothing can make life awkward for werewolves, for whom the most comfortable state is to be in wolf form. In an environment where we're relaxed, sometimes we don't even realize we've changed. There's a shift of light, and suddenly there's a full-grown wolf standing next to you. It's difficult to change form while dressed. At the same time, adult werewolves become conditioned to associate clothing with being out in public among humans. It becomes less of an issue for us as the weather gets colder, but for southern packs, clothing is handy as a reminder to stay on two feet.

You would think it would be weird to see your male relatives running around naked all the time, but really, you stop noticing. It's sort of sad, really. You've seen one penis, you've seen them all.

I had to stop saying that in front of my mother, because she said it was something a hooker would put on a business card.

Cooper flopped down on the couch, throwing his arm over his eyes. Mo slumped next to him and buried her face in his shoulder. There was a fond little twitch to his lips as he nuzzled his nose along her brow line.

Gag me.

"It's seven-thirty!" I exclaimed.

"Maggie, as much as I appreciate your dropping by to call us lame, please get to the point," he muttered. "Keeping in mind that if you raise your voice above a whisper—" He stopped and gave a jaw-cracking yawn while waving his right palm at me. "Hand of God."

"Yeah, yeah," I muttered, showing my big brother exactly how much he intimidated me. "I thought you should know that Nick doesn't think you're a werewolf."

Cooper sat up, his brow furrowed. "But that's a good thing, right? Problem solved, you can go home now."

"He thinks *Mo* is a werewolf," I said, biting my lip and waiting for the reaction that would, indeed, wake up my niece.

Cooper locked eyes with me, looked over at his wife, grinned at me again, and then laughed so hard he nearly toppled off the couch.

"Bwahahahaahaha!" Cooper guffawed. "He thinks . . . he thinks . . . *Mo*?"

Mo threw up her hands. "I don't see why it's *that* funny!"

Mo's indignant hiss was just what I needed to double over laughing. "Grr!" I gave a exaggerated fake growl. "I'm Mo, fierce predator. I could catch you if my designer thong wasn't riding up!"

Cooper laughed. "Or how about, 'I'm Mo, the baking werewolf. I'll stuff you so full of chess squares you won't be able to run away!"

"Are you done?" Mo asked in a dead, flat voice.

Cooper sucked in a breath. "Sorry, baby, it's the sleep deprivation. It's getting to me." His face flushed as he spluttered. "Nope, I have one more." Mo scowled at him. He bit his lip, suppressing a snicker. "I'm done."

She scowled. "Can we get back to why Nick thinks I'm a wolf, please?"

I wiped at my eyes while she stared daggers at both of us. "Whew. Sorry, I have to catch my breath. He, ahem, he thinks John Teague turned you into a werewolf and then you were on some sort of Wolfman rampage across the countryside," I said, rubbing the ache in my side.

"And what stopped my rampage, exactly?" she asked dryly.

"Oh, Cooper," I said, a giggle escaping my tightly pressed lips. "He saved you from yourself. And we, your loving human in-laws, are helping you suppress your homicidal urges."

"Well, that's awfully nice of us," Cooper said blandly.

"Actually, we can use this," Mo said, sitting up, getting that "I've got a project" expression that always scared the hell out of me. "I'll just start eating raw meat, standing out in the street, howling at the moon. It will totally throw him off."

"Yeah, and then we'll go into Susie's attic, rattle some chains, and make him think the house is haunted," I said, rolling my eyes.

"Susie Quinn's place?" Cooper asked.

"Yeah, he's renting it."

Mo frowned. "That's sort of ghoulish. Besides, how would we even get into Susie's attic?"

"You know, I hadn't considered that. I got sort of hung up on the fact that this means he's going to be here for a while. Which is bad."

"Well, it's not good," Cooper said, scratching his bare stomach and shuffling into the kitchen. "I'm getting something to eat. Mags, pecan pie?"

"I'm insulted you have to ask," I told him as he unloaded one of Mo's calorie-laden pie plates from the fridge. He cut two huge slabs and brought one to me.

Mo eyed the pie with longing, obviously thinking of the postbaby weight she was still shedding. "I hate you and your damned werewolf metabolism."

Cooper offered his wife a little bite of pie, which was quite a concession for a wolf. We generally don't share food if we can help it. She took a tiny bird-like nibble, which we all knew wouldn't satisfy her. But the gesture on Cooper's part was the important thing.

As was his habit, Cooper asked about Mom, Samson, Pops, the cranky aunties in the bridge club, and the kids who kept dipping tobacco behind the school. I told him that I'd solved the underage "chaw" problem the same way Pops had when he caught Cooper and Samson dipping when they were twelve. I let our young cousins Ricky and Benjamin finish off the can of Red Man they'd swiped from my uncle Steve, indulging until they were an unpleasant avocado color and finally upchucking violently while they paid Steve back for the stolen can.

"They'll never dip again. Trust me." Cooper shuddered. "And how's Aunt Billie doing?"

The teasing smile evaporated from my face. "Good days and bad. Alicia says she'll be lucid one minute and then freaking out the next. Or she just sits in a chair staring into nothing. I always seem to stop by when she's having a bad spell, and sometimes I find myself trying to find reasons not to go over, which, of course, makes me feel even worse for taking advantage of Alicia and Clay."

"You've got a lot on your plate," Cooper told me, squeezing my shoulder. "And I know your ego and your God-given stubbornness make you think you can do it all. But it's natural to want to try to find ways to lessen the load. Billie's family, and you're going to do right by her no matter what. Don't feel guilty for letting Alicia and Clay shoulder some of the burden. They're her family, too. You're no good to anybody if you're worn down to nothing."

"I know," I admitted softly, picking at the pie.

"I would say I'm proud of how you're handling yourself as alpha, but I'm pretty sure you'd sock me one for being a sissy," he said, nudging my arm.

I nodded but nudged him back.

"Speaking of Clay, how are you two doing?" Cooper asked, trying and failing to seem nonchalant.

"We're fine," I said, my brow crinkled. "Why?"

"Because Lee dropped by yesterday. With a moose carcass," he added, chuckling nastily. "I just thought maybe Clay should be told about his competition."

I groaned, which made Cooper that much happier.

Big, brawny, and without discernible brain function, Lee Whitaker was my uncle Frank's brother-in-law's son, raised in a pack eighty miles west of the valley. He'd been thrown in my face as a potential mate since I was, oh . . . born.

We went out on two measly dates, one of which was dinner at his mother's house. And Lee seemed to think our getting married was already sewn up. He tried to monopolize my time at any and all gatherings between our packs. I once spent an entire Memorial Day pretending to have pinkeye just to keep him away.

Lee had good intentions but was dumb as a post. He also had some strange ideas about what he would be "entitled" to as my husband. He seemed to think I would be just handing the reins of my pack over to him, that I was just waiting for a big, strong man like him to sweep me off my feet so I never had to worry my little head with decisions like what to eat for breakfast or whether to go outside.

Clearly, he had never paid attention when I spoke.

If he hadn't been Uncle Frank's favorite nephew, I would have just beaten the hell out of him and sent him on his way. But Uncle Frank, my dad's brother, had always been "sensitive" about his position in the pack. He resented the fact that Cooper had assumed the alpha role so young and felt that he hadn't been given a fair shot. Which was sort of ridiculous, because he wasn't even in the running. He protested— loudly—when Eli took over Cooper's leadership role and became an all-around pain in Eli's ass. Believing that I would one day marry Lee and give him some sort of power base within the pack had kept him quiet under my leadership. So, I put up with Lee and his blithe advances and contented myself with giving him minor injuries whenever he tried to touch me.

"I've meant to ask, is there a significance to the moose carcass?" Mo asked. "Beyond 'ew'?"

"Lee is officially opening negotiations for Maggie's paw," Cooper said, his eyes glinting gleefully.

I huffed, gritting my teeth. "That's so insulting, and just like him. He shouldn't be coming to you to negotiate for my hand. He should be coming to *me*. I'm your alpha, not the other way around. Not to mention the fact that he's a big pain in my ass, and I will never, ever . . . ever, marry him."

"Not even if he was the last fertile werewolf on earth?" Cooper prodded.

I growled. "He would have to be the very last," I muttered. "And I would look into artificial insemination."

Cooper nearly choked on his pie, trying to contain his laughter.

"I'm glad you're enjoying yourself," I barked.

"I really am," Cooper said. "Just so you know, I told him that if he wanted to marry you, he was going to have to talk to you about it. He just shrugged and said he'd get around to it."

"Well, this was completely unhelpful. I'm leaving now," I told them. "Enjoy the many, many hours left in the evening, none of which you will spend sleeping. And I don't mean that in the fun way."

"That was mean," Cooper told me. I blew him a raspberry and waved good-bye to Mo. As I walked out, I made like I was going to shut the door quietly, then slammed it at the last minute. I counted to three and waited for the baby to wail.

Just before I phased, I heard Mo mutter through the door, "If we'd moved to Australia when I suggested it, this wouldn't be a problem."

THE NEXT DAY, Nick still hadn't called. I'd gone from making excuses for him to sitting at my desk, enjoying imagined scenarios where he might have been digested by a bear.

I ran past Susie Quinn's place on my way home from Cooper and Mo's . . . just because it was on my way. Seeing the warm, homey light shining through the windows, I'd paused. I'd sat on my haunches at the edge of the tree line. And I'd felt like a creepy stalker. But through that disquieting interest, I'd felt better, settled, to be sitting there, knowing he was inside, safe and well. When Cooper and I had started talking again the year before, he'd described his compulsive habit of running past Mo's house while he was wolfed out, feeling at peace for the first time since he'd left the valley. He said it was like the primal part of his brain was leading him there every night, just to be near her. He'd been torn up for years over leaving home, and with Mo, he was given a little glimpse of tranquillity. And when they stopped being idiots and admitted that they were crazy for each other, that contentment had become part of his everyday life.

After watching Nick's house, I'd woken up and felt calm, warm. I usually woke up thinking of all the things I had to get done, my mind racing and raring to get started. But the moment my eyes had popped open, I felt . . . light, I guess. I stretched under the covers and smiled into my pillow, reveling in the feeling of serenity washing over me.

Crap.

I forced myself to jump out of bed, to go through my normal routines. I kept trying to recapture my normal patterns and feelings. I knew it sounded like one of Mo's lame pop-psychology rants, but in the absence of that anxiety, I was a little depressed. I'd never realized how much pressure I put on myself. The idea that Nick was somehow a solution to a problem that I didn't know I had was upsetting.

My mental self-torture was interrupted when my cousin Will stuck his grizzled brown head through my office door. Will was one of my gruffer cousins, quick with the sarcasm and quicker to attack if a packmate was threatened. He'd married Angie, a wry, blond female from a Seattle-area pack, and produced two towheaded little boys, the only wolf boys to be born to our pack in the last five years.

"Hey, Maggie," Will said, tossing me a Baggie of Angie's famous oatmeal-raisin cookies. I opened the bag and inhaled the heavenly, spicy fragrance before shoving one into my mouth. Angie was known to shove dozens of cookies into Will's coat pockets before he left for the day. If he hadn't married her, he probably would have had to fight Samson and half the valley's male population for her, just for the potential cookie privileges.

"I was just running along the east border, and there's a hiker up there. Seems harmless enough, but I thought you'd want to know."

"Blond?" I asked, frowning. I held my hand far over my head. "Yea tall? Looks like a hot, annoying Viking?"

"I don't know how to respond to that," Will said, shaking his head, taking a cookie for himself. "Not without you making fun of me later. But yeah, I think that would cover it."

I snorted. "Did he see you?"

"Nah, I was being all stealthy-like," he said, grinning. "I'm like a ninja with fur. Quiet, quick, and a mind like a steel trap." He tapped his temple and winked at me.

"Yes, steel traps are scary and dangerous, too," I muttered.

He laughed, and I told him to go on home. I shed my clothes, phased, and ran toward the east border. I might not have been as big as Samson or as strong as Cooper, but no one in the pack could match me for speed. Still, I kept my pace even, light. I didn't want Nick to hear me coming.

What did he think he was doing? Forget the all-out rudeness of coming to my valley—again—without so much as stopping in town to let us know he was tromping around in our backyard. He was supposed to be touring the eastern Wheeler range. What was Nick looking for? He thought Mo was the wolf, so what was he doing up there instead of in Grundy?

Werewolves in the movies always had some convenient crypt or basement where they locked themselves up during the change. Did he think we had some bunker carved out for Mo in the woods somewhere? Did her family think we spent three nights a month tossing her rabbit carcasses and hoping for the best? The more I thought about it, the more his whole "Mo as a werewolf" scenario insulted me. Nothing about Mo screamed predatory or even vaguely threatening, unless you cut her off from chocolate. I was the tough one. I was the one who could take care of myself. I'd spent most of my life defining myself by those qualities. Why didn't he see them in me?

This level of introspection could not be healthy. This was why I avoided self-help books.

I found him sitting on a rock, overlooking the valley. There was a backpack beside him on the ground, and he had a big coil of neon orange rope attached to it, with some carabiners and a few climbing blocks. He'd said he was a climber; was he planning on rappelling down the rock wall? That seemed like a rude thing to do in someone's backyard without permission.

At the moment, he seemed content to sit. He could see everything from this spot, the green expanse of the valley walls, the thick forest that sheltered us from the harsher winds coming down the mountain and provided the rich supply of game we needed to keep the pack fed. It was a spot Cooper often used for "thinking," a.k.a. "getting the hell away from Maggie and Samson for a few minutes of peace." I'd come here a few times, but I always got my best ideas while running.

And there sat Nick, scribbling in that notebook again with a silly grin on his face.

Under the shelter of low-hanging spruce, I sat on my haunches and watched him. I watched the light and the wind play against his hair. Damn it, the sight of his wire-rim glasses sliding down his nose was bringing out some sort of professor fetish that I didn't even know I had. My heart did this weird skittering thing, as if it was going to jump out of my chest and run away. I really needed to get this thing under control,

He turned suddenly and saw me.

The smartest thing to do would be to bolt, as a real wolf would do. But I just sat there frozen, staring at him. His face. There was such an expression of joy there, stretching his smile from ear to ear. I wasn't one to throw around pretentious phrases like "child-like wonder," but it was the only way to describe his face. Moving with slow, deliberate steps, he hunched down and stretched his hand out toward me.

Innocent wonder or no, if he tried to scratch behind my ears, I was so going to bite him.

"Mo?" he whispered, smiling down at me. "Is that you?"

I huffed and stepped back. He retracted the hand.

"Wait!" he called as I backed into the tree line. "Mo?"

Mo? He looked at me that way, left me hanging for days on end, and now he thought I was *Mo?* I growled, the low, threatening sound resonating deep in my chest. This was beyond messed up. He flirted with me in human form and had a weird little were-wolf crush on my sister-in-law.

Wasn't this a story line in one of those lame-ass teen-vampire movies?

I was the one who'd spent weeks doing a sad little avoidance shuffle around him. And he was thinking of Mo? Not happening.

I cantered back over to him, huffing at him to get his attention. We locked eyes, and I did my best to glare at him, which is difficult to do without eyebrows. He narrowed his gaze. "You're not Mo, are you?"

Too damn right, I wasn't. I huffed again and pivoted in the opposite direction, to make him think I was leaving. Then I feinted left. Nick only had a second to turn before I lunged, sinking my teeth into his nicely rounded butt cheek.

"Yipe!" he cried, clutching at his ass. "What the? Hey! Come back here!" He hobbled after me, wincing in pain.

I made a sort of whickering sound, spitting out a chunk of the denim from his jeans. He gaped down at me. I sniffed, stuck my nose in the air, and trotted home, feeling a lot better about the situation.

THE FARTHER I got from Nick, the more that heavy guilty feeling crept into my chest. I wasn't used to feeling remorse. It sort of sucked. Maybe I should go back and check on him. I slipped back into my jeans and sweater inside my office. I would just amble up there and pretend I was taking a long walk around the valley. I'd just make sure he made it to his truck OK and then come right back. I slipped on my boots and was bounding out of my office to do just that when I heard a sly voice to my left.

"Maggie, Maggie, Maggie."

I cringed.

There stood the pretender to my throne, all overdone muscle and wavy black hair. If Nick was my Aragorn, Lee was Lando Calrissian: handsome, confident, and about as trustworthy as a used-snowmobile salesman.

Lee quirked his full lips as he struck a casual pose against the wall of the community center. I was thankful that my body seemed as annoyed by Lee as the rest of me, and whatever hormones had been surging through my blood had now retreated like low tide. Clearly, despite the many lures of Lee's exterior, my primal brain had some taste.

"Maggie, Maggie, Maggie," Lee said again, because he was incapable of saying my name just once. He winked down at me with his wide brown eyes. And once again, I cursed Cooper and Samson for getting all the height in the family.

"Lee." I acknowledged him, my voice as flat as Aunt Winnie's ass.

"I had an interesting conversation with your brother the other day."

I bared my teeth, making him take the slightest step back. "I heard about that."

"So, Cooper told you we settled things?"

"You didn't settle anything. Because Cooper isn't going to arrange my marriage. I'm afraid you're going to have to deal with me."

He shrugged, and his voice dropped to this weird cross between seductive and condescending, as if he was trying to lure me into his van with candy. "I was just following the rules, Maggie. Cooper is the rightful alpha and the oldest male member of your family."

"Do you really think that's the tack you should take with me?" I demanded.

"Look, baby, when we're married and you've grown up a little, you'll see how silly you're being." When I stared at him, shocked speechless for once, he added, "Uncle Frank says you've had a human hanging around."

"And?" I asked, wondering how Uncle Frank had heard about my interest in Nick and how many other pack members were talking about it.

"Well, I don't know how I feel about my girl

spending time with a human," he said, stepping close enough that he could almost run the tip of his nose down the side of my face. I resisted the urge to shrink away. "You never get that smell out of your clothes."

"What I do is none of your business, Lee."

"I'll never understand why so many of our females are letting humans sniff around them," he continued, as if I hadn't even spoken. "I mean, why dilute the blood? Just look at your brother's little girl. She could have been the pride of the pack. And now what's that pup good for?" He sniffed dismissively. "She's not even breeding stock. She'll live a quiet little life as some human's wife, and no one will care. What a waste."

I tried hard to remember that from Lee's perspective, he wasn't saying anything offensive. His pack was a little more "conservative" than mine. He was repeating the opinions he'd heard his whole life. And he just wasn't bright enough to keep them to himself.

But I guess the way I was gritting my teeth gave me away, and Lee said, "Oh, don't pretend that you and Cooper are back to being attached at the hip. I remember how you talked about him after he ran off. You can't say you're any prouder now that he's a coward *and* a dead-breeder."

I scowled at his use of a rarely spoken epithet for a dead-liner's parent. I bunched my hand into a fist and had it half raised when Clay stuck his head through his front door.

He saw the fist and the pissed-off, uncomfortable

look on my face and frowned. "Mags, you all right?"

I lifted an eyebrow. Enter Clark Kent or, at least, Val Kilmer as Batman. My packmates rarely asked me if I was OK, particularly the males. They usually assumed I was fine, as long as I wasn't griping at them or hitting them in some way. But somehow Clay had managed to ask without making it sound patronizing, as if he was about to swoop in and rescue me. And it was sort of nice. The decency of the gesture made me feel a genuine rush of affection for him. "I'm fine, Clay. Thanks."

This was a completely inappropriate time to be thinking about nibbling on Clay's earlobes.

"More competition, Maggie?" Lee asked, giving Clay a long appraising look before dismissing him with a sniff.

I gave Lee a dead-eyed stare. "Clay is a member of our pack."

Lee shot a scathing glare at Clay. My lips quirked into a twisted smile. Lee was all swagger and smirks until he realized he was on an even playing field.

"He doesn't have the close family ties that I do."

"Which some people would consider a good thing," I muttered.

Clay stepped out of the house and took none-too-subtle steps toward us, positioning himself at my side. Despite the comfort of his presence at my elbow, I wanted to tell him not to bother. Lee was all lazy, no action. In the years I'd known him, he'd never once been in a real fight. He backed off the moment he realized he might have to make an effort to cover his own ass. But he wouldn't hesitate to, say, attack a lone human wandering around our valley in some misguided attempt to prove himself to me. There was no way I could go check on Nick now. My chest sort of ached at the thought, and I rubbed my hand against my sternum absentmindedly.

"Maggie and I go way back," Lee told him. "*Way* back. We'll be married and mated any day now."

Clay arched his eyebrows and smiled at me. I shook my head. Clay snickered.

"She tries to deny our love." Lee trailed a finger along my cheek. "Makes her feel like she's playing hard to get."

Clay growled. I barely resisted the urge to clamp my teeth down on Lee's offending digit, but I put a restraining hand on Clay's arm. As much as I appreciated it, it would hardly do to have him "sticking up" for me. It would make me look weak, and that was exactly the sort of thing that got around to other packs.

"Ah-ah-ah, Lee, we've talked about this," I said, clucking my tongue. "Anything that touches, I get to keep."

But as I said, Lee was none too bright, and he seemed to like the idea of staking his claim in front of Clay. He kept rubbing his freaking hands along my cheek. So I wrapped my fingers around his, yanked his hand palm up, and jerked his arm. He yowled and dropped to his knees. I smacked him on the back of the head for good measure.

The arm would heal, probably by tomorrow morning. But it would keep him from phasing until then, keep him from snooping around the valley and stumbling onto unsuspecting humans who had probably made it to their trucks by now.

I walked away, hooking my arm through an astonished Clay's as we walked into his house. I wanted to visit Billie before we headed home for dinner.

"Good talking to you, Lee," I called over my shoulder.

His voice was hoarse as he choked out, "You, too, Maggie."

5

Humble Pie a la Mo

THE NEXT DAY WAS Saturday, which meant a long run, in human form, for me. Sure, it was easier and more fun to run as a wolf, but I liked the challenge that came with running on two feet. Plus, it was really difficult to keep an iPod clipped to fur.

I had a hard-packed dirt path worn up to the north point of the valley, beside the river, through a dense thicket of pine trees. It was rare that anyone joined me on my Saturday runs. As much as I loved running with my pack, I liked that it was just me, the wind, and the scent of pine. Every girl needs a little time to herself to hash things out in her head, even if my problems were a little more complicated than "Which dress should I wear tonight?" or "I need something waxed."

Waxing was sort of a moot point for me.

I was reaching the hardest part of the incline

up the valley wall, when a strange presence in the woods stopped me in my tracks. I lifted my face to the wind and waited, fighting the instinct to phase, just in case it was Nick again. I scanned the trees. This didn't smell like Nick. It smelled like . . . nothing. It was like an olfactory blank space. The little hairs on my arms and neck rose as I felt the scrutiny intensify, as if whoever it was was trying to decide what to do. I stood my ground, waiting.

Eventually, the presence faded away, and I shook off the feeling. It was just before noon when I jogged up the steps to find my mother standing at the door with the cordless phone.

"It's for you, hon," she said, kissing the top of my sweaty head. "It's your brother. He doesn't sound happy. I'm making waffles for when he's done yelling at you."

I groaned, stretching my aching legs and pressing the phone to my ear.

"Would you like to explain to me why Nick Thatcher showed up at the Grundy clinic last night with a bite wound on his ass?" my brother demanded without bothering to say hello.

Shit. I'd forgotten about Nick. After the Lee incident, Billie had had another spell, in which she claimed strangers were breaking into her house every night and moving things around. I ended up spending the night with her while Dr. Moder monitored her at the clinic. If nothing else, it helped give Alicia some rest. Dr. Moder had forced me to leave at around four A.M. I crashed and completely blanked out Nick's mangled butt cheek.

"I was provoked." Cooper was silent on the other end of the line, so I continued, "He saw me, and he thought I was Mo. He was looking at me like I was Christmas morning, and then he called me by Mo's name. Mo would have done the same thing."

Cooper didn't dignify that with a response. "You're lucky he's telling everybody around here that he had a run-in with a stray dog. I don't know why, but he doesn't seem to want to make a fuss. If he had been anyone else, he would have called the *Weekly World News* as soon as his butt cheek got stitched up."

"Stray dog?" I spat. "Stray dog!"

"Maggie, you were the one who said we should stay away from Nick. And then you not only let him see you in wolf form, but you bit him? What were you thinking? *Were* you thinking? You could have seriously hurt him."

"By biting his ass?"

"Mo says there are lots of important nerves and stuff back there. She was laughing too hard to get a lot of information across. I'm serious, Mags. I'm not cleaning up this mess, you got it? You're always going on about you being the alpha. Great, you're the alpha. *You* take care of this." He slammed the phone down.

I yanked the receiver away from my ear, wincing. My dramatic eye roll was interrupted by a knock at the door. "What now?"

I opened the door to find Mo, holding one of her sinful brownie cheesecake pies. Two of my favorite desserts combined in a chocolate graham-cracker crust.

"Are you guys guilt-stalking me?" I huffed, closing the door behind me so my mother wouldn't overhear. Mo, used to this sort of response from me, only smirked and stepped out of my way. "I told Cooper biting Nick was a mistake."

Mo's coal-black eyebrows winged up. "So that *was* you. Nice, Maggie. Excellent job keeping a low profile."

I growled at her. "So, you drove all this way, bearing pie, to make sure Cooper's lecture sank in?"

"Cooper doesn't know I'm here. I'm on the clock." She pressed the pie into my hands and then pulled a note out of her jacket pocket. "Nick called the saloon last night—thoroughly hopped up on pain meds, I might add—and begged Evie to arrange for your favorite food to be delivered to you ASAP. Offered her an obscene amount of money and then rambled on about you being 'Uhura pretty' and how you were ignoring his calls and he had to find some way to get through to you. I guess he knew the way to that teeny-tiny Grinch heart of yours is through your stomach."

"Uhura pretty?" I repeated.

Mo shook her head, exasperated. "I gave up trying to understand men around here a long time ago. Are you going to read his note or not?"

Bobbling the heavy pie tin, I opened the little white envelope. I read Evie's neat block print aloud. "Thinking of you, Nick. P.S. I think you may need to check your voice mail. It's full."

I frowned. Voice mail? I hadn't looked at my cell phone in days. Not since I drove to the Glacier.

Aw, hell.

As usual, I'd left the phone in my truck. I only used it when I was driving, and I tended to forget about it otherwise. I plopped the pie into Mo's hands and ran to retrieve my dead phone. Mom was hugging Mo while I bolted back to my room to connect it to the charger on my dresser. I had five missed calls. And three voice-mail messages. All starting the day before, from a weird area code that could only be Nick's.

"Hey, Mom, when Nick asked for my number, which one did you give him?" I called, not really wanting her to answer.

"Your cell phone," Mom called back. "I thought you'd probably want any messages he left you to be private."

I heard Mo give a soft snicker.

Well, now I felt horrible. I'd marred perfectly good ass cheeks for no reason. It was as if I'd sneezed on the *Mona Lisa.*

Mo was sitting at the kitchen table, drinking tea, while my mother mixed more waffle batter. "Mom, I'm going to need those waffles to go. I'm driving to Grundy."

"Driving?" Mom asked, cracking a half-dozen eggs into her mixing bowl. "Today's your running day."

"I owe Dr. Thatcher an apology . . . or something."

Mo hid her smirk behind her teacup, and Mom's gaze narrowed. "For what?"

I took a precautionary step back. "It was just a

misunderstanding, Mom. I might have hurt his, uh, pride a little bit."

"Just his pride?" Mom asked pointedly.

I smiled innocently and dashed for the shower.

"You know, you're going to have to get better at lying if you're going to survive as a public servant," Mom called after me.

THE DRIVE TO Grundy was spent coming up with really awkward apologies for biting Nick on the ass. And then I remembered that Nick didn't know I was the one who bit him on the ass and that saying so would tip him off to the whole "world of werewolves" thing. Maybe I could just continue to let him think Mo bit him on the ass. That wouldn't make things awkward.

The smart thing would be to send a detached, polite thank-you note for the pie or ignore him completely. But I felt this new, unpleasant gnawing sensation in my chest. I actually cared about what Nick thought of me. I worried about him thinking badly of me. I felt guilty for hurting him, not just little pangs of regret but full-on spasms of "why did I do that?"

I was maturing emotionally. *Ew*.

OK, pie. I'd stick with the pie. He'd taken the time to order me pie while he was laid up on a doughnut pillow. That he'd send me something edible was oddly touching. Courtship in this part of the country rarely centered on flowers and perfume. Nick had made an effort, and he'd put some thought into it. And that was doing strange things to my ability to produce coherent thoughts. By the time I pulled my truck into Nick's driveway, I'd come up with "Thanks for the pie."

Brilliant, I know. I was considering a career in speechwriting if this whole werewolf-leadership thing didn't work out.

I forced myself out of the truck and considered Susie's former home. "Susie Q" was the town's former postmaster and the first victim of Eli's weird string of attacks. I'd like to think that she was just a victim of opportunity, that Eli had stumbled across her as she was letting her ridiculous little wiener dog, Oscar, out to pee. Because the possibility that he spent time stalking a harmless, though eccentric, middle-aged country music fan was plain icky.

Susie saw the world through Dolly Parton–colored glasses, you might say. Platinum blond and blessed with more boobs than sense, Susie wore tight western shirts and jeans that looked painted on. But when it came to running the post office, she'd been all business, save for the fact that she kept Oscar in the mailroom for company.

Mo took Oscar in after Susie moved in with her daughter to recover from her injuries. When Susie's daughter claimed to be asthmatic and allergic, Mo kept him. As a rule, werewolves don't keep dogs. There are food-competition issues. However, Cooper considered it a mission of mercy. Susie was awfully fond of doggie sweaters.

Shaken from my reminiscing by the sound of a TV clicking on inside the house, I raised my hand to knock. But I lost my nerve, turning on my heel and preparing to dash for the truck. I'd taken a step when I heard the door open behind me.

Double damn it.

"Maggie?"

Nick was looking all cute and rumpled, wearing sweats and a Tribhuvan University T-shirt. His hair was mussed, and he was limping a little, but he didn't look too bad.

"Hi," I said hesitantly. "I just wanted to say thanks for the pie. That was very thoughtful. And I didn't get your calls. I left my phone in my truck a few days ago, and the battery died. I hardly ever use it; I don't know why Mom gave you that number. Well, uh, see ya."

"Wait," he said, wincing as he stepped toward me. "Uh, if I'd started calling sooner, I might have gotten you before the battery died. I actually hiked by the valley to try to work up the nerve to try to talk to you, when this happened."

"Why did you wait so long?" I asked, trying to keep the demanding tone at bay.

"Holding on to some scrap of my male pride?"

"Says the man holding a special sittin' pillow," I noted.

"It's a small scrap," he said, leading me into the house. The hitch in his stride needled at me. Watching him struggle down the hall, I wondered how he'd made it back to his truck from the valley. And I felt a cold flush of guilt and fear spread through me, thinking of what might have happened to him if he hadn't been able to get to the truck. The image of him sprawled on the dirt, defenseless, unable to get to help, tore a hole through my chest, leaving me swaying dizzily against the wall. I took a deep breath, and Nick heard the huffing sound. He turned, his brow furrowed.

"Hey, are you all right?" he asked, closing his fingers around my bicep, the warmth of his hand seeping through my sleeve. "Your face just went really pale."

I let a long breath stream out of my nostrils, marveling at the electric tingles traveling from his hand to my arm, easing the ache in my chest. I gave him a shaky smile. "I'm fine," I promised him, looking up and gaping at my surroundings. "I'm just allergic to suede and rhinestones."

Susie's house looked as if she'd decorated from Roy Rogers's garage sale. The sofa was covered in denim-colored suede and had Bedazzled pillows made of red bandanas. There were posters for old country-western acts such as Hank Williams Sr. and Patsy Cline on the walls. There was even a longhorn skull over the mantle, where most of us would put a moose head or a particularly impressive fish.

The only sign of Nick's presence was a pair of night-vision goggles on the wagon-wheel coffee table and a laptop on the kitchen table, surrounded by books piled in wobbly stacks. They made a nice holding pen for the random pages of loose-leaf paper strewn around, covered in Nick's neat block lettering. There were little sketches in the margins, of wolves, of the moon in various stages. I laid my keys on the table and picked up one of the more complicated pictures, a pair of wide, heavily lashed eyes. I tore my gaze away from the little drawings and smirked at the cow skull. "I had no idea that you were such a huge country-western fan."

He shuddered. "I'm not, but apparently, Susie's daughter wanted to leave the house furnished for renters."

"Meaning she didn't want the cowboy look encroaching on her carefully decorated McMansion," I said, snorting. He shrugged. "Doesn't it make you feel a little weird, living in Susie's house while reading about her attack?"

"Not really. It keeps it more real for me, reminds me that I'm dealing with actual people. Susie seemed like a nice lady. She didn't deserve what happened to her." He was watching my face for signs of change, deception.

I gave him a placid smile. "Susie is a nice lady, and she's lucky to be alive. Abner Golightly, another nice person, wasn't so lucky."

He chewed his lip thoughtfully. "I know we've gotten off on a, well, bizarre foot here. I know you think I'm nuts. And I know that you're an unusual girl, so the usual dating tactics aren't going to work with you. So I'm going to lay all my cards on the table, since that's something you seem to respect. I like you. A lot. I like that you're contrary and know how to say what you think. And you're beautiful and strong and a little peculiar."

"Peculiar?"

"I love peculiar," he assured me, edging slightly closer, his voice husky. "Peculiar is sort of my thing."

Bolder now, he moved closer, bringing with him

that delicious scent of man and spice and woods. I watched his cobalt eyes come closer and closer to my face as he leaned toward me. His mouth was a hair's breadth away from my lips. I was torn between praying he would kiss me and hoping he wouldn't, so my life wouldn't get even more complicated. I whispered, "You're very confident, Dr. Thatcher."

"I'm faking most of it," he assured me as he leaned closer bit by bit.

Behind him, I saw Susie's less-than-plasma television showing a very young William Shatner romping with a green-skinned chick in a silver bikini. On the top of the entertainment center, I saw a DVD set labeled "Star Trek: The Complete Original Series." The man had driven thousands of miles away from civilization, and he'd brought his favorite DVDs. I couldn't decide if that was adorable or idiotic.

"Why am I not surprised?" I exclaimed. "You're a Trekkie."

Just call me Maggie Graham, Moment Ruiner.

Startled, Nick blushed as he pulled away and looked toward the screen. "I simply enjoy the aesthetics and storytelling involved. I don't take it to the creepy fan-boy level."

"Really?" I smirked at him. "How many conventions have you been to?"

"Three, but only because my college roommate dragged me . . ." he spluttered. "Fine, there was a fourth incident as well. But just because the guy who played Chekov was auctioning off one of his communicators for charity."

"Mmm-hmm."

"You know, even when you look past the great story lines and the compelling characters, the show is worth watching because it was groundbreaking. *Star Trek* was one of the first network shows to reflect America's emerging youth counterculture. At the time, television was a wasteland of picture-perfect nuclear families and white-hat-wearing cowboys. There were no flaws, no textures. It was one of the first shows to really examine class warfare, racial justice, sexual equality, the role of technology in society," he said, ticking the subjects off on his fingers as he got more and more flustered.

I cannot explain why the "professor" tone he used while passionately extolling the virtues of geek porn sent tingles to my special places. All I knew was that I was having a hard time staying on my side of the couch. So, instead, I feigned disinterest and snickered. "And it was the first network show to feature half-naked alien chicks dressed in aluminum-foil swimwear."

"OK, fine, now we're watching it." He nudged me down onto the couch and slowly lowered himself onto a special doughnut pillow. I sank into the soft cushions, watching as he manipulated the DVD system he'd obviously installed on top of Susie's TV. Susie was sweet but not exactly techno-savvy.

He clicked on some episode called "The City on the Edge of Forever," and the theme music started. From a little cooler he kept near the couch, he offered me a pack of Sour Patch Kids and a Coke. I wondered where to put my hands. Well, I knew where I wanted to put them, but I think that would probably be a felony if I did it without warning him first. I crossed my arms over my chest for safekeeping.

This was strangely pleasant. I'd never done DVDs as a dating activity. I didn't bring guys home. I didn't force them into awkward interactions with my mom or brothers. Because that could end badly. And bloodily.

I was hyperaware of Nick, the warmth from his body, the hints of his scent wafting toward me, luring me closer to him. His arm was stretched over the back of the couch as he struggled to find a comfortable position to sit. His fingers played with the ends of my hair as we watched Captain Kirk kick ass and make intergalactic booty calls. I found Spock oddly hot, though, considering my recent nerd-hag leanings, this wasn't surprising.

Still, three episodes later, I wondered aloud, "Why would anyone on the crew put on a red shirt? Honestly, it's like they're standing in front of their closet, and they're thinking, 'Yellow? Blue? Nah, today's a good day to die.'"

"Red shirts meant you were part of the operations crew, who spent most of their time in the engine room or on security duty, off-camera, so the audience didn't care much about them." Nick tilted the bowl of popcorn we were sharing toward me. "The writers needed a way to ramp up the violence without killing off characters people were fond of."

"Like on *The A-Team* or *G.I. Joe*." I nodded. "When the bad guys would shoot and shoot at the good guys but never seemed to hit anybody?"

Nick's face was a mockery of solemnity. He clutched my hands to his chest. "Marry me and have my babies."

My voice was a little shaky when I chucked a licorice rope at him and said, "In your dreams, Thatcher."

"Well, until humans start procreating like seahorses or penguins, you would be the designated egg bearer."

"You just can't help yourself, can you? You have to be the smartest person in the room."

"Doctor of zoology. It's what I do," he said as he popped a few more gummy candies into his mouth.

"Nerd."

"Oh, come on, you love it," he said. When I lifted my eyes to the ceiling and shook my head, he gently tucked his fingers under my chin and brought my face level with his. "You like that I'm smart. You like that I'm different from most of the guys you know. You even like the fact that I could be just a little bit crazy. Otherwise, you wouldn't be here."

My eyes narrowed at him. Damn it, he was right. But I wasn't about to admit that. It would give him too much power. So I gave him a speculative look. "You're a very direct nerd," I mused.

"I just want us to be on the same page," he said, leaning close to me.

Despite my saner, sensible half's screaming at me to back away, to get my horny wolf ass back to my truck, I stayed still, feeling more like prey than predator for the first time in my life. He was cautious in his approach, just barely brushing his lips over my own, the faintest whisper of flesh against flesh. I sighed, mingling my breath with his. His thumbs traced lightly over my cheekbones, down the line of my jaw. I wrapped my arms around his waist as he drew me closer, parting my lips with the tip of his tongue.

Boy and howdy. I felt warm from the toes up, like the first flash of heat that comes just before phasing. And I couldn't seem to keep my hands still. They kept moving over the small of Nick's back, holding him to me.

I was lost, and it felt nice. No worries. No responsibilities. Just warmth and peace and a pleasant coil of pressure building in my belly.

"Maggie," he whispered, and my heart thundered in my ears. When his fingertips grazed the hollow of my throat, I jumped, my own fingertips digging into the rear of Nick's sweats. I felt papery bandages crinkle underneath the cotton. Nick yelped. My eyes went wide. I remembered with a flush of guilt that I'd been the one to hurt him. As a wolf. While he was investigating us. And all of the reasons not to be anywhere near Nick came crashing down on me again.

Shit.

I gasped and scrambled back.

"What?" he asked. "It's not that bad. We can work around it."

"I've got to go," I said, leaping off of the couch and backing down the hall.

"Maggie, wait," he called as I stumbled out the front door. I got two steps to my truck before I realized I'd left my keys on Nick's table. I glanced back to the door, where Nick was limping into the frame.

"Oh, screw it," I grunted, and took off running down the driveway.

"Maggie!" he yelled, but I was already on the highway, sprinting toward home.

I was running at my top human speed, having put a couple of miles between Nick's driveway and my feet. A light rain had started to fall, misting over my damp cheeks. Running in my human shape felt right, as if I was bleeding poison from the ragged human wound in my chest with every step. I needed to go through this as a woman, not a wolf. Obviously, my more animal instincts weren't leading me in the right direction.

I couldn't put my whole pack—hell, my whole species—in jeopardy because a man happened to curl my toes and give me arm tingles.

My hair clung in damp ropes to my cheeks as my feet ate through the intense climb up the winding mountain road to the valley. It was late September, and the sharp bite of the air was leeching the warmth from my bones, leaving me shivering in my soaked jacket and jeans. The raindrops grew bigger, splashing into my eyes, making me wish for my hat. I would have phased and run the rest of the way, but these were my favorite boots, soggy as they were, and it was a bitch to keep replacing my clothes.

I had to find the positive. I needed this. I needed to feel foolish and humiliated and crazy. It was like cauterizing a wound. The next time I thought about throwing myself at Nick Thatcher, I would remember this feeling, and it would turn me off faster than Lee bragging about his nunchuck collection.

I doubted Nick would want to see me again for a while anyway, I told myself. He probably thought I was nuts. Normal girls didn't respond to delicious, earth-shattering kisses by running away down an Alaskan highway. Maybe I was nuts. This was like some episode of not-so-temporary insanity. Even if he was this decade's answer to Fox Mulder, I couldn't afford to throw myself at good-looking humans just because I got tingles in special places. I needed someone like Clay, someone who understood all the weird drama that came with being a wolf, who could help me continue the line. Nick needed . . .

I slowed my pace to what a human runner would consider jogging. Thinking of the kind of woman Nick needed and deserved put that hole back in my chest. I rubbed a hand over my aching breastbone, feeling suddenly out of breath. A man like Nick deserved a woman who was smart. A woman who would be nice to him, all the time, who would be pretty and soft and sweet. Who didn't wolf out and bite him on the ass.

I'd never had a crisis of self-esteem. I'd never minded not going to college. I'd never minded not having a skill set, as Mo did with her cooking. All I knew was the pack, and so far, it had worked out for me. Some people would find that depressing, limiting. But I thought it was a nice way of simplifying my life. And now it felt as if it might not be enough, and that was terrifying.

Behind me, I heard my truck's engine rumbling. *Shit.* I wiped at my eyes. Considering his butt-cheek injuries, I hadn't expected Nick to come after me. I'd expected to have to call Cooper to pick up my truck.

"Maggie, stop!" he yelled out of the driver's-side window. I slowed to a crawl, for me, and eyed him warily through the window.

I could just keep running. Hell, part of me wanted to phase right there and make tracks for Canada. But Grahams didn't shirk away from problems. We didn't run. Well, Cooper did, that once, for a few years. But he eventually came back.

None of this inner coaching was helping, as Nick was still staring at me through the rain.

"What are you doing?" he demanded.

"I'm fine!" I told him. "I'm halfway home. Just leave me alone."

"Are you crazy?" he yelled. "It's pouring. It's going to be dark soon. Get in the truck!"

I tipped my head back, blinking as I watched the dark clouds swirling overhead. The rain wouldn't be letting up anytime soon. And I didn't relish the idea of jogging all the way home with Nick trailing me at idling speed, yelling through my window.

"Damn it," I grumbled, stomping toward the truck. He leaned over and popped the passenger door open, wincing in discomfort.

"Oh, you must be kidding. This is my truck. Scoot over," I told him, opening the driver's door.

He carefully moved over to the passenger seat. I watched him settle against the bench, his face contorting, and I felt that twinge of guilt again.

"Why in the hell did you take off like that?" he yelled, pulling me close. My clothes slapped wetly against his, and he dug his hands into my snaggled hair. "What the hell was that? If I move too fast, you tell me. You don't run off."

I frowned. I'd been yelled at before. And I'd been hugged, but not at the same time. Weird.

"And how did you get so far?" he asked, pointing the truck's heat vents toward me and cranking up the thermostat. "What are you, a champion sprinter?"

"Well, you gave me a pretty good head start," I told him.

"Yeah, I couldn't get your truck started," he mumbled. "And it's hard to steer . . . and slow down. Your brakes are making really weird noises."

"The clutch is kind of tricky," I confessed as he pulled at the sleeves of my wet jacket and made me shrug out of it before I slipped the truck into gear. "I think Cooper and Sam rebuilt the transmission a few too many times."

"Why not just get a new truck?" he asked.

"It was my dad's," I said as I pulled a careful U-turn and pointed the truck downhill toward Nick's place. "He died when I was really little. I barely knew him. And I just like the idea of having something that used to be his."

The rain was pouring now, sheeting down the window in rippling waves. We rarely had what you'd call heavy rainfall, so the roads were slick with a layer of newly rehydrated oil and dust. I could hardly see through the windshield for the rain flowing down the glass, but I could tell that the landscape was moving by faster than it should be. I tapped the brake, but the truck didn't respond. It rolled along faster, building speed.

Nick cleared his throat. "OK, Maggie, I know you want to get home, but you need to slow down."

I pushed the brake with more force. "I'm trying."

"If you were trying, the truck would be going slower," he insisted.

I pressed my foot down harder, but the truck kept coasting along. The tires squealed slightly as I rounded a corner. "Hey, Nick," I said, trying to keep my voice calm. "Did you notice anything weird about the brakes on the way out here?"

He shook his head. "Besides the noise? They were a little sluggish, but it was uphill most of the way. I didn't use them much."

I grunted as the end of the truck bed swiped an outcropping of rock while I took a curve. Nick's eyes went wide with alarm. "Nick, I need you to pull up the emergency brake. Hard. I'd do it, but I think I need to keep my hands on the wheel."

Nick nodded and scooted toward me. As he wrapped his hands around the brake lever, I braced myself for the jolt of the wheels stopping.

"This isn't bad," Nick assured me as I eased around a minor curve. "I once drove a Jeep down the Yungas Road in Bolivia; it's the most dangerous road in the world. I came around a corner, and there was a logging truck stalled out—"

"Would you please shut the fuck up and pull the fucking brake!" I yelled.

"I am pulling it!" he exclaimed, tugging the brake arm up. Nothing happened. We locked eyes. Nick's gaze flashed toward the road. "Look, just anticipate the turns; we should slow down enough to come to a stop."

"We're heading downhill. We're *picking up* speed! Did you get your PhD online?" I cried.

"Hey, don't yell at me because you're panicking!"

"I'm not panicking!" I yelled.

We came to a particularly nasty turn, almost forty-five degrees overlooking a deep ravine. My heart thumped in my throat the closer we rolled. I pumped the brake furiously, hoping for some last-minute Hail Mary solution. I tried to turn the wheel, but the curve was just too sharp. "Hold on!" I shouted as he braced his arms against the dash.

The truck careened down the embankment, side-swiping trees and bouncing us back against the rear window separating the cab from the camper top attached to my truck bed. The truck pitched left, and my head cracked against the driver's-side window. I closed my eyes, letting the pitch and roll of the cab flop me around like a rag doll as I concentrated on not throwing up. We finally slid into a bank of trees and skidded to a stop.

"Shit! Shit! Shitshitshitshit!" I yelled, my eyes squeezed shut.

A few moments later, careful fingers pried my fingers loose from their death grip on the steering wheel.

"Maggie, the truck's stopped. You can stop murdering the English language now," Nick said. He gently turned my head to examine the rather impressive swelling on my temple. I winced and hissed as his fingertips brushed the throbbing skin.

The passenger side was wedged against a pair of trees at the bottom of a ravine. Frankly, it was a miracle the truck hadn't flipped. God bless solid, preplastic American auto engineering.

"Are you OK?" I asked, gripping his wrists. "How's your ass?"

His lips quirked. "I'm fine. I'm worried about you."

"And I'm worried about your ass," I told him, a sudden wave of dizziness washing over me. "I'm really sorry about that," I said, tracing my hand along his cheek. I smiled, feeling sort of loopy. "You have such a nice ass."

He chuckled as I leaned my forehead against his. "You cracked your head pretty good, huh?"

I nodded, cringing at the pain that spiraled out of that small motion. I dug into my pocket for my newly recharged cell phone. I had a healthy battery but no bars. "No cell-phone reception out here. You?"

"I paid an obscene amount of money for 3G network coverage." He shook his head.

I carefully stuck my head out through the shattered window, staring up the steep rock and earth wall that separated us from the road. Nick could barely walk. There was no way I was making it up that incline in human form in this rain. I considered knocking him out and phasing so I could run for help. But knocking someone unconscious sort of made rescue efforts irrelevant. Plus, the last time I ran with a concussion, I woke up in Juneau, naked in the parking lot of a 7-Eleven, with no clue what day it was. I could forget where I was running, and he could end up stuck out there for who knew how long.

"We're not getting out of here anytime soon," I told him.

"So, what, we wait for morning or for the weather to break?" he asked, looking back into the truck bed.

I nodded. "Whichever comes first. There's some blankets and stuff in the back. We're going to need to cover the window. It's still fall, technically, but it's going to get cold tonight."

I pushed the back window, which Sam and Cooper had custom-installed. It was just wide enough to shimmy through, though Nick was going to have some trouble with his injuries. I was glad that I'd recently cleaned out the truck bed. The camper top wouldn't allow us to stand or move around much, but at least we had shelter from the wind and rain. I passed the blanket and some duct tape through to him and started putting together a pallet. I'd insisted that everyone in the valley keep emergency kits in their cars, for situations like this. But I'd been expecting something more along the lines of a blizzard or a zombie invasion, rather than failed brakes and an impromptu slumber party with my human crush.

I gnawed my lip and considered the situation. My truck was old, but it was well maintained. Samson took a look at it every few months, inspecting the rebuilt engine, the aging axles, and the brakes, which he'd replaced last winter. It didn't make any sense for the brakes to crap out like that. Samson was goofy and lazy, but he was a solid mechanic. Also, as far as I knew, he didn't want me dead. Of course, that might change after I went home and put a boot up his ass.

"Well, this is cozy," Nick said wryly after struggling through the camper window. He pulled one of the blankets off the pallet and wrapped it around my shoulders. "Maybe I should have you redecorate Susie's place for me."

"Funny," I muttered.

"I know this is going to sound like a line, but I think we need to get you out of those wet clothes," he said, pulling my boots off. I pushed his hands away and yanked them off myself. "It's going to get cold in here, even with the blankets."

"I have an extra set of sweats in here, just in case," I told him, not bothering to add that they were there "just in case" I woke up naked in a strange place after a run, which was sort of an occupational hazard.

"I'll turn around," he said.

I arched my brows, then laughed as he dutifully turned his back and covered his eyes.

When you spend so much time around people who pay no attention to nudity, you forget niceties like modesty. It was sort of strange, but a refreshing change from guys who paid no attention when my boobs were exposed to God and everybody. It was nice to have a little mystery about me . . . you know, beyond the furry issue.

I peeled the wet shirt over my head and slid into the warm, dry sweatshirt. It felt absolutely delicious against my skin. It took a bit of effort to fight my way out of the wet jeans, but it was worth it to pull on the dry sweatpants.

Now that the adrenaline was wearing off and I was seventy-five percent sure we weren't going to die, I was suddenly so tired I felt as if I'd just run a marathon. I pulled my hair into a messy bun on top of my head. I wasn't going to win any beauty contests, but I was comfortable and warm. I couldn't want much else.

"You decent?" he asked.

"Depends on who you ask," I retorted.

He turned, pulling the emergency bag open. "And for dinner, we have our choice of protein bars that taste like peanut butter or protein bars that taste like chocolate and dirt. Paired with a lovely domestic bottled water."

"I think I'm going to go with the peanut butter," I said, shuddering. "The chocolate and dirt one lives up to its reputation."

"Excellent choice," he said, tossing the packet to me.

I stripped off the foil and shoved most of the protein bar into my mouth. Between the run and keeping warm, my body was starved for calories. His eyes went wide, and I swallowed. I tended to forget my table manners when I was hungry.

"I eat when I'm nervous," I told him.

"How's your head?"

"Feels like there's a drunk marching band in there," I said, gingerly rubbing my temple. "And the tubas are way off-key."

"Well, your pupils look good, but we should probably keep you awake for a while, just in case you have a concussion," he said. "Talk to me. Why'd you run off like that earlier?"

"You couldn't think of something a little more small-talkish before diving right into the deep end?" I griped.

"What's your favorite color?" he asked.

"Blue." I sighed, staring up into his eyes and hating myself for being such a sappy masochist.

"What do you think of the Red Wings' chances this season?"

"They'll be fine until the Avalanche take the ice," I muttered, biting off another hunk of protein bar.

He snorted. "OK, then, why did you run off earlier?"

"I don't like how you make me feel," I said, my lips somewhat loosened by exhaustion, warm dry clothes, and the weight of the protein bar in my belly.

His eyes widened in alarm. "I'm sorry. I don't mean—"

"No, I mean I like you, too much. You make me forget. You make me feel like you're more important than anything, and I can't let that be."

"Why not?" he asked, pushing my hair behind my ears.

"I have to take care of everybody," I said, yawning.

"And who takes care of you?"

I smiled at him. "Me."

"Nobody takes care of themselves all the time."

"Who takes care of you?" I asked.

He grinned suddenly. "Me."

"There you go." I blinked again, letting my eyes droop closed.

"No, no," he said, pinching my arm lightly. "Stay awake."

"Ow," I grumbled, swatting at his hand. "OK, fine. Tell me something. Anything. Tell me anything. Where are you from?"

"I'm from Reno, originally," he said, tucking a blanket around my shoulders. "My mom ran out on us when I was five or six. Didn't give much of a reason, but she'd made it clear that she didn't like being a mom nearly as much as she liked getting loaded or going to the casino with her friends."

"You don't believe in personal-history small talk, either, do you?" I asked wryly.

"I'm hoping you'll reciprocate," he said. "I always thought Dad was just putting up with her, but he sort of fell apart after she left. I'd never seen him drink more than one beer at a time, but he started drinking the better part of a six-pack as soon as he came in from work. I was handling the bills and signing my own report cards by the time I was eight. Dad lost one job and then another, so we started moving around. I think the highlight of my truancy report was the year I spent more time out of school than in it. Still, my grades were good. And by the time I hit high school, I was able to get a job, start sharing some of the load. I figured I could keep us in one town for a while, so I could go to school. We ended up in Darien, Connecticut, of all places. I went to class in the mornings and then did whatever I could at night, loading groceries from trucks, convenience-store clerk, mucking out stalls at a dairy farm, sawing limbs for a tree trimmer—which is how I developed an interest in climbing, by the way.

"Dad died in the middle of my senior year, liver failure. Mom sent a registered letter asking if he'd kept up his life-insurance payments. I had a guidance counselor who actually cared about her job and helped me get a full scholarship to a minor state school."

"That's impressive," I told him.

He shrugged. "I had enough grant money to stop working and just be a student. It was the first time I remember being able to just sit and study and read. And that's all I did. It kind of freaked my roommate out. I wasn't used to living with someone who liked to talk. I think Dane was convinced I was going to go postal on him, but two months into the semester, he put in this *Star Trek* DVD. I'd never seen the show. I started asking questions. And that's all it took. He was really into comics, sci-fi, role-playing games, and he shared it with me. He dragged me to all these conventions and meetings. It was fun. I'd never really had a friend before. So I just went along. Kind of pathetic, isn't it?"

"No. It's sort of sweet."

He looked faintly embarrassed. "Dane was always going on about this online multiplayer game software he was designing. It was different from anything we'd ever seen, an Internet-based joint experience among gamers all over the globe. A fully developed world where they could chat, build their characters, and, most important, pay subscription fees and buy upgrade packages. He spent every cent he had on hard drives for his 'rendering farm.' He told his former jock dad he'd joined some hard-core gym, swindling Daddy Dearest out of a few hundred a month, which he has paid back in spades, by the way. The game looked great, but he was having trouble coming up with character options and story lines. He was a genius with code but crap at storytelling. I filled in the gaps. I'd just taken a class in mythology. I'd served as dungeon master for a couple of our D&D games."

"I don't even want to know what that means."

He poked me in the ribs, his mood lightening. "It just means I wrote the story lines for the game. Pervert. Anyway, I wrote a bunch of different scenarios and created a colorful cast of characters. I based them on the stories we studied in class. I took a little Celtic mythology, some Greek, some Norse, some faerie lore, swirled in a little Tolkien, and voilà, you had Guild of Dominion."

"Wait a minute, are you telling me you helped invent Guild of Dominion?" I exclaimed. "My delinquent cousin Donnie lives for that game! We didn't see him for three weeks when you offered that upgrade package with the scantily clad elf ladies!" I gasped, slapping at his arm. "Are you loaded, Thatcher?"

"That's an incredibly rude question, but yes, I am."

Hmm. I'd never met anyone with money before. Evie was the most affluent member of our clan, though we wouldn't dream of asking her for anything. I wondered whether I should be embarrassed that he'd seen my house, my little village in its sometimes charming state of semishabbiness. Then again, he drove a truck that was almost as old as mine. He wore flannel and jeans, and other than insisting that there was a deep metaphysical meaning to *The Prisoner,* he didn't put on airs. If he could deal with the fact that I didn't have much, I could deal with the fact that he had a lot. "Good, then I don't feel bad about you springing for dinner later."

He chuckled. "Dane beat his competitors to the market by about six months. He was a hit. I did some freelance work for him during his first year in business, writing gaming manuals, cheater guides. I was glad to have the extra money and figured that was where it ended. Imagine my surprise when I was presented with a five-percent share in his company. I was able to retire at twenty-five, just from the dividends. Dane was as happy as a pig in shit running his company. I transferred to a much better school and finished my bachelor's. I was able to study whatever I wanted, and I decided to stick with folklore. I liked to look at the way people explained the world around them. And the more I looked, the more I saw patterns in nature, in reality. It made me question how much of myth was real. And *boom*, I knew what I wanted to do with the rest of my life. I wanted to find the connections between fact and the fantastic."

"But what do you do with it?"

"I write journal articles about the people and the stories I've studied," he said. "Some of them are published in well-respected academic journals. I've written a book or two. For the most part, I just like traveling around and learning about people. Everything was cool until Dane and I went to speak at a gamers convention in Vegas a couple of years ago. Some old friend of my mom's was tending bar at the convention center. She called my mom, let her know I'd come into some money. Next thing I know, Mom's calling me, says she's missed me, wants to reconnect, sob sob sob. I was working to get my PhD in folk studies. I'd just bought my own place, and I had the room. I actually sent her a first-class plane ticket. Isn't that stupid?"

I ran my fingers along his earlobes, applying faint pressure at the tips. "No, you wanted her to see what you'd become, what you'd made for yourself, what she'd missed."

"Yeah, it only took about a week for dear old Mom to swipe my ATM card, pawn everything that wasn't nailed down, and hightail it to Vegas."

I winced. "Ouch."

"Yep."

I squeezed his hand. "That's a very sad story," I assured him. "I mean, you actually have a PhD in folk studies?"

He scowled at me, though he was obviously trying hard not to laugh. I measured a small distance between my thumb and forefinger. "It's a little funny."

"Damn your powers of sarcasm-slash-cuteness," he grumbled, relaxing against me, letting me wrap my arms around him. He nuzzled my neck. "What about you? Where'd you go to school?"

"I went to high school in the valley," I said.

"And then?"

"And then I stayed in the valley. I didn't go to college."

His blond brows furrowed. "Why not? You're articulate, smart, scary as hell. You could have given the professors a run for their money."

"Well, that's just it," I told him. "We didn't really have the money. I made really good grades, scored high on those college aptitude tests. Cooper tried to get me to sign up for scholarship programs and grants. But I wasn't interested."

"Wasn't interested" was a major understatement. Cooper's attempts to force me into leaving the valley to go to the University of Alaska led to one of our legendary brawls. He'd lost three fingertips and part of an ear. But I didn't think that was the sort of thing I should share.

Nick and I talked for hours, until my throat was dry and my tongue felt swollen. It was hard, editing myself. I wanted to tell him everything. I wanted to tell him what it was like growing up in what was more of a wrestling league than a family. I wanted to tell him that I'd never reacted to anyone the way I reacted to him. I wanted to tell him about the mating urge and how it made me crazy for him, how I was expected to marry another wolf.

But every time I was on the verge of telling him, I'd get quiet and let him talk for a while about the places he'd grown up. Florida, Arizona, Texas, Georgia, California. I couldn't imagine seeing so many places—the desert, the mountains, the beach. I envied him that, but at the same time, it broke my heart that he'd never had a real home. I couldn't imagine living without a place to run back to, without people who—as much as they annoyed and needled me—loved me and accepted me for what I was. How did he live like that?

"China is like a hundred different countries in one. Crowded cities, sweeping mountains, huge, vast open plains, Scotland, India. India is so hot that you can actually taste the air, like spicy cotton candy," he said. "Scotland was nice; the people were friendly. I'm pretty sure that's where I ended up getting the tattoo, which just goes to show you that you shouldn't get into drinking contests with people who have their own class of whiskey named after them." He turned his back and pulled up the hem of his shirt to reveal a red lion on his shoulder, the kind you might see on some old English battle flag.

I thought maybe it wouldn't be such a bad thing to see those places. I wouldn't ever want to live anywhere but the valley. But it might be interesting to go where Nick had gone, to see what he'd seen. But my opinion was probably being swayed by the fact that he was practically shirtless.

Long after the sun set and the rain stopped,

Nick finally decided that I could fall asleep without danger. I stirred in the middle of the night, feeling pleasantly warm. My fingers were curled around his collar. His skin smelled like sleep and spice. I brushed my lips along his throat. He mumbled, still asleep, and swiped his fingers across his chin. I snickered. I kissed the little divot in his chin, edging toward his mouth. I pressed my lips against his, soft and deliberate, so I wouldn't forget what it felt like. He moaned. I did it again, then raked my teeth against his plump bottom lip. His hands slipped under my chin, keeping my face against his. His thumbs grazed my cheekbones to my hairline.

I fell asleep again, content.

I woke up hours later, Nick's face hovering in front of mine. His eyes fluttered open, and I could see the morning sun reflected in them. He grinned down at me. His eyes went wide. He scrambled back, whacking his head against the window.

I looked down to where my arms should have been and saw paws covered in black fur.

I was a wolf.

Shit and double shit.

6

The Best Laid Plans
of Men and Morons

"**Maggie?**" he asked, reaching out to touch me and then pulling his hand back, remembering the bite mark on his butt cheek.

Werewolves rarely phase during sleep, but sometimes it happens after a serious injury. We heal faster in our wolf state, and sometimes our bodies want to give us a little push toward running at full speed. I must have hit my head a little harder than I'd thought, I mused as I forced myself back into my human shape. I quirked my face into an awkward sort of cringe. "Hi."

"It's all real?" he choked out. "Werewolves? Ghosts? Vampires?"

I nodded. "Well, I don't know about vampires, but werewolves definitely. And ghosts, probably. I thought you knew all this."

"Yeah, but there's a difference between knowing and *knowing*. I feel so stupid," he said. "You're a werewolf, like me?"

"Well, Mo's not, but I am. And Cooper and Samson and my mom and most of my family. Do you see now why I don't want you investigating the wolf stories?"

"*You* bit me on the ass?"

"Yeah, sorry about that. I was a little upset."

"Upset?" he repeated. "Upset!"

"Stop repeating that."

"I'm—I'm sorry! I have so many questions for you," he said, patting his pockets for his notebook. "How often do you change? Obviously, your cycle isn't tied to the moon. Does it hurt? Is the transition painful? I mean, there was a sort of glow, and then you were just there in your human form. I always thought I would see your bones stretch around and change shape, but it's just like a trick of light, isn't it? What about your diet? Your sleep patterns? Can everyone in your family change? Is it passed on the mother's side or the father's side? Or both?"

I stared at him, my eyebrows raised. "I see you're over the scarred-ass-cheek thing."

"Temporarily. " He chuckled at his own goofiness. "I just can't believe you're real." He sort of dove for me, clasped my face between his hands, and closed his lips over mine. I moaned into his mouth, threading my fingers through his hair.

I pulled back, surprised.

"Is that not OK? I mean, this isn't because of the wolf thing. Obviously, it's an added bonus. But I've wanted to do that since the minute I met you, and now I can't seem to stop."

I basically tackled him and pressed myself against his body. He rolled me onto my back. My clothes were torn from the transition, and I felt my breasts pressing against the rough fabric of his jacket. My nipples puckered, tingling from this strange new sensation. This was so much farther than I'd been before. Sure, I'd been naked around men; it sort of came with the territory. But I'd never been touched like this, never touched someone to seek out this kind of pleasure.

He traced the lines of my thighs with his fingertips to bring my legs over his hips. He ground into me, his denim-covered—*oh, my God!*—pressing into my hot, uncovered . . . lady business.

I really had to start using grown-up words.

Every cord of muscle in my body felt as taut as a bow string. I was full, plump, ripe, warm, wet. My body sang with want and needs soon to be fulfilled.

I hooked an ankle around his calf, arching into him. He moaned, gripping my hips and leading me into a slow, steady rhythm against him. He gently ripped the remains of my shirt and peeled it away, tossing it aside. I pulled his T-shirt over his head. A heavy silver medallion, threaded on a rawhide strip, bounced against my collarbone as he pushed my hair back from my face. It felt as if every part of him was reaching out for me, taking me in. I ran my thumb along his lower lip. He playfully bit down on the tip of my thumb as I tried to unbuckle his belt with the other hand. It was a trickier maneuver than you'd think.

I whispered kisses across the hollow of his throat. He splayed his hand across my stomach, rubbing slow, tentative circles down until he reached the nest of curls covering my waiting—

Damn it.

Outside, I heard paws thumping against the damp ground, jarring me out of whatever spell we'd woven in that warm little space. My brothers had tracked me down.

My eyes widened as I looked down at my own naked skin, Nick's half-undone pants. I'd almost—we'd almost—I shrank back from him. He frowned as I eased out from under him.

"Stay here," I told him. He leaned forward to kiss me, but I ducked, reaching into the bag to pull the extra, extra sweatpants out. I climbed out over the tailgate.

The rain had stopped, leaving the woods with that cold, smoky-clean smell. The horse-sized russet-colored male was Samson. Cooper was the large black specimen. I tossed the sweatpants at them. "Hey, guys. Took you long enough to find me."

They phased simultaneously. Cooper looked furious. Samson looked as if his head was about to explode.

Awesome.

"What were you thinking?" Cooper demanded. "Mom's worried sick. She called last night freaking out because you hadn't shown up. Samson and I have searched every run path between here and the valley. Why didn't we think of looking in ditches for some improvised truck treehouse? And I just realized you couldn't call because you had a wreck. Sorry, it's taking me a little bit to work through the mind-numbing terror." Cooper threw his arms around me. "Are you OK?"

Samson joined the group hug by nearly knocking us both over.

"Midget, you reek of . . . guy." His eyes narrowed as he caught Nick's scent. "Dr. Girlie Face? You spent the night 'stranded' with *Dr. Girlie Face*?"

"I'll kill him," Cooper growled

"Not until after I kill him," Samson countered.

They both lunged toward the truck. I caught them by the scruffs of their necks and pulled them back.

"You're not killing anybody. We got into a wreck. He's injured. I whacked my head. I couldn't phase to run home and leave him alone. He was a perfect gentleman."

Samson and Cooper locked eyes. "We kill him anyway," Cooper said. Samson nodded.

"Come on!" Cooper exclaimed when I shoved him back. "This is a time-honored tradition! Older brothers hurting and/or scaring the crap out of their sisters' boyfriends. It's the whole point of having a little sister!"

"Cut it out, Coop! And he's not my boyfriend!"

"But—but!" Samson sputtered.

"Fine, fine," Cooper conceded. "We won't kill him because he's interested in you. We'll kill him because judging by the way your clothes are clearly thrown on, I'm assuming that he saw you naked or saw you phase. Either offense warrants me knocking the crap out of him."

"I phased while I was asleep." I cringed. "I whacked my head pretty hard and must have needed the beauty sleep."

Cooper nodded. "Damned inconvenient."

"So, he knows our secret? Much better reason to kill him," Samson said, rubbing his hands together gleefully.

I snapped at him, "Samson, shut it. We just have to think this whole thing through. Now is not the time for one of the nasty, bloody overreactions you end up apologizing for."

"Not this time, Maggie. This time, I have a well-thought-out three-step plan."

"Hi, guys," Nick said, limping around the side of the truck. "Look, there's no reason we can't—"

Crack.

Nick made a startled "uhf" noise. His eyes rolled back, and he sank to his knees. Samson was standing behind him with a tree branch in his hands.

"Did I knock him out?" Samson asked, raising the tree branch over his head to strike Nick again.

"Are you crazy?" I yelled, dropping to the ground next to Nick to check the wound on the top of his head. "You could have killed him! This is your plan? What are steps two and three? 'Find a shovel' and 'Dig a hole'?"

Nick was well and truly unconscious. But his pulse was strong, and his breathing was even. I sprang up to my feet and punched Samson in the nose, knocking him flat on his ass.

"Told you she liked him," Cooper said.

"Ow! What the hell, Maggie!" Samson grunted,

cupping a hand around his bleeding nose. "That really hurt!"

"It was supposed to hurt, dumb-ass!" I yelled, flexing my bruised fingers. "What is wrong with you?"

Samson swiped at his nose. "This is just step one. Step two is we take him to the clinic in Grundy. We call Buzz to report the accident. And then we tell Nick that he hit his head really hard during the crash, and if he saw anything, like Maggie turning into a werewolf, it was probably just a bad dream. You know, the result of his concussion."

"Have you been watching soap operas again?" I demanded.

"It's actually not that bad of a plan," Cooper said. "And if he goes around telling everybody he saw you turn into a wolf, he'll just get laughed at. It will discredit him. People will think he's loony."

My chest ached a little at the thought of Nick being mocked by locals. But I had to admit it wasn't totally misguided, as plans went. It was far better than Samson's idea for getting us out of trouble when we knocked over Mom's china cabinet, which centered on faking a robbery by carnies. "There are four steps in your three-step plan," I muttered.

Samson brightened, and tossed Nick over his shoulder like a sack of potatoes.

"Would you be careful with him?" I yelled.

"I don't think we're going to be able to save your truck, Mags," Cooper said, trying to distract me from fluttering around Nick's unconscious form like an overwrought soccer mom.

I sighed, prying the tailgate open, knowing that my scent, mixed with Nick's, was now billowing out of the truck full-force. My face flushed hot, and Cooper pretended to be fascinated by some moss on a nearby tree.

"I don't think there's a wrecker on earth that will be able to haul it out of here," I said, grabbing my bag. I rescued the necessary paperwork from the glovebox and claimed a couple of CDs from the floorboards. I took my dad's Saint Edmund medal from its honorary spot on the rearview mirror. The lot was stuffed in my emergency bag. I slid my still-damp boots onto my feet, as it seemed we would be walking home human. I stood at the edge of the ravine and stared at my former transportation. It felt as if I was losing my last connection to my dad.

"It's OK, Maggie," Cooper said, wrapping his arms around me. "I'll get you an older, shittier truck when we get back to town."

"Ass." I coughed to cover the sniffle caught in my throat and punched his arm.

"Can we get going?" Samson demanded, shifting Nick's weight. "I've got things to do."

"No, you don't," I scoffed.

"We've got to get Samson a girlfriend," Cooper said. "Speaking of which, what exactly happened between you and Dr. Girlie Face last night?"

"Nice attempt at a segue, but it's none of your business."

"But you're, you know, being all careful with him. Being protective. You don't do that."

I rolled my eyes. "I'm not a monster, Coop."

"Maggie, you once left a date at the emergency room with appendicitis because you didn't want to miss the previews for a Steven Seagal movie." I glared at him. "I'm not saying it's a bad thing. It's sort of nice to see this softer side of you. But, uh, Maggie, please understand, this is a conversation I never, ever wanted to have with you, but Samson was right. That guy's scent is all over you, and vice versa. You two obviously got . . . pretty close last night. And it seems like we interrupted something when we showed up."

"No comment."

"Thank you," he said, shuddering. "It's just you've always said you were going to . . . you know, with another wolf. I just want to make sure you're not rushing into anything. Of course, keep in mind that I don't have a lot of room to throw stones here, since I pretty much leaped into a relationship with Mo without even thinking of looking. And you're my baby sister, so I prefer not to think of you even doing that until you're, oh, eighty or so. Or when I'm dead. Whichever comes first."

"Cooper, stop."

"Thank you," he breathed.

"No, you're right. You interrupted something. And it would have been a mistake. I realized that as soon as I snapped out of the haze I was in. I let my hormones and all that 'we almost died' adrenaline get the better of me."

"He seems like an OK guy," Cooper admitted. "I mean, I have to hate him a little bit, because it's my brotherly duty. But as guys who want to nail my sister go, I guess you could do worse. Like Lee."

"Nice."

"So, are you going to see him again?"

I shook my head and chewed on my bottom lip. Nick was changing me, making me weak, distracting me. Making me irresponsible and putting me *this* close to making life-altering decisions on a whim and a whiff of pheromones. I hadn't even thought about my family the night before. I didn't worry about whether my mother was worried about me or if Pops's heart-cath results had come back from Dr. Moder yet. All I could think about was Nick. That was unacceptable. I had people counting on me. People I loved and to whom I owed far more loyalty than some random guy I'd know a few weeks. I shrugged, trying to give Cooper my most convincing nonchalant sigh. "No. I'm done. This is over."

CAMPED OUT IN the uncomfortable waiting-room chairs in the Grundy clinic, I stared at Nick's face for most of the night. Dr. Patterson, who spent two days a week at the Grundy clinic, assured me that the "blow to the head"—Samson's dumb-ass idea—probably didn't do any long-term damage. The masochist in me wanted to take in as much of Nick as I could while I could, because what I was about to do would keep me away from him for the foreseeable future. I kept thinking of a passage in the final act of *Romeo and Juliet,* something about "Eyes, look your last!"

Devoting any thought to the words surprised me, since I'd loathed being forced to read about two spoiled, lovesick kids in high school. But I think I finally got why Romeo was so desperate and unbearably whiny while crouching over Juliet's body, even if my own situation was far less emo. He was trying to savor what was no doubt a scary, extremely crappy moment, because he didn't know what the future held.

"I don't need deep thoughts right now," I moaned, pressing my fingers to my temples.

"My head." Nick whimpered, the paper underneath him crinkling as he squirmed on the clinic cot. "What happened?"

"I was driving us to your place, and I lost control of my truck."

He blinked at me a few times and then gingerly nodded his head.

"We rolled into a ravine," he said, moaning as I handed him a glass of water. I had Dr. Patterson's number, but I held off on calling him back to the clinic just yet. Nick sipped the water and carefully tilted his head back to the pillow. "You OK?"

"I'm fine." I nodded. "And you hit your head on the window."

"No. You hit *your* head," he said, squinting at me. "I had to keep you awake. Kissed you. And when I woke up, you'd changed. I woke up, and you were a wolf."

"You must have hit your head pretty hard, huh?" I said, forcing myself to give him a sympathetic smile.

He blinked at me, frowning. "What?"

"You hit your head in the accident. You must have had some crazy dream."

"It wasn't a dream. You were there. We spent all night talking. And Cooper was there, eventually. And Samson."

"And the Tin Man and the Scarecrow, too?" I asked, struggling to keep the wry smile on my face. This hurt. It hurt so much to make him feel crazy, stupid, anything less than the sweet, brilliant man who kept me awake to prevent my brain from leaking out my ears.

"Don't try to play this off, Maggie. You're a were-wolf."

I burst out laughing. "No, Mo's the werewolf. Oh, wait, no, it's me. I'm the werewolf. Or maybe it's my mom or Great-aunt Tilda." I sighed, fighting to keep my expression placid.

Of course, Great-aunt Tilda was one of the most intimidating specimens of geriatric wolfdom you could ever come across. But that was beside the point.

"Nick, this whole thing with werewolves has just gone too far. I humored you at first, because it was kind of quirky and charming, but it's just weird now."

"You're telling me that I didn't wake up next to a little black wolf this morning, and that wolf didn't phase into a very human you?"

"I'm telling you that we were in a car accident, and you have a pretty severe concussion. Beyond that, I don't have one clue what's going on in your head."

"I know what I saw. You don't have to worry. I'm not—I won't tell anyone."

Oh, how I wished I could believe that.

I frowned at him. "There's nothing to tell."

"No, look, I remember. We were at my house. We were watching *Star Trek*. I kissed you. And you ran away."

"I ran away from your house because I was upset. Because I have a boyfriend."

Nick sank back against the mattress, recoiling as if the wind had been knocked out of him.

I twisted my hands together, trying desperately to look like a guilt-ridden girlfriend, the kind you couldn't trust to go on spring break with her girl-friends. "I started dating Clay a little while ago. He's good for me. He's a close friend of the family. Part of the reason I came to see you was to tell you that I can't accept things like pie from you. I'm a one-man sort of woman. I don't play around like that. Between that and the wolf thing, I don't think we should see each other anymore. Don't come by my house. Stay away from my family. You're creeping me out."

"I thought . . . I thought we were . . ."

"It's not like that, Nick. You just misunderstood."

Oh, God, this was making my chest hurt.

"Then tell me what it's like!" Nick shouted. "You know, I don't know what pisses me off more, you denying that there's anything between us or you denying what you are. Do you know how much people would give to be able to do what you do? To be special? To be able to escape?"

"Oh my God, are you like one of those weird guys who post sexy sketches of half-animals/half-ladies online?"

"The term is 'furry,' and no, I'm not. I don't like you because you're a wolf. I like you because you're strong and funny and loyal and smart. You're special in a lot of ways. Being able to morph into a wolf is just one of them. And certainly not the one I will tell my friends about."

"Why do you know the term for people who are sexually attracted to—You know what? Never mind. None of this matters, because it's all in your head."

He smirked at me in that ridiculously cute way of his. "Of all the things I just said, what you picked up on was my vast knowledge of sexual preoccupations?"

Under normal circumstances, that would have made me laugh my ass off. But I needed to pretend to be a normal girl, with normal tolerances for dirty jokes.

"I like you, Maggie. Why are you fighting so hard against liking me back?"

"You think I'm a mythological creature!" I exclaimed.

"OK, if I was willing to drop the werewolf thing, if I was just to become another tourist up here, enjoying the Alaskan scenery, would you reconsider?"

"You wouldn't do that. You can't. The supernatural crap, it's your whole reason for being. It's what makes you . . . you. And I wouldn't ask you to give that up."

"So, I'm damned if I do and damned if I don't?"

I stood up and slid into my jacket. "I'm sorry. Please, don't call me. Don't show up around my valley. Stay away from me and mine. Please."

"Maggie, don't—"

But I'd slammed the door before he could get out of bed.

AFTER I'D HANDED over my clothes and bag, Samson and Cooper let me run home solo. Given the way my face was all pinched up, I think they knew I needed some time alone. I ran until I thought my lungs would burst. I collapsed to the ground outside town, phasing to human and lying on my back.

I lay there, staring up at the pine needles shifting over the endless expanse of blue.

I could smell a badger shuffling in the underbrush. I hated badgers; they were like sour-smelling, crotchety old men who could claw your face off. I considered chasing it just for the hell of it, but I just didn't have the energy.

I had to pull it together. I couldn't go home like this, all frazzled and twitchy. I took deep breaths, pulling the air down through my toes. I closed my eyes and went to my happy place, the ferry from Bellingham. My mother took me on a rare visit to her family in Seattle when I was seven, and I'd spent most of the three-day trip sitting on the deck, with my legs dangling under the railing, my face in the wind. It gave my mom fits, seeing me that close to the edge, but she couldn't keep me inside.

I'd never been anywhere before, really, and I remember marveling at how big the world was. How you could actually taste salt on the wind. How the spray from the ocean broke down to almost nothing and whispered across my face like kisses.

That's about as poetic as I got.

Nothing I'd done since had ever been as peaceful or as right. Every time I was stressed or just needed a few minutes to myself, I closed my eyes and put myself right back on that boat. And I felt better for it.

The moment I closed my eyes, I could almost feel the tilt and roll of the deck under me. I leaned my chin on the cool aluminum rail and watched the whitecaps lap against the hull. I smiled, deciding to give myself just a few more minutes before I returned to reality.

"Hi."

I looked up to see Nick standing over me. He sat down next to me without benefit of a dough-nut pillow, so I figured I'd managed to slip into a dream state. It didn't stop me from being really annoyed.

"What the hell are you doing in my happy place?"

He smirked at me. "I was this close to getting to your happy place, so if that's an invitation, I accept."

My dream version of Nick was pretty perverted.

"What are you doing here? This is where I go to get away from things that bother me."

He looked offended. "I bother you?"

"A lot."

"I don't think that's true."

"How would you know?"

"Because if you were really upset with me, you

probably would have dreamed me with a hump or a debilitating, itchy disease."

"Well, you're not wrong," I muttered. "So, what, you think you can show up here and put in a good word for reality Nick?"

He shrugged. "How should I know? It's your happy place."

I muttered, "Well, you could at least do this with your shirt off. What are you doing here, anyway?"

"I think there are probably some things you left unsaid earlier, and your brain is just giving you a chance to get it out of your system."

"No, that couldn't be it."

"Fine," he huffed, pulling his T-shirt over his head.

My eyes went wide at the sight of finely sculpted abs lightly dusted with a little gold happy trail. "God, this is going to be so much worse if you look like that in real life."

"Oh, it's even better," he assured me.

"Bastard." I sighed. "I'm sorry. I'm sorry I have to lie to you. And I'm sorry I have to make you feel crazy or unsure of yourself. I wish I could help you, but I just can't. As much as I think you could mean to me, I can't put you ahead of the people I love. You are a smart, funny, strange, drop-dead-gorgeous man. And I would like nothing more than to get to know you a hell of a lot better. But I think it's better this way."

"But none of that had anything to do with you, or you being a wolf, or how you feel. It's about everybody else."

"Exactly."

"So your reasons are bullshit. You're so afraid of expressing how you really feel that you'll use any excuse to stay away from me. You've never had someone interested in you and only you. And you're so afraid that's not enough to keep me around that you'll do anything to avoid finding out one way or the other."

"I don't think my figments are supposed to mouth off to me," I grumbled.

"I was never much for rules."

"Tell me something I don't know," I muttered.

"Butterflies taste with their feet."

I raised my eyebrows.

He shrugged. "I bet you didn't know that."

"Oh, for fuck's sake. You can't help yourself, can you?"

"Well, I don't think you'd want a lesser version of me in your happy place," he said, giving me a cheeky little leer.

I snorted and closed my eyes. "Good-bye, Nick."

I felt a featherlight touch on my shoulder. "Good-bye for now, Maggie."

I woke up with a start.

Well, that was helpful.

My head throbbing, I sat up, wondering how long I'd been sleeping. The sun was hanging low over the mountain range. I sat up, feeling more groggy than refreshed. This was not the point of the happy place. Stupid Dream Nick and his verbal riddles consisting of stuff I already suspected.

I stretched my arms over my head and popped

my back. Sleeping on the ground might connect you with the earth and all that crap, but it was hell on the vertebrae. Sure that my mom was worried enough to chew through phone books by now, I jogged toward home. I felt a fresh flush of guilt as I entered the village. This must be what parents felt like, returning to their kids after a long weekend away. I was a short step from giving every member of the pack a tacky T-shirt and a teddy bear. But at the moment, all I wanted was a hot meal, a large one, a hotter shower, and my bed. My front door was in sight when I heard my name called.

"Maggie!"

I turned and saw Clay jogging down Main Street toward me. I groaned inwardly, bidding that hot meal a mental farewell. But I took a deep breath and turned to him with a genuine smile on my face. Clay was a good guy and considerably less of a pain in the ass than most people I knew. He deserved my undivided and nonirritated attention.

I sighed as I watched him lope to an easy stop in front of me and give me one of those heartwarming grins. In a good and decent universe, my choices would be limited to Lee and Clay, and the decision would be relatively easy: Clay and his cute little chin dimple by a landslide. I huffed, thinking about stupid, shirtless Dream Nick and the "grindy" encounter in the back of my truck. I had to do something to get him out of my head. I had to show him that I was serious about staying away from him.

"What would you think of going to dinner with

me some night?" I asked Clay before he could say anything.

Clay hesitated. "Uh, I was just going to tell you that part for the snow blower came in yesterday. What did you say?"

"What would you think of having dinner with me Friday?"

"That would be great," he said, smiling hesitantly. "We could try that new pizza place in Burney."

"Actually, I was thinking of the Glacier. We could see Mo and Cooper. It would be fun."

Clay looked confused but shrugged. "Who am I to turn down one of Mo's burgers?"

"I'll pick you up?" I offered, then suddenly remembered that my truck was at the bottom of a ravine. "Hmm. No, wait, I think you'll have to drive."

7

Say It with Pastry

ON FRIDAY MORNING, I walked outside to find a tow truck unloading my truck in the little side lot by the community center. It hurt to see the scraped, dented side panels, the huge crater the trees had left on the passenger's side. The fender was bent to hell where the truck had tugged it up the incline. It was a wonder the tow truck had managed to winch it up from the ravine at all.

I could still smell Nick's scent, mingled with mine, wafting from the rear compartment. The scent made all previous empty chest aches feel like a mild tickle. I actually had to bend over and brace my hands against my knees as the tow-truck driver lowered the winch and gently dropped my poor baby to the concrete. He stepped out, a rangy, weathered man in his forties, wearing blue overalls that stated his name was Wesley.

"Hi, can I help you?" I asked, straightening and doing my best to function like a normal person. "Did the state police send you?"

"Nope," he said, unhooking a chain from under my truck's tires.

There was something off about his smell; he definitely wasn't human. He wasn't a werewolf, either. He was definitely a were but something little, which was sort of funny, given that he looked as if he was blown out of a straw. I sniffed again. A weasel? *Oh, come on.* This guy was a were-weasel that ran around with "Hi, my name is Wesley" stitched on his shirt? Some people had no sense of irony.

"OK, do you just drive around the wilderness rescuing random were-creatures' stalled vehicles?" I asked, my tone just a little bit snotty.

"Nope."

"Do you ever say anything besides nope?" I asked.

He shook his head. "Nope."

I laughed, which made his lips twitch. "The bill's taken care of. Your cousin Caleb says you should call him."

With a chortle at my shocked expression, he drove away, taking the north road through the preserve. I dashed into my office to grab my cell phone and dial Caleb's number.

"Y'ello?" my cousin and packmate mumbled into the phone, using his "being held hostage" voice, which he only used when he was conducting surveillance.

"Hey, cuz! You got a mullet yet?" I sang cheerfully into the phone . . . because it annoyed him.

He sighed. "Hi, Mags."

"Everything OK?" I asked. Normally, Caleb, who spent his time on the road using his werewolf senses to track down society's misfits for a handsome fee, loved a good Dog the Bounty Hunter joke. "Who was the were-weasel who just dropped my truck off? And how the heck did he manage to yank it up a forty-percent incline?"

"Wesley's done some work on my truck," Caleb said. "He replaces a lot of my windows."

I snorted. As a not-quite-legitimate bounty hunter, Caleb came into contact with people who did not like being delivered back to the people they owed money to. And sometimes they took out their "feelings" on his truck.

"He's a good guy. And he gets into those hard-to-reach places. Samson called, told me what happened to your truck. I thought Wesley could lend a hand."

"Well, thanks, I appreciate it. But is it causing you pain in some way? Why do you sound so weird?"

"Wesley took a look under the truck when he was hooking up the chain. He said your brake line looked worn. But not from use or age. He said it looked like something sharp had been scraped over the brake line over and over until it was ready to rupture. Maggie, have you pissed anybody off lately? Besides Cooper? Or Samson? Or Mo? Or your mom? Or—"

"I get it, I get it," I grumbled, considering the question. "Honestly, other than that little problem last summer with Eli, I haven't gotten into any more scrapes than I normally would."

"That's not saying much." He snorted.

"Thanks," I muttered. "Seriously, I've been a rel-atively nice girl." Caleb snorted again. I shot back, "I said relatively! So, what, you think someone tam-pered with my brakes because I was a smart-ass to them? Or maybe it was a rabbit out for revenge for all the little bunnies I've eaten? Seriously, I rarely leave the valley. Who would mess with my truck?"

"I don't know, Mags," he said. "I just think you need to be careful."

"I live in a veritable fortress, surrounded by burly protective relatives willing to kill for me. And not to mention, I sort of kick ass myself."

"Yeah, but you're not invincible," Caleb argued.

"Fine. If I see a rabbit dressed in camo trying to jimmy the screen door with a hunting knife, I'll call for help."

"Somehow I get the feeling you're not taking me very seriously." He sighed.

"And you would be right," I told him. "But I will keep an eye out, I promise, just to humor you."

"Thank you," he said.

Caleb kept me on the phone for another twenty minutes, asking about various relatives, which meant he had to be worried. He tried to avoid talking on the phone whenever possible. I hung up, unsure what to think. How likely was it that someone had tampered with my brakes?

I shrugged out of my jacket and slid under the frame. There were clods of dirt, pine needles, and dead grass spotting the worn chrome. I inched my way under the axle . . . and realized I didn't know nearly as much about big engines as I thought I did. I recognized the bottom of the transmission and the fuel line. I found the brake drum and followed the thumb's-width plastic rope with my fingertips. It was smooth and unmarked until it reached the point lowest to the ground. I frowned. It wasn't cut, exactly, but it was definitely damaged. And the tear didn't look like something that would occur over a long period of time. As far as I could tell, I'd hit some debris on the road and ripped it myself, which wasn't surprising, considering the tumble the truck took off the road.

I leaned closer to inspect the rupture in the line and picked up the faint scent of dryer sheets, the sort of clean, floral fabric-softener stuff my mom was always using. I chuckled. Wesley didn't look like the April Fresh type. But maybe he had a concerned she-weasel mate at home.

I heard two of my older uncles arguing loudly between their front stoops over a borrowed power tool. Apparently, they'd decided to use other power tools to settle the dispute, so I crawled out from under the truck. Distracted by senior citizens armed with band saws and extension cords, I abandoned my defunct vehicle and didn't give the brakes another thought.

NICK SENT ME a freaking apology pie.

Several, in fact. First, it was apple-raisin, then Mo's famous chess pie, then French silk, each delivered to my door every day by my decreasingly bemused sister-in-law.

"I'm charging him mileage," Mo told me as she

walked through my front door and placed the chocolate "too fluffy to look real" meringue masterpiece
in my hands. I could see the delicate little chocolate
shavings speckling the crusty brown dome through
the plastic carrying case. Mo slapped the note into
my palm. It just said, "Please."

This was the saddest pie of all. The previous
pies had at least told me Nick was sorry and that he
wanted to start fresh.

"He's moved on to meringue," Mo said, shaking
her head. "This does not bode well."

"I honestly don't know how to respond to this,"
I said, taking the pie into the kitchen. Mo collected
the empty pie tins from the counter. Pie never lasted
long in our house. Samson had taken to stopping by
the house every night to make sure no pie was left
behind. As long as Mo was making daily deliveries,
he said I could stay mad at Nick forever.

"I'll talk to him," I promised her. "Even though I
really don't want to."

"You should," Mo countered. "He asked this
morning if I could get enough peaches to make a
cobbler."

"No one says they're sorry with cobbler."

"Yeah, 'cause saying it with pie is super-normal,"
she retorted.

WORKING WITH MY hands generally helped me sort
through whatever had me wound up. The weird
swooshy, acidy feeling that twisted through my chest
whenever I thought of Nick or Clay had me taking
apart the village's snow blower piece by piece.

At least my emotional turmoil was serving some purpose. Part of the problem with having an aging population was elderly werewolves' increasing inability to negotiate icy streets and sidewalks. We couldn't afford to replace the snow blower, but we also couldn't afford the cost of adding a Broken Hip Wing onto the clinic. Hence my need to squeeze one more year out of the twenty-year-old snow blower.

I'd replaced the belts, the oil, and the spark plugs and was now praying that it wouldn't literally blow a gasket or part of my hand as I fired it up. I grinned like a madwoman when the diesel engine roared to life. Then a cloud of black smoke spiraled up from somewhere just out of reach, and I heard the first signs of stalling.

"Stupid, useless piece of crap!" I yelled, the sound of the engine whining and sputtering to its death covering the worst of my curses.

"It's nice to see that some things, like your naturally even temper, never change."

I looked up and saw my grandfather standing in the doorway, clearly amused.

"I thought I would come by and pay my favorite granddaughter a visit," Pops said, winking at me.

At eighty-two, Noah Graham was sort of the Robert Redford of the Alaskan werewolf community. He was still blessed with a headful of iron-gray hair and the blue-green eyes Cooper had inherited. He also appeared to be in his early sixties, which was one of the perks of being a werewolf. Our bodies are resilient because of the constant phasing, lots of collagen. As long as we keep up with the sunscreen, we can look young well into our golden years.

But we aged, like everybody else. Pops had had what Dr. Moder called a "minor episode" the year before, which scared the hell out of all of us. We'd all babied him shamelessly, which irritated his independent soul. He finally blew up and tossed a quart of chicken noodle soup at my aunt Maisie. That was when I knew he was getting better.

Pops and I had always had a close relationship. Most girls confided in their mothers when they were worried about a test or upset with a friend . . . or going through "weird new body parts" anxiety. I relied on my grandfather. Cooper and Samson went to him with their problems, and I figured I should, too. So far, with the rare exception of what we will only call the Training Bra Incident, it had worked out pretty well.

I kissed his cheek. "Don't let your five other granddaughters hear you say that."

He shrugged as he hitched himself into the seat of a defunct tractor-mower. "Well, you're each my favorite in some way."

"Nice save, Pops." I snickered, handing him a bag of the Reese's Pieces he favored. "How are you feeling?"

"I thought we agreed that you wouldn't start every conversation that way," he said, cocking a gray eyebrow at me.

"Force of habit."

"I'm fine," he told me, tugging my hair gently. "How is the search for a new truck?"

"Stalled," I griped. "Bad pun intended."

"You know I enjoy bad puns."

I chuckled. "I haven't had time to go look for another one. Fortunately, I don't leave the valley much, except to visit Grundy. I can run there, so it's not a huge deal."

"Yes, I know," he said quietly. "I saw your aunt Billie earlier. She seems to be having a good day. She was playing Legos with Paul and Ronnie."

"She thought they were Eli and Cooper, didn't she?" I asked.

"Probably," he said, nodding. "But she was happy and smiling. And at this point, we should be grateful she can have days like that. Alicia told me to thank you again for sending the aunties over to help at night while she bathes the boys and gets them to bed. She says it's been a big help."

I shrugged. "That's why we're here. Nobody should have to shoulder all that responsibility alone." Pops smirked at me. "Oh, hush," I told him. "We're not talking about me."

"Alicia also mentioned that you went on a date with her brother the other night."

"Are we going to braid each other's hair now, Pops?" He gave me the stink-eye in response, so I sighed and said, "I went out on a date with Clay. And it was fine."

"And you're making it sound like a trip to the dentist's office."

"Why does everyone want to talk about my personal life all of a sudden?" I grumped, jumping and inspecting a wrench on the other side of the room.

"Have you talked to any of those curious souls about your personal life?" he asked. I shook my head. "Are you likely to?" I laughed and shook my head again. He held out his hands and waved his fingers, as if to say, "Bring it on."

I sighed. "I like Clay. On paper, he is the perfect mate for me."

Pops nodded. "Clay is a good boy. He's kind, he thinks before he acts, he takes care of his family—"

"Do you want to date him, Pops?"

Pops frowned. "We should have never encouraged you to speak. So, if Clay has balanced your pros-and-cons list, why aren't you out there running with him, instead of hiding in this shed?" He smiled at me, triumphant. I never have been able to fool Pops.

I picked at the engine grease under my fingernails. "There's another man who seems interested in me. And he confuses me, mostly, but I like him, too . . . almost against my will. And I can't do anything about it."

"Dr. Thatcher?" he asked, grimacing. "You know, Maggie, there's nothing wrong with you dating a human. It's mating with one that's the problem."

"Why put the energy into dating someone if you can't mate with them?"

"The fun of it?" he suggested

"Obviously, it's been a while since you've dated, Pops."

"I do all right."

"Ew."

"You know that we want you to be happy, Maggie."

"Yeah, but when has telling someone to do what makes them happy ever resulted in a good decision? Remember when we told cousin Todd to do what made him happy and he came home with recently augmented boobs?"

Pops gave me a stern look but was working hard to keep the snickering internal. "As I was saying, we want you to be happy. But you also have to think of what's best for the pack," he said. "Do you know why you're the alpha?"

"Because I got more votes than Samson?"

Pops chuckled. "Because you see underneath. You cut through the layers of . . ."

"Bullshit?"

"I was going to say politeness," he deadpanned. "And say what you think. It's an undervalued quality for humans, especially in a woman. But after the initial sting, people appreciate hearing the truth."

"I have a feeling I'm about to get hit with some of that truth," I muttered.

"I know you don't like the idea of mating and marrying. And I know you hate it when one of the aunties declares she's found the perfect male for you. You're afraid that you'll lose the independence you've built up. And you're afraid of spending your life with someone who's not going to make you happy. But you have to settle down sometime. It's part of your responsibility as pack leader. You set the example, provide stability for the pack. And there aren't enough werewolf males running around out there for the taking. If you think you could make a life with Clay, you should start now."

A tiny, petty voice welled up somewhere in my gut and grumbled that Cooper hadn't bothered setting an example. He'd tied himself up nice and tight to the first human to break that thick cement shell he'd built around his heart . . . and his brain.

As if he sensed my resentment, Pops added, "You've always been the strong one, Maggie. We both know Cooper wasn't ever going to be ready to lead the pack, not really. I want him to be happy, and I'm glad that he found Mo. But it's always been you. You're the one who can make the hard decisions. You're the one strong enough to make your own happiness, even if it's not exactly what you wanted. I will love you no matter what you decide, but I can't help but hope that you'll make the choice that those around you could not."

"No pressure, huh, Pops?"

He kissed my forehead and ambled toward the door. "If you want easy advice, ask a different grandpa."

"I don't remember 'asking' for your advice," I muttered.

LATER, I WAS wandering home for a late lunch, wiping my hands on my overalls, and wondering if it would be weird for me to do repair work nude just to avoid the stains. I passed the community center and noticed an odd, acrid scent on the air. I followed it toward my office door and saw the first curling gray tendrils of smoke winding their way out of the splintered door glass. The motion of my yanking the door open pulled a cloud of thick smoke right into my face. I spluttered and coughed, pushing my way through to the growing plume of flame blooming from my desk.

Even through the choking gray haze, I could see that my office was trashed. The filing cabinet lay on its side, drawers torn out. My shredded files were strewn across the floor like wounded birds.

Someone had put my wastebasket in the middle of my desk, crammed it full of my paperback books, and set them on fire. The plastic walls of the basket were starting to soften and melt as the flames reached toward the ceiling tiles. Covering my mouth and nose with a bandana, I grabbed the fire extinguisher from the wall and doused the whole flaming mess with white foam. The sterile-smelling chemicals sprayed across my desk and hit the wall with a muted *splat*. After giving the wastebasket one long, final blast, I took out my work gloves to protect my hands while I heaved the smoking remains out into the parking lot.

I left the door open and propped all of the windows to let the smoke vent. I wiped my streaming eyes with the bandana and searched the ceiling for the blinking light of the smoke detector. As the smoke cleared, I could see the frayed wires dangling from where the device had been yanked from the wall.

I moved closer to my foam-covered desk, opening the drawers and finding the petty-cash box intact and the village checkbook still locked up tight. I ran to the other rooms of the center but found that the damage was limited to my office space.

How had this happened without my hearing anything? *Gah, the music.* Between my too-loud worship of all things Journey and the noise of the engine, I wouldn't have heard a Mack truck parking in my office.

Mom and a few of the aunties appeared at my door, gasping in shock at the mess and the smoke. Ignoring their murmurs, I strode out into the street, working up a decent head of steam while I worked through what might have happened. The kids were in school, and most of the adults were at work or indoors. We ran perimeter checks on occasion, but it's not as if the valley was under twenty-four-hour guard.

I heard the school bell ring down the street, announcing the end of lunch, and paused. The high school kids were allowed to run home for lunch if they wanted. Between the werewolf stuff and the regular human adolescent roller coaster, their bodies went through more food than could be easily carried to school. It was easier for them to run home and scarf down as many calories as possible just to get through the day. "Free lunch" left them unsupervised for a good hour of the day, but we tried to emphasize trust and personal responsibility in the pack. Obviously, that had come back to bite us on the ass.

I marched to the school building and called all five high school students to the office, which was basically the supply closet at the end of the classroom. If I was going to question one of them, I would question them all. Frankly, if one of them had anything to do with the fire, their friends were smart enough to distance themselves by ratting them out.

Cousin Teresa gave the little kids busy work and sat with me while I marched the teens away.

Their chatter and teasing died the minute I walked into the tiny room. The kids sat up a little straighter and put on their serious faces. They eyed me solemnly, all long, coltish limbs combined with baby cheeks and huge eyes. Of the five, only three, Ricky, Rebecca, and Benjamin, were able to phase, but they all recognized the authority of the pack leader. They knew that disrespect and sass would get them into trouble with me and then again with their parents. It was a double whammy of adult supervision.

My eyes narrowed at Benjamin and Ricky, the chewing-tobacco enthusiasts whom I'd forced to overindulge to the point of vomiting. They were good kids but had been known to cause more than their fair share of trouble. This included accidentally setting my workshop aflame with a badly timed M-80. Had their pyromaniac antics escalated to intentional damage? Were they trying to get back at me for the puking?

"Do any of you have anything to tell me? Something to do with my office?" I asked, giving each of them my best motherly glare. The kids' eyes went wide, and their mouths clamped shut. "Look, if you did it because you thought it would be funny or you're upset with me about something, it's not OK, but I get it. I did a lot of stupid stuff when I was a kid. But it's better to go ahead and fess up to it and take your licks now than to lie. Because then I'll be pissed at you."

Silence. "No one knows who gave my office the arsonist's makeover?" I asked.

Teresa gasped. "Someone set fire to your office?"

Benjamin, the oldest of the group, shook his shaggy brown head. "Honest, Maggie, we wouldn't do something like that. My dad's still pissed at me for the chaw thing."

"And we're afraid of you," Lila added.

The other kids nodded solemnly. I gnawed on the inside of my cheek, focusing all of my energy on keeping my frustration and temper in check. I believed them, which meant that my anxiety over the whole episode had just doubled. It wouldn't do to explode all over these kids just because I didn't get the easy answer that I wanted. Breathing slowly through my nose, and getting a nostril full of the smoky stink rising from my jacket, I sighed. "When you were on your way home for lunch, did you see anything strange or see anyone who isn't part of the pack wandering around?"

The kids shook their heads.

"We just heard that crappy old-timer music you like blaring from the shed," Ricky said, smirking at me. Ricky was the resident smart-ass, which sort of endeared him to me. Rebecca, his twin, elbowed him in the ribs.

My mouth twitched. That smart-ass little answer was exactly what I needed to snap my mood back into place. I kept my voice level but serious. "OK, until I say otherwise, I want you guys to keep an eye on the little kids," I told them. "And if you see anyone you don't recognize walking around, tell the nearest pack member. Don't try to approach them yourselves." I saw Benjamin bristle a little. "Even though you are all clearly bad-asses."

Benjamin smirked, appeased.

"Well, how about we skip the history quiz this afternoon?" Teresa suggested. The kids whooped and hollered. Teresa added, "And as a community service project, you can go over to the center and help Maggie clean up her office."

"Aww." The kids groaned.

Teresa lifted her brow.

"I mean, yaaaay," Ricky said in the least convincing cheerful voice ever.

I laughed. "I'd appreciate it, kids."

"Shouldn't you call the cops?" Teresa asked as the teens filed out of the room.

"I sort of am the cops around here," I reminded her. Teresa had lived in Portland for a while, after getting engaged to a male from one of the local packs. She lived there for two years, an incredibly long engagement for a were, before deciding that he wasn't a good match, and moved back home. Her mother had told my mother that the bastard had called it off and mated with a human.

City life had left Teresa a bit out of sorts. She was used to public transportation, restaurants, movie theaters, cooperating with the human authorities. . . .

"Oh, right," she said, frowning. "It's just been so long since we've had any sort of trouble. I sort of forgot the procedure."

"It's OK. Thanks for sending the kids over. I'm pretty sure I have a brigade of aunties helping me already, but the kids will make the job go faster. Do you need anything here at the school?" I asked as she walked me out of the schoolhouse. "Supplies? Snacks?"

"Nope, we're pretty much covered, as long as I can get the Gilbert kids to stop chewing on the nap-time mats."

"I miss nap-time." I sighed.

"Who wouldn't?" She chuckled, waving me away.

When I arrived at the office, the smoke had all but disappeared. Mom and the aunts and gathered outside the building, whispering among themselves, while the kids worked.

"What a mess." Mom sighed, kissing my cheeks and checking me over for obvious wounds. "Are you all right?"

"I'm fine," I promised, wiggling out of her grasp. There were people watching, for goodness sake. "And I'm not sure what happened. We might need to have a pack meeting later, OK? Can you all tell your families?" The women nodded earnestly. "For right now, how about you go home and let the kids do the heavy lifting? Burn off a little of that energy."

I heard my aunt Bonnie, Ricky's mother, whisper, "Please, Lord," as the ladies dispersed.

I walked into my office and found that Rebecca, the most organized soul in the group, had already started sorting through the papers and trying to salvage some of my ripped file folders. Ricky and Benjamin were in deep conference regarding which caustic substance would best clean the smoke marks from my ceiling.

After convincing them that hydrochloric acid was probably overkill, I directed the others to help me gather my paperbacks and throw what couldn't be saved into the Dumpster out back. As I leaned over to right my slashed office chair, I caught the faint whiff of a familiar scent. Something clean and floral under the smoke.

Fabric softener. The same sort of April Fresh scent that had lingered on my truck.

I leaned closer, inhaling. It was new, definitely not something that had been clinging to my chair that morning. I tried to circulate through the room and subtly sniff the kids to check if maybe they'd cross-contaminated the chair with their moms' laundry habits.

But kids today, what with the *Dateline* sex-predator exposés, notice when an adult sniffs them. Frankly, that made me feel better about the kids' survival instincts. And it ended up being an exercise in unnecessarily creepy futility, because none of them smelled April Fresh. Spring Meadow? Mountain Breeze? Sure. But not a whiff of April Freshness.

I didn't know what to make of it. I believed the kids when they said they didn't barbecue my office. And we hadn't had a stranger wander into town for random vandalism in, well, ever. And I couldn't shake the odd coincidence that the undercarriage of my truck had smelled like dryer sheets. Who the hell would want to cut the brakes on my truck? Or toss my office? One act seemed rather serious, while the other just annoyed the hell out of me and cost me a new wastebasket. And who the hell used so much fabric softener that it obliterated all other traces of their natural scent?

Eli. The pack's former alpha would have thought of something like that as he was terrorizing and attacking people near Cooper's home in Grundy— Susie Quinn, a couple of teenage hikers, Abner Golightly. Cooper had been convinced that he was doing it himself, that he was having some sort of wolf blackout, which was exactly what Eli wanted him to think.

Cooper had a harder time remembering his time as a wolf than most of us. The more time a wolf spends with the pack, the clearer memories are during the phasing. There was a sort of collective memory among us, which could be unfortunate, given some of the stupid shit Samson pulled while on four legs. Since Cooper had spent nearly two years away from the pack, he was practically an amnesiac. When people started dying and Cooper thought it was possible that he could hurt Mo, he thought his only option was to leave.

Eli would have pulled something sneaky and backhanded like messing with my truck or setting fire to the "seat of my authority."

But Eli was dead, which left me without a suspect list.

8

Battle Scars

I CIRCULATED THROUGH THE VILLAGE, warning the older members of the pack to keep an eye out. And able-bodied pack members were going to be running perimeter a lot more often. We didn't want the police traipsing around the valley. I couldn't run fingerprint analysis on my own truck or my office door. So, beyond increased patrols, there wasn't much I could do.

And that's what had me on four legs, running along the lip of the valley on a Monday evening. Well, I was supposed to be running along the edge of the valley.

After Uncle Frank mentioned our possible intruder problem, Lee had shown up with "reinforcements," big burly males from his pack to help run patrols. I think he saw it as some sort of courting gesture, a "see how well we will all work together when the two packs are in-laws" thing. He kept trying to organize us into pairs and send the troops to "strategic locations" in the valley, but he didn't know where those points were. And again, he just wasn't that smart.

The meeting spiraled into a chaotic mess, and it took Samson bellowing "Shut the hell up!" at the chattering mob of weres before I could get everyone calmed down and paired off.

Of course, Lee refused to be paired with anyone but me. But I'd managed to ditch him just outside the village while he was distracted. I took off through a tight passage under a bunch of scrub pines. He was too big to fit through and hadn't managed to catch up to me in more than an hour.

Wandering aimlessly in the dusky, purpling woods, I wondered where Clay was. He'd been paired up with Teresa. I'd planned on partnering him with Samson, but my cousin suddenly had to pee during the assignments. He came back in just as Alicia stepped through the door, eager for a day outside since my mother had offered to watch the boys. And somehow, conveniently, Samson was the only wolf left without a partner.

My big dumb cousin could be downright devious sometimes. His interest in Alicia was an interesting development. It was a little strange, as werewolf males didn't typically spark on widows, particularly widows with children. But if Alicia made Samson happy, I'd help negotiate for her paw myself.

On the other hand, Teresa was showing clear interest in Clay, which was a problem. Clay and I had gone on two dates so far, and we'd had a great time together. Clay could take my mind off the stresses of the pack, but I didn't forget myself completely. It felt safer being with him than the constant emotional carnival ride I seemed to be stuck on with Nick. But how was that was going to work with Teresa? I hated to think of her seeing us and feeling jealous, upset, alone. She'd already been screwed over by Cupid once. Maybe I could try setting her up with one of Lee's packmates. Some of them seemed smarter than he was, though not as handsome.

I was considering the various blind-date candidates when I caught the April Fresh scent of fabric softener lingering on the wind. I bolted after it blindly. Tactically, it was a stupid thing to do. But after tumbling that scent over and over in my head for nearly a week, it drew me like a beacon. My legs seemed to devour the ground as I raced through the trees, following the scent all the way to the town limits of Grundy.

I was running toward Cooper's house, my feet crunching on the frosted ground. The faint, shadowy outline of the moon was rising high over the trees. I lost the scent somewhere near the little brook that babbled through Cooper's backyard. It just disappeared. I slowed to a trot and tried to find some hint of it on the breeze, but I got nothing.

Suddenly, the hair on the back of my neck rose with some electric charge. The faintest trace of that smoky-moss and Sunday-lunch smell wafted around my head. Nick was somewhere near.

And he wasn't alone.

I dashed through the underbrush, charging head-long toward Nick. I broke through the tree line to find him sitting in the clearing, talking in a conversational tone to a huge tawny male wolf that was staring at Nick as if he were on the menu.

Seriously, what does it take to keep one human alive? It was as if he was the anthropological Evel Knievel.

I growled, announcing my presence to the male timber. Keeping his eyes on Nick, the wolf rounded his body toward me. He wasn't about to give up Nick, which had me worried. Most sane wolves try to shy away from human contact whenever possible. This one was treating Nick like prize prey. Using one last quick burst of running energy, I threw myself between man and wolf. I felt Nick retreat behind me, as if he'd finally caught on that something wasn't quite right.

I widened my stance, making myself look as large as possible, and growled. The timber's lip curled away from his fangs, and he grumbled back. He advanced, thinking that because I was smaller, I would back down. I stepped forward, thumping my head against his chest and throwing my shoulder into him. He snapped his jaws, trying to catch my neck, but I'd slipped back enough to give me room for another shove. He shifted his weight, feinting left and then dashing right. I held, sinking my teeth into his foreleg and dragging him away from Nick, none too gently. He retreated slightly, only to rear up on his hind legs and come at me with its front. I ducked, then leaped up, pushing at his stomach until he fell onto his back.

The male leaped to his feet, gathering at his haunches to lunge at me. I braced myself for the impact and instead ended up dropping to the ground as a high-pitched shrieking noise made my head feel as if it was imploding. It was every annoying sound combined—nails scratching on a chalkboard, tires squealing, my aunt Edie singing. I pressed my head against the ground, rolling my ears against the dirt, just to try to block it out. The noise lessened just a little, allowing me to raise my head.

I looked back to see Nick, on his knees, holding what looked like an air horn. His face tensed as his eyes connected with mine. Did he recognize me? Did he know? Could I persuade him to throw that freaking horn into the woods and never use it again?

The wolf beside me rose wobbily to his feet and seemed to be trying to mount another attack. Cringing, Nick blasted the damn horn again, knocking my legs from under me. I lay there for what felt like hours, praying for the pressure in my ears to subside. The other wolf got tired of writhing on the ground in agony, shook his way to his feet, and dashed off. As soon as he was out of the clearing, Nick laid off the "pain horn." I whirled around to find him patting the ground for his glasses.

Honestly, I could have strangled him, but at the moment, I didn't have any thumbs. He reached his hand out, as if he was going to freaking pet me. I barked sharply at him and phased in mid-step.

"What in the name of holy hell where you *think-*

ing?" I demanded. "Do you have *any* idea what could have just happened to you? Do you have instincts that might *not* lead to your certain death?"

Nick gaped at me, a goofy look of astonishment and happiness twisting his moonlit features. "You're a werewolf!" he exclaimed.

Damn it. I hadn't meant to phase back in front of him. I'd just been so mad at him for putting himself in such a stupid situation that I'd put myself in the best form for yelling.

Honestly, I gave up. There was no way to keep Nick from finding out about us. He seemed to have some sort of unholy gift for putting himself in exactly the right place at the right time. He was just going to keep doing this sort of thing until he got himself killed. Maybe it was better this way . . . but there was no way I was going to admit that. I held my arms across my chest self-consciously and glared up at him.

"I knew it!" he cried, half accusing, half triumphant.

"Fine, fine," I spat, throwing up my arms. "I'm a werewolf. Happy?"

"Actually, yes, a little bit," he admitted, sliding his glasses onto his nose.

"What the hell is that thing?" I asked, snatching the little air horn out of his hand.

"Oh, uh, a friend of mine in the bio department at U Dub came up with that," he said sheepishly. "He's still testing it as a defense system for hikers. It works at a decibel level and frequency that are almost debilitating for canines. If you come across a wolf on the trail and use it, the wolf will either run off or be too distracted to chase you when you run away."

"He'll make a fortune," I muttered, slapping it back into his hand.

"I'm sorry. I didn't know it was you. I was just trying to break up the fight—" Realization suddenly dawned on Nick's face. "Oh, hey, wait a minute, so that means that whole scenario with the nudity and the kissing and the rubbing in your truck—that really happened!"

I blushed. Blushed! I never blushed, and here it felt as if my cheeks were going to burst into flames. "No, it didn't!"

He grinned winsomely. "Trust me, I keep very careful mental records of the beautiful women I've seen naked. And you are a very memorable entry in my—"

"If you say 'spank bank,' I will literally knock teeth out of your head."

"I was going to say—" He stopped in mid-sentence, suddenly aghast. "Where does a nice girl even learn a term like 'spank bank'?"

"I'm not a nice girl. And I spend a lot of time with barely postadolescent men," I said, rolling my eyes. "Look, can we have this conversation somewhere a little less secluded and open to attack? What are you even doing out here?"

"I heard Alan make some crack about this being a high-traffic area for the wolf sightings. I came out here to investigate. I saw the wolf . . ."

"And you assumed it was a werewolf and not, say,

an actual timber wolf that could rip your throat out and leave your bones scattered all over this clearing?"

"I thought it was Cooper," he said, paling. "Oh, shit, was that a real wolf?"

"No, that was a werewolf," I said, shaking my head and eyeing the tree line.

"So, why are you so upset?"

"Because I didn't know him."

WE ENDED UP stumbling our way back to Nick's, although Cooper and Mo's place was closer. I didn't want to have to explain to my brother that I'd phased in front of Nick *again* or endure Mo's superior little smirks.

I called Samson to tell him I would be away for the night and to watch the borders of the valley for strangers. He was confused, but I was using my "don't question me" tone, so he agreed. I turned back to Nick.

I crossed my arms over my chest, feeling oddly naked. Well, I was naked. But I felt more naked than usual. How was I going to do this? I wondered. What would this mean for my family? How much of this was I telling him because I wanted him to understand the pack, and how much of it was I telling him because I wanted him to understand me?

We basically stood in his front hall and stared at each other. I turned on my heel and walked into his kitchen. On the wall, he had a map marked with red pins at the attack sites. He had tried to mark the estimated hunting range, with a list of average wolf-hunting ranges posted on the wall next to mileage estimates from each attack site to Mo's house. He had our accident scene marked with a blue pin. He had two huge lists written on two sheets of legal paper. One was marked "Proven" and was completely blank. The other was titled "Total Bullshit—Probably" and included "full-moon phasing," "bipeds," "bitten vs. born," and, finally, "silver bullets" with a question mark next to it. And there was a stack of little notebooks, each one filled with scribbles.

"Technically, silver bullets will kill us," I told him. "And so will real bullets. Bullets kill pretty much everybody."

He nodded and pulled out a Sharpie to make a note on his chart. "Good to know."

"You don't have any other little James Bond gadgets I should know about, do you?" I asked, eyeing the air horn, which he'd tossed onto the counter. "A gun that'll launch a net over me? Cufflinks that shoot bear mace?"

"Nope. That would be pretty cool, though." His lips twitched a little when I glared at him. "But obviously not appropriate."

Snickering, he tossed me a pair of old basketball shorts and a Reidland High School Greyhounds T-shirt. I turned my back to slip into it.

"What the hell is that?" he asked, suddenly very close behind me, running his fingertips along three slashing scars down my back.

"Angry bear. I was on a run with my brothers at Eagle Pass," I murmured. "I was young. I thought I was the biggest, baddest thing on the mountain. The bear reminded me otherwise, when I got too close to her cubs."

"But you heal so quickly; I seem to remember something about that," he said.

"Sure, we heal, but we still scar. It's not like we're vampires." Nick's face lit up with delight and a million questions, so I had to add, "As far as I know, vampires are not real."

"Damn it," he grumbled as I pulled the shirt over my head and slid into the shorts. Nick lifted my leg and examined the waffle pattern of tiny dents along my thigh. He quirked an eyebrow.

"Never piss off a porcupine, no matter how jolly he may seem," I explained gravely. "Cartoons are very misleading."

He pointed to another long white streak on my shin.

"Softball game, sliding into second. Samson wouldn't get out of the damn baseline."

He laughed, then traced his fingers along the faint trio of short lines just over my throat. "I'll get to that one," I told him. His brows furrowed. "Ask me anything," I offered. "I'll tell you all about us, and then I'll tell you why you shouldn't share what I tell you with other people."

His face lit up as if I'd just offered him the Holy Grail, a Babe Ruth rookie card and Megan Fox's phone number.

Just to take the look off his face, I added, "That reason includes the words 'because I'll kill you and make sure no one ever finds your body.'"

"I can live with that." He nodded, making little "hurry up" motions with his hands.

"No, no," I told him. "I don't start the explanations until you have your little notebook and a number two pencil and all that crap. I don't like interruptions."

Patting his pockets frantically, he ran for his notebook, and it was clear that he had pages of carefully scripted questions. His eyes scrambled over the pages for a few moments before he finally looked up at me, pushed his glasses up on the bridge of his nose, and said, "How?"

"How do we change?" I asked. He nodded. "It's just genetics. Some people have good balance or are really good at making egg salad. We can change into abnormally large wolves."

I explained to Nick that there were packs all over the world. Our pack happened to be descended from people who lived in the valley. An outsider crossed the frozen oceans, made his way over the mountains, and married a valley woman. He must have come from Russia or northeastern Asia, where there were a lot of packs. Either way, something about the mixing of their bloodlines produced the first wolf-sons, two huge, burly, probably pretty hairy fellas. There was a terrible winter, and the hunters couldn't get enough food for their families. People were starving. The Northern Man's elder son wished for the strength of the wolf, so that he could provide for his family and neighbors, and he wished so strongly that he was able to phase. And then his brother, seeing what the elder could do, joined in. They were able to hunt up enough food for the whole village and store some away, which was almost being a millionaire in the those days. The other villages kept asking how they did it, but my ancestors were smart enough not to tell. Instead, they shared what they had and prevented jealousy, which was pretty damned ingenious. I like to think my family invented public relations.

"Phasing just became a way of life," I told Nick. "They had a lot of kids, all of whom could transform. So could their kids, and their kids, et cetera, et cetera. And here we are."

He was silent, his eyes all shiny and bright like a kid's on Christmas morning.

"I'm starved," I said, motioning at his cabinets. "Do you mind?"

He shook his head. I took a carton of eggs out of his fridge and heated a pan. I opened his spice drawer and was shocked to find garlic salt that was at least five years old and what might, at one point, have been nutmeg.

"Mo would be appalled by this," I told him, clucking my tongue.

"I'll subscribe to the Spice of the Month Club if you keep talking," he promised solemnly.

"Well, don't do that online; you'll be shocked by your search results." I cracked eggs, beating them lightly. I poured them into the pan and took a hunk of cheddar cheese from the fridge. I sniffed to make sure it was mold-free. I wasn't a cook. I didn't have the knack or the time for it. Plus, my mom never let me near her stove. You melt one microwave, and the woman completely loses her sense of humor. But at the moment, it felt nice to move around the kitchen, to keep my hands busy and give myself some time to work through what I wanted to say.

"Can you make toast?" I asked.

He nodded, coming out of whatever contemplative fog he'd been in. "So, is the pack set up like a real wolf pack? Is there an alpha male?" he asked, sliding wheat bread into the toaster.

"Actually, there's an alpha female," I said. His jaw dropped. I grinned and pointed to myself.

"That is so hot," he groaned. "Not to be a chauvinist, but how do you get dozens of big, burly guys and older, stubborn ladies to listen to your every command? Don't they resent being bossed around by a woman?"

"Well, Dr. Dolittle, as you well know, there are lots of matriarchal setups in the animal kingdom, including killer whales, bees, and elephants. Mother Nature isn't completely chauvinist," I said, chuckling. "It's not typical for werewolves to be led by a female, but in the absence of the rightful alpha, Cooper, it was the pack's choice. The alpha serves as a sort of leader for the village. While the lesser pack members have property rights and general free will, all major decisions must be filtered through the alpha couple. Or would be, if I had a mate."

When he frowned, I could almost see the "sounds like a cult" wheels turning in his head.

I added, "I know it sounds weird. Wolves work together to make sure that everybody in the pack is fed, safe. They're conditioned to work in harmony under a clear social rule. They need a single voice to lead them, the alpha. So when the alpha tells you to do something, even if you know what he's asking is stupid or dangerous, you'll do it. And you're happy to do it, because it's for the good of the pack. You need that community, the family, to feel complete. It's a little harder for me, because I'm not the rightful alpha. Sometimes I have to appeal to my pack's collective common sense and, well, their fear that I'll kick their asses, to get my way."

"So, if the pack is so important, why did Cooper leave?"

I lifted an eyebrow and flipped an only slightly singed cheese omelet onto a plate. I poured more eggs into the pan and grated more cheese. I forked a huge mouthful of omelet into my mouth. "You really don't know how to ask softball questions, do you?" I asked around my food.

"Well, it's not like I don't share!" he exclaimed, handing me a piece of buttered toast, which I promptly devoured. "Now that I know that the truck interlude was real, I know I told you about my crazy childhood. I can break out the stories about being left in the family station wagon while my mom gambled for twelve-hour stints. We can play the 'whose childhood was more screwed up? game. Because I've never lost."

I countered, "My dad was shot in the head by research scientists because they thought he was going to eat them."

He pursed his lips. "So, you are a contender."

Oh, hell. If I was going to do this, I was going all

in. He was probably going to find out anyway. My mom would probably tell him over tea and cake. I took a deep breath and told him my story, that when I was sixteen or so, another pack came to the valley and tried to take it. Cooper had only been alpha for about a year. I guess at the time, I didn't realize how young Cooper was. He was my big brother and always seemed so grown-up to me. But he was practically a kid, and not only was he taking care of me and my mom, but he was running the pack, too. Looking back, I'm sort of ashamed that I didn't see how much stress he was under. But I was young and, well, stupid.

Late one night, this other pack showed up and dragged me out of my bed into the street. I explained, "The alpha, this huge guy named Jonas, held me by the back of the neck and told Cooper that he'd wring it like a chicken's if we didn't just hand the valley over and disappear."

"Like Roanoke?"

I squinted at him.

"Colonial Virginia . . . whole community disappeared into thin air. It's like the first unsolved mystery of the New World." He held up his hands as I flipped the omelet onto his plate. "I'll tell you later."

I rolled my eyes. "Anyway, these numb-nuts had apparently hunted their own packlands into nothing, and the valley is known to be a particularly sweet setup in the were community."

He frowned while he chewed. "I assume that's a werewolf faux pas?"

"Territory is all we have sometimes. You just don't do that. Werewolves are genetically programmed to protect their packlands, to stay close. Ripping a pack away from that is just evil. A wolf's brain is hard-wired to protect a certain area of land, to hunt there, to live there. And that's the way it's been for our pack for almost a thousand years. So, if they'd managed to snake it out from under us, imagine fighting against that kind of draw, every waking moment of every day. It would be torture. The sick thing is, if they'd come to us and asked if they could stay, I know Cooper would have let them. Hell, he did offer them a place, even when they threatened us. He's just that kind of guy. He's better than me, kinder."

"Eh, you're not so bad."

I pressed my hand over my heart. "Thank you, really, the praise, it's heartwarming."

"You know that you're fantastic," he said.

"Thanks. Back to my story. So, Jonas is shaking my head so hard I can actually feel my brain bouncing around in my skull. And I'm just laughing my ass off, because I know any minute, my brother's going to open a case of whoop-ass on this guy. I could almost taste the fight, and it was going to be beautiful. I was so caught up in the anticipation that it took me a minute to realize Cooper was just standing there. He was frozen. It hadn't even occurred to me that he wouldn't know exactly what to do. I mean, how stupid is that?"

"Everyone idolizes their big brothers," he said, shrugging, pushing my hair over my shoulder. "What happened?"

"I kicked Jonas in the balls and called him a jerkoff."

He snorted. "Well, of course, you did."

I shrugged. "I figured it would wake Cooper up, draw him into the fight. And man, Jonas was pissed. He phased faster than you could blink and went right for my throat." I dragged my fingers over the faint white lines left behind by his claws. "I thought, *Bring it. If Cooper isn't going do his job, I'll do it.* But damned if Cooper didn't phase and shove me out of the way. I tried to circle around, get at Jonas myself, but Cooper wouldn't let me. When I finally got a shot in at Jonas, I jumped at him too early, and the fucker pinned me. I would have felt like an asshole, except he had his teeth at my throat. I was too busy panicking." I twisted my fingers around the blankets and looked down. This was the part of the story I hated. The one I'd never talked about with anyone but Mom and Cooper.

"Go on, Maggie, please."

"Cooper knocked him off me. And he, um, he killed him. You know what they say about cutting the head off the snake? Well, it just pisses the rest of the snake off. The enemy pack circled on Cooper. They were going to tear him apart, and he took them all on. He killed all of them. He wouldn't let any of us near the fight. Except for a straggler male who tried to jump on his back. I killed him, without even thinking about it."

Nick was quiet, picking at the remains of egg on his plate. "Does it bother you?"

"Oh, hell, no," I exclaimed with false, exaggerated cheer. "It's awesome to know I've taken someone's life, that I'm responsible for taking a wolf out of this world, when there are so few of us left. My mom brings it up every Thanksgiving, so the whole family can relive the memory."

"I'm glad you're taking this seriously," he dead-panned.

"Cooper had a hard time with it. He had night-mares. He lost weight, stopped running with the pack. He didn't want to be near any of us. He couldn't bring himself to touch our mother, wouldn't even hug her, for the longest time. He said he was afraid of what he was, of what was inside him that let him kill people, even if it was in defense of the pack. If I'd known anything back then, I'd have known he probably had PTSD or something. But I thought he was being dramatic and stupid. Every-body tried to talk to him, to tell him how proud we were, how proud my father would have been. But nothing stuck. He just sort of retreated into himself. The pack suffered. It was like mass depression or something. Nobody wanted to run or hunt. Without a leader, we were more vulnerable than ever. I got scared, and I was hurt . . . and that's not something I work through very well. There was a lot of, um, lashing out."

"Imagine," he said dryly.

"When Cooper talked about that night, he made it sound like he'd done something unforgivable. And that meant what I'd done was unforgivable, too. I'd depended on him to be everything, a brother, a father, and to have him snatch that away . . . well, needless to say, I got pissed. I mean, who did he think he was, being all tortured and selfish when we needed him? He was the alpha. He had a responsibility to us, and he was just pissing it away. I wouldn't have wasted it. I knew that much. And that little seed of resentment started to grow and take root.

"Cooper decided we were better off without him and moved to Grundy. I went a little crazy. And for years, I kept expecting the hurt to go away, even just a little bit, but it just seemed to get worse.

"My cousin Eli air-quote 'reluctantly' stepped in to take over the pack. He'd been a sort of kindred spirit. He always said he was just holding Cooper's place until Cooper came back. And I started to resent that, too. Without Cooper, I was the strongest in the pack. I was the fastest. Except for Eli, I was probably the smartest . . . which wasn't saying much. Once we were back on our feet, I didn't see why Eli should be holding the place at all. I thought I was ready to take Cooper's place right then. And why shouldn't I? He didn't want it, so why shouldn't I have it?"

Nick lifted his eyebrows.

"I know. But I was eighteen. How level-headed and mature were you at eighteen?"

He shrugged. "Well, I was living on my own and putting myself through school."

"As a person, I sort of sucked," I admitted. "For years, I was just horrible to Cooper. Every time he came around, I made it as painful as possible for him. As in, I took parts of him off. It wasn't enough for him to be run from his home. I didn't think he was hurting enough. And it helped that Eli was there, pouring poison in my ear. 'See,' he said, 'Cooper's fine. He's making a life for himself. He's not even sorry.' And then Mo came along. Cooper was the one who saved her from John Teague. Mo figured out what he was, and she didn't care. She loved him. I saw how happy she made him. And somehow that made it worse.

"I figured, I was hurt, so he should hurt more, you know? Eli fed into it, and I didn't realize how deeply I'd fallen. He pulled the strings, and I danced. He said all the right things in all the right ways. Turns out Eli was the one who brought Jonas's pack down on us in the first place. Sort of an 'I'd rather serve at the right hand of the devil' thing. When that fell through, he settled for running the pack himself. But he didn't think Cooper had moved far enough away. He was afraid Cooper would get over his guilt and come back."

I explained Eli's reign of terror, the attacks, and how they drove Cooper away from home, family, and the woman he loved. But when Mo was pregnant with Eva, Eli realized that Cooper was never going to leave permanently, that people in the valley would always be waiting for him to come back. He snapped. He went after Mo. He figured Cooper wouldn't want to go on without her.

"If we hadn't gotten there in time . . . well, it was Mo. Given that she was swinging a wrench at Eli when we showed up, she might have had a chance," I admitted.

"Wow."

"She's kind of a bad-ass under the apron," I said,

smiling fondly. "You know, this might be the most words I've ever strung together in my life. I don't think I like it much."

"You should do it more often. You say really interesting stuff," he said, taking our plates to the sink.

"This is the part where I tell you that your body will never be found." I walked across the living room and flopped onto the couch. "Werewolves don't share their secrets with humans often. And if you screw me over, I'll have to kill you. Not ha-ha, 'joking around' kill you. It will mean the actual end of your having a pulse."

He blanched, as if during all of the information I'd just dumped on him, he'd forgotten that he wasn't going to be allowed to share it with anyone.

"But this is what I've been waiting for my whole life!" he shouted. "Proof of an intelligent species besides humans! Proof that the folk tales, the fairy stories, the things that go bump in the night, they could all be real! This is one of those moments that redefines how we see our history. It's electricity, the Rosetta Stone, and Darwin's theory all in one!"

"All of which made the men who discovered them incredibly famous," I noted dryly.

"That's why you think—I don't give a shit about being famous! Hell, I've already got more money than I know what to do with. I just want people to know what's really out there, what's possible. That there's more to life than what we've been told."

"Stop and think. You're not the first human to

know about us. Do you honestly think I would tell you this and just let you run to the nearest wacko tabloid? Do you think I would let you unveil the existence of my species on a whim? This is one of those sacred-trust sorts of things. We let you into our lives, and you keep our secrets . . . or we kill you. It's not a particularly friendly sacred trust."

"So, why tell me in the first place?"

"To keep you from wandering around in the woods, getting yourself eaten by random apex predators." I sighed, scrubbing my hands over my face. "You're one of those guys who won't stop until they stumble right into the path of certain death. You want to know everything. Well, I'm willing to share that with you, but you won't be able to tell anybody about it. You have to decide which is more important, knowing everything or knowing a little and being published . . . and then dying. I can't emphasize that last part enough."

"I—you—I can't possibly decide something like that right now!" he exclaimed.

"Well, you kind of have to."

"Can I have some time?"

I considered. There was a possibility that he could use that time to run to said tabloid. But he didn't have photos or recordings, just some scribbled notes that made him sound like a crackpot. I nodded, edging toward the door. "Sure."

"Is it weird that after all the death threats, I still sort of want to kiss you?"

I nodded again. "A little."

He chuckled and leaned in anyway. Opening the

back door, I pressed my hand against his chest and gave him a gentle shove back. "I can't."

"Why? I happen to remember, now that I know I wasn't having a concussion dream, that we've already done this. Several times. And a little more, now that it's coming back to me."

I smiled ruefully. "I just can't. If you decide that you can live with the consequences of knowing about us, I'll tell you why."

"That's sort of cruel."

I sighed. "Welcome to the wacky world of werewolves."

2

Are Eyelash Curlers Banned by the Geneva Convention?

THE NEXT FRIDAY NIGHT, I climbed out of my mother's SUV, pulling uncomfortably at my skirt and cursing the day I was born with two X chromosomes.

Yes, I was wearing a skirt.

I'd finally made time for another date with Clay, and it just happened to be the biggest social event of the season. Such as it was. Every year, Evie and Buzz hosted the Big Freeze at the Glacier, a sort of big last hootenanny before winter set in. The first heavy frost of year always came pretty early, in what most lower forty-eight residents would still consider fall. And although it would be weeks before the snows truly set in and made travel difficult, the people of Grundy put on their Sunday best and gathered for beer, dancing, and general merriment. For most of the people who lived on the fringes of town, it was the last chance to socialize before winter hit. I rarely went, since it was basically a way for unattached men and women of Grundy to find the person they planned on shacking up with during the cold months.

Normally, Evie scheduled the party right before the almanac forecast the first freeze. But this year, she and Mo had rescheduled at the last minute because some Food Network guy was coming by to film a segment about "Hidden Gems of the Northwest," and they wanted to hold the party before the crews arrived. Clay had been pretty understanding when I told him that our date was suddenly semiformal and that I would have to meet him there, since I was dropping my mom off at Cooper's so she could babysit. Which was just one more reason to like Clay.

Mom knocked on Cooper's door, because she didn't want to be "that" mother-in-law. I rolled my eyes and opened the door, despite her scolding. Cooper was standing in the living room, eager to hand the baby off before she could spit up on his good shirt.

"Hello, my sugar pie!" Mom cooed at Eva, who was all pink and rosy and recently bathed. That would last all of five minutes. As Mom snuffled and nuzzled her pride and joy, Kara and Mo came out of the bedroom and screeched to a halt. They were staring at me.

"What?" I said, looking down at my sleeveless black knee-length sheath. "You said to dress up. I'm wearing my dress."

"Is it your designated funeral dress?" Kara asked,

adjusting the strap of her own low-cut royal-blue number.

I huffed out an annoyed breath. I caught my mother, my own flesh and blood, standing behind me, nodding.

"Come on, sweetie, we only have an hour or so to make this work," Kara said, pulling at my elbow.

"Make what work?" I demanded.

Mo and Kara hooked their arms through mine and dragged me toward the bedroom. Mo wasn't playing fair. She knew I wouldn't do anything in front of Kara. She knew I couldn't just shake her off, phase, and run. Cooper came ambling out of the bedroom, looping his tie around his collar.

"Cooper! Help!"

The coward turned on his heel and walked into the kitchen as if he hadn't seen me getting frog-marched by the estrogen squad. "Hey! Don't act like you don't hear me! Seriously! Remember that time I hid a salmon in your truck and it stank for a month? Child's play! My revenge will be swift and terrible. Damn it, Cooper!" I yelled as they dragged me into their den of girliness.

They threw me into a chair near Mo's bathroom and spread out torture devices on the bathroom counter. They glared down at me like supervillians trying to pry information out of James Bond.

"She's got such beautiful skin," Kara said, lifting my chin and talking about my face as if I wasn't even in the room. "No sense in covering it up. We just need to play up the eyes, tame the brows, and gloss the lips. A good, strong blood-red, I think."

I snorted and muttered something about a quick hunt on the way to the dance, and Mo gave me the stink-eye. Without warning, they pounced. My dress was whipped over my head, and my hair was pulled out of its ponytail. The next half-hour was a haze of stuff rubbed on my face, my hair yanked, and my body pushed and pulled at as if it wasn't even mine. I was tweezed. A lot.

"Can't do much about the painfully sensible shoes," Mo muttered as she safety-pinned the sides of my dress to give it a "silhouette." "It's too cold out for sexy shoes."

"Tell me about it. The one thing I miss about home is being able to wear peep-toes year-round," Kara griped, giving my hair a gentle yank to remind me to keep my head up. She was arranging my hair into some weird cinnamon-bun shape on top of my head. I only hoped I wouldn't walk out of there looking like Princess Leia . . . then again, Nick might dig that.

But I didn't care what Nick liked, I reminded myself. Clay was my date. Nick was the guy who was currently considering whether he could be a silent witness to my family's wolfy weirdness.

I hadn't heard from the good doctor in a few days, and given the fact that the valley hadn't been overrun with teams of commando scientists, I took that to mean that he was still considering my proposal. I'd had twinges of panic that first day after the "big reveal," wondering if I'd made a huge mistake in trusting him. But the silence of the last few days had been a sort of balm. Surely, the first twenty-four hours after hearing something like that were the hardest to keep it a secret. But I couldn't go looking for him to ask him what he decided. Every time I did that, I ended up naked in some way.

This might be harder than I thought. I frowned.

Kara stepped back to look at her handiwork. "She looks like a grumpy ballerina."

"It's a little too . . ." Mo took out the pins and shook my hair out, slicking it back with some citrusy goo. "That's better. More tousle, less froufrou. She needs a smoky eye."

"That sounds painful," I said, and was ignored. I shied away when Kara came at me with what looked like a cross between pliers and a speculum. "What the hell is that thing?"

"It's an eyelash curler."

"How are you going to curl my eyelashes when that thing rips them all out?" I demanded, jerking my head away when she moved toward me with the sinister-looking device.

"Hold still, and it won't hurt," she said, clamping it down on my lashes.

"Owowowow!" I yelled, my eye watering as she pulled the lid away from my eyeball and crimped the hairs. "You're a damned liar, Kara Reynolds."

"Beauty is pain, babe," Mo advised me. I snaked my hand around Kara and took a swipe at my sister-in-law. Since *she* could freaking move, she just danced out of the way.

"Well, just focus on your breathing, and you should be fine," Kara said wryly as she went for the other eye.

"You stay away from me, you psycho."

"You can't just walk around with one set curled. It looks weird," Mo protested.

"It can't make that much of a difference," I shot back. Mo rolled her eyes and thrust a hand mirror in front of my face. "Oh, I guess it does."

Since the lift and curve of my newly pressed eyelashes really did make them look bigger, I dutifully sat still while they put three shades of gray eye shadow on my eyelids, followed by eyeliner . . . then they wiped the whole thing off and started from scratch because it was "too much."

"What's that called?" I asked as Mo painted a bright, bold red across my lips.

She checked the little label on the end of the lip-gloss tube. "Cabaret." I frowned, so Mo added, "As in, 'life is a'?"

"When you wonder why we don't always understand each other, it's because of jokes like that," I told her. Mo huffed and slicked my lips with gloss.

I wasn't allowed to see a mirror. Kara kept muttering under her breath about killer cheekbones and "lucky bitch who doesn't even appreciate her teeny-tiny pores." Finally, they stood staring at me, trying to figure out what to do next.

"Maybe we could . . ." Kara trailed off.

"No, she's perfect," Mo said, stopping Kara's hand as she reached toward me with the powder brush. "Doing anything else would make her overdone."

"I think I hate her," Kara said. Mo shrugged.

They turned me around to face the mirror.

I was me but different. My hair looked as if I actually planned for it to fall around my face in dark waves, instead of all messy and wind-blown. My eyelashes felt all stiff and goopy, but they looked damn good. The cinched-up dress showed off the few curves I had, and the satiny red scarf Mo had tied around my dress made my waist look tiny. Don't get me wrong, I like me. But seeing this hotter, femme incarnation of myself was very cool.

"Let me get this straight. You guys spend an hour scrubbing and polishing your faces, putting on three layers of makeup, and fiddling with your hair so you can like me after I take most of the makeup off?" I asked, grinning at them.

"Yep, definitely hate her," Kara decided.

Mom gasped and scrambled for a camera when I emerged from Barbieville, USA.

"Mom," I moaned.

"Oh, hush, you're gorgeous. And it's not like you went to your senior prom. Give me a chance to fuss."

"This is *why* I didn't go to my senior prom!"

Mom snapped picture after picture, from every angle conceivable. Only Eva's spitting up in my mother's hair persuaded her to stop. I mentally doubled the amount I'd budgeted for Eva's first Christmas present.

"Mom, it's just a party. There's no reason to make a big deal out of it," I told her. "It's just another Friday night at the Glacier."

*   *   *

AND I THOUGHT SO, right until we got to the edge of town and I lost my nerve. I wasn't about to change for some stupid guy. Even if he was hot and available and a werewolf, I didn't want Clay to think he had that kind of power over me. Screw this; the minute Mo was in the door, I was going to phase and run home.

Eyeing the way I was gripping the truck door, Mo warned, "You do that, and I'm telling Samson you were too chicken-shit to go to a silly dance."

I grunted, growling at her and shoving a couple of warm, cheesy mini-quiches into my mouth.

"I hate you," I muttered as Cooper parked his truck in front of the Glacier. "I hate the both of you."

"And me, too?" Kara asked.

"You, too," I muttered. "Welcome to the family."

"I'm so touched." Kara sighed, with her hand over her heart.

"Well, hate me while you're carrying in that tray of mini-egg rolls, OK?" Mo asked, handing me one of a dozen carefully wrapped parcels of appe-tizers for the party. "But eventually, you will agree that you look hot and I am right, I have always been right, and I always will be right."

"It's best not to argue with her when she's like this," Kara told me. "She literally remembers every single occasion she was right. She still brags about warning me against fluffy bangs in tenth grade."

"But you went ahead and did it anyway," Mo snickered. "And now, who hides her sophomore yearbook like it's homemade porn?"

"I'll pay you ten bucks to see the yearbook," I offered Mo.

"Done," Mo said, grinning. Kara scowled at us both. And it struck me that, other than the facial torture devices and hair shellac, hanging out with girls wasn't that different from hanging out with the boys. They didn't care if I cursed at them. We called each other names and threatened each other regularly. That was pretty much my top three activities with my male packmates. I wasn't ready to let them paint my toenails, but maybe I wouldn't respond quite so rudely the next time Mo asked me over for a movie night or something.

As we came through the door, goodies in hand, Alan sidled up to Kara and kissed her cheek.

"Hey, sweetheart, who's that with you—" Alan started as I took off my coat and turned toward him. "Holy shit!" he exclaimed. The room got quiet as everyone turned to see what had made straight-arrow Alan curse. I heard glass crashing to the floor and looked to see Buzz holding a dishrag in one hand and a shocked expression on his face.

"Thank you," I muttered to Alan.

Clay looked very nice, if not uncomfortable, in a crisp white shirt and red tie. He'd obviously taken time to get his sandy hair in some order. Clay and Cooper eyed each other and gave each other a distant but not unfriendly nod, which I thought was pretty normal for brother-date interactions. At least, Cooper didn't start cleaning a firearm in front of him.

"Hey, Mags."

"Clay," I said, waiting for some comment as he eyed me from head to toe.

"Wanna get a beer?" he asked, having to shout a little now that the band Evie and Buzz had brought in from Dearly had started a bad rendition of "Looking for Love in All the Wrong Places." People were moving toward the dance floor in twos, doing dance steps I knew I was in no way qualified to execute.

"Sure," I said, a little taken aback that he hadn't even mentioned that I wasn't wearing jeans and flannel. Was he setting me up for some sort of joke? "So, uh, you don't have anything to say, something smartassy about my dress or the stuff on my eyelids?"

He shrugged. "You always look this good."

"Oh, I like you," I said, smiling at him as he put his arm around me and walked me to the bar.

Across the room, Nick was talking to Alan, Kara, and Darby Carmichael, a checker at Hannigan's Grocery. Darby was a tall brunette with a heart-shaped face and big caramel-brown eyes. I'd never really paid much attention to her before, but now, given the way her fingers were curling around Nick's arm, I sort of hated her. With the fiery passion of a thousand suns.

Nick saw me with Clay and frowned. He looked down at his beer, and I could see his hand flex around the bottle.

Ha, right back at you, Doc.

"Wanna get a table?" I asked. "I'll grab the beers."

Clay grinned and waved at Mo as he claimed one of the booths near the pool tables.

"Maggie, what are you doing?" Mo asked, smiling around the question and waving back at Clay.

"I'm here with Clay."

The line of her mouth did this weird pretzel thing, which was pretty funny. "I thought you were going to meet Nick here."

"Why would you think that?"

"Well, Cooper mentioned that you two were getting close. Or 'got pretty close to something.' I don't know. He flushed beet-red and started to mumble about concussions. I love him, but I don't always understand him," she said, frowning.

"Well, he neglected to mention the part where I told Nick that us getting close was a hallucination brought on by head injury."

"Yeah, he did leave that part out," Mo said, chewing on her lip. "This is why we need to spend more time together. I need unfiltered information."

"Well, I'm sorry your makeover efforts for Nick were in vain."

"Oh, honey, that wasn't for Nick. We've been itching to do that for a while. It had to be done, for the good of mankind," Mo told me. I frowned. Mo made a gesture toward her upper lip. "Mustaches are for porn stars and Tom Selleck, not young ladies."

"Fuck you very much, Mo."

"Don't kiss my daughter with that mouth. I'm afraid of what she'll pick up."

I made a sour face at her as I sauntered back toward the table. As I was walking past the restroom corridor, there was a yank on my arms. I was rather proud that I didn't spill a drop of beer as Nick pulled me into the little hallway.

"Hands! Hands!" I exclaimed, shrugging out of the hold he had on my arms. He held up his hands in a defensive position but didn't step away. He kept his voice low, quiet, as he murmured, "Sorry, I didn't know how else to get your attention."

"How about 'Hey, Maggie, how about we have a conversation that doesn't involve lurking near a men's room?'"

"That probably would have been better," he agreed. "So, I wanted to tell you, I'm in."

"I really don't know how to respond to that."

He rolled his eyes. "I mean, I'm willing to give up the possibility of ever telling anyone about your family, if you let me study your pack. I want to know everything there is to know about you. It would be worth it, just to have my questions answered. I give you my word, it would be for my own personal enlightenment. I will never tell a soul."

The intensity of his voice, the close proximity of his mouth to my ear, sent a shiver down my spine. I cleared my throat, backing away as much as the wall would allow.

He continued, "We don't even have to tell your family what I'm doing. In fact, their behavior would probably be more natural if they didn't know why I was there. You can always tell them we're dating."

"I can't tell them that, because they know that I'm already dating Clay."

The confident nonchalance he'd been using melted away, and he seemed honestly bewildered for a moment. "You were serious about that? I thought you were just trying to put me off at the clinic."

"I was trying to put you off at the clinic with information that's true. We've been out a few times," I said, shrugging. "He's a nice guy, a member of the pack. And that's important."

"Why?"

I looked down the corridor to make sure none of the other guests was within earshot. But given the head-splitting volume at which the band was playing, it wouldn't matter if they were. "Fewer and fewer of us are mating with werewolves. We're basically breeding ourselves out of existence. There are more dead-liners—that's what we call our relatives who can't phase—living in the village than pack members."

"Hold on, hold on," Nick muttered, patting his pockets for his little notebook. He settled his glasses on his nose and found a pen. He took a deep breath and smiled at me. "Explain."

"Well, wolves mate for life," I said in a low, soft voice. "Werewolf mates are claimed with a bite, which is sort of ceremonial, or through flat-out impregnation. Our genetic material is what you might call obsessive. Once our bloodline mixes with someone, something in our bodies just won't let us make babies with anyone else. It's a one-mate-only opportunity. It's why you don't see a lot of remarried widows of childbearing age in packs. Their new husbands won't be able to have children of their own."

"So, you're all virgins when you get married?"

I waffled my hand back and forth. "Most are, but

there are exceptions. We can have sex with someone and not be mated to them . . . but since werewolves, particularly the females, are hyperfertile, having sex means you're probably going to end up pregnant either way. So most of us don't risk knocking up a random one-night stand."

"So, you're a virgin."

"I'm not talking to you about this."

He held up his hands. "Purely scientific interest."

"No comment," I grumbled.

"Subject is uncooperative," he murmured, scribbling.

"Subject can't believe you're taking notes about my virginity," I shot back.

"So, what does any of this have to do with you dating Clay instead of taller, smarter, more charming candidates?"

I snorted. "When I get around to having kids, I need to pass the wolf genes forward. And for a good shot at that, I need to mate with a werewolf. Our pack is dying out. Werewolves everywhere are dying out. We're an endangered species. I can't risk being with somebody unless I know for sure that I can produce a werewolf with him."

"But you said there are dead-liners who come from two wolf parents, right? So, there's no guarantee."

"I have to at least try. I have a responsibility to my people, Nick. How could I live with myself ten years from now, fifty years from now, when there aren't any more wolves born to my pack? If I let this go anywhere, if I let myself get involved with you, and we couldn't produce a wolf, it's not like I can try again with someone else. I can't take it back, you see?"

"No, frankly, I don't see why that would be so bad."

"Because if I do, what kind of example am I setting? I'd be telling my people that duty and responsibility take a backseat to being happy? That putting yourself first is more important than the long term? I've got people counting on me, Nick. Look, I like you, a lot. I like spending time with you. But if we're going to keep seeing each other, it can only be as friends."

"Bullshit." He took the beer bottle I was throttling out of my hands. I think he was afraid I would chuck it at him. "That's bullshit, Maggie. If you don't want me, fine. But don't go blaming some breeding obligation for you running."

"Running?"

"Running scared," Nick challenged.

"You don't know anything about me except what I've told you. And I've told you more than I should. You can at least pay me back by not calling it 'bullshit.' I thought they taught you better at all those fancy schools, cultural sensitivity and all that crap."

"I'm not calling your beliefs 'bullshit,' I'm calling your hiding behind them so you don't have to deal with me 'bullshit.'"

"I don't have to stay here and listen to this," I spat, snatching the beer from him. "I told you what you wanted to know. Now, either stand by your word, or go straight to hell."

"Well, let me move aside so you can *run* away." With a mocking little bow, he stepped aside and cleared a path to the barroom.

"You're an asshole!" I spat as I brushed by him.

"You're a stubborn brat!"

"Good! I guess that will make it easier for you to get over this lame little crush on me!"

"Well, we're on to a great start on this 'friends' thing, aren't we?" He grunted as I stomped away. He caught my arm and ignored my protests as I tried to free myself, practically dragging him along with me. He turned me toward him, my nose nearly colliding with his chest. His free hand floated just over my shoulder, as if he knew that touching me would send me over the edge toward decking him.

"I'm sorry," he muttered, his mouth hovering close to my ear. I shivered but played it as a squirm to get away from him. "I'm sorry that I'm not handling this very gracefully. I want you, Maggie. But if he's what you want, I'm not going to stand in the way." I shoved past him, but he caught my arm again.

"What are you doing? You said you wouldn't stand in the way. This is standing in the way *and* dragging me around like a rag doll, you jackass!"

"Clearly, I was bluffing!" Nick exclaimed. "And you called me on it, so good for you." He grabbed my arms and shoved me against the door. His body pressed against mine, and the weight felt so good. Instead of pushing his shoulders away, as I intended to, I found my fingers wrapped around his collar, pulling him closer. His hand snaked around to the small of my back and bunched the fabric of my dress, until I could feel his fingers brushing against my ass.

His mouth was hovering so close to mine I could feel his breath fanning over my lips, and I instinctually flicked the tip of my tongue over them. He moved closer, and just before his whiskers brushed over my hypersensitive skin, I pressed the flat of my palms against his shoulders.

"I can't," I said softly.

He rested his chin against my temple and whispered, "He's no good for you."

"Neither are you," I said, stepping sideways, away from him. "Besides, aren't you on the verge of being engaged to Little Miss Express Lane?"

"Darby's a nice girl."

"Well, Clay is a nice guy. You just don't like him because you're jealous."

"Yeah, I wish I had a forehead that proves our genetic link to Cro-Magnon man." I glared at him. He sighed. "OK, fine, that was petty. And I am jealous. What am I supposed to do? He's a likable guy, and he can do the one thing I can't."

"Find his glasses without the aid of the state police?"

"And that's the delicate charm that calls me like a siren's song," he said, his lips twitching into a smile.

I murmured, "This is it, Nick. We can be friends, or we'll have nothing. Your choice."

"You're not making this easy for me."

I huffed out a laugh. "I'm not supposed to."

"If it means that I can spend time with you, I'll call myself your friend. I'm not going to stop hoping for more. But I'm going to wait for you to come to me."

"That won't happen," I said, to myself as much as to him.

"We'll see," he said, wriggling his golden-blond eyebrows at me.

I rolled my eyes and turned away, leading Nick out of the hallway.

Unfortunately, Clay had gone to the bar to look for his wandering date and was talking to Darby. I tried to plaster a pleasant expression on my face as I slid into the empty space on his left. He breathed a sigh of relief.

"I thought you'd crawled out the bathroom window to escape," he said, taking the beer and bussing my cheek. He stopped for a moment, inhaling. He shot a suspicious look at Nick, who had sidled up behind Darby.

"I'm more of a 'cause a distraction with a bar fight, then sneak away through the back' sort of girl," I teased, watching Nick warily as he put his hand at the small of Darby's back. Without warning, I had the irrational desire for the power to make her spontaneously combust with my mind.

"Clay, have you met Nick Thatcher?" For now, I was omitting Nick's job description. It would get around to the pack eventually, but it might help if the pack got to know him and trust him beforehand. Still, Clay's smile was sharp, and not all that friendly, as he reached forward to take Nick's hand. I guess he picked up on more than just my scent on Nick. I sighed and took a step farther away from both of them. Darby and I watched as the boys seemed to be competing over who could squeeze more circulation out of the other's fingers.

"Well, this isn't awkward," Darby muttered. Despite myself, I shared a commiserating little grimace with her.

"I'm Maggie, by the way. I don't think we've ever really met."

"Darby," she said, shaking my hand in a way that didn't leave me wincing, like the boys were doing now.

"Darby works full-time at the supermarket," Nick told me. "She just got promoted to assistant manager."

I threaded my arm through Clay's and smiled affably. "Clay is a mechanic. We keep him pretty busy around the village, but there's nothing he can't fix. It's taken a load off of Samson."

"Darby's studying for her master's degree online, in social work. She wants to help kids like herself who grew up in the foster-care system," Nick shot back, his tone a little bit more aggressive than proud.

"Clay is helping his sister raise her two children while they care for an ailing elderly aunt," I retorted as Clay began to look distinctly uncomfortable under my "praise."

"Darby takes in retired rescue dogs. She's adopted two German shepherds through a state shelter program," Nick said.

Damn it. That did make me like her a little more.

"OK, I think it's time to get out of firing range,"

Clay said, pulling me toward the dance floor. "Darby, it was nice to meet your résumé."

She snickered and waved as Nick glowered at us.

"So, what was that?" Clay asked, spinning me around and slipping his hand to my waist. He stared over my shoulder to where Nick and Darby were chatting companionably. I gritted my teeth and stepped back, so Clay would have to turn me away from them. "Were you two dating or something?"

"No, he's a friend," I grumbled. "A friend who is a giant pain in my ass."

"You want I should get rid of him?" he asked in his best New Jersey accent. "We could make it look like an accident."

"That's what I said when I first met him!" I exclaimed as Clay snickered and pulled me closer. My head tilted up, and my forehead brushed the line of his jaw. Seriously, when did God stop giving men jaws like that? I muttered, "But I guess cold-blooded murder is wrong and all that junk."

Clay's eyes flickered with some emotion I didn't quite understand. His smile faltered. And it was as if some invisible mask had been pulled away from his face. He caught himself, it seemed, and lifted the corners of his mouth again. "Well, if you need help burying the body, I'm handy with a shovel."

I chuckled. "Good to know."

"So, let's talk about something more interesting," he said, sliding his fingers along the bare skin of my shoulders, leaving a little trail of sparks in his wake. "Let's talk about you."

"Oh, you must have read a book on how to charm lady wolves," I said.

"I'm not a proud man," he said. "There were Cliffs Notes involved."

God help me, I actually giggled as he swayed me around the floor. The rest of the night was like that. Clay made me feel comfortable, more comfortable than I think I'd ever been with a guy. He kept me talking so much I hardly noticed we were dancing. He was light on his feet and managed to step out of the way if I was on my way to stepping on his toes. He didn't even break his stride when I tried to lead a time or two, just went with the flow.

I know he noticed when I tried to subtly brush my nose along his collar, but he was too polite to say anything. He smelled like citrus and sage. And I pulled him a little closer, so I could hold that pleasant, distracting scent in my head.

It surprised me when I looked up and realized we were among only a few stragglers left at the party. Everyone but Mo, Cooper, Evie, Buzz, and Nick had headed home. Nick was standing at the bar, drinking a beer, and trying very hard to make it look as if he was talking to Cooper and not watching us. Cooper wasn't making any pretenses. He was watching Clay like a hawk.

"It's later than I thought," I said, laughing and suddenly realizing that my feet were *killing* me.

"I could give you a ride back home," Clay offered. On hearing this, Nick and Cooper both stood and not so subtly moved closer to us.

"I appreciate it, but I rode with my mom. And

she's at Cooper's watching the baby. I need to drive her back tonight. But I'll walk you to your truck," I said, frowning at Cooper as we passed on our way to the door.

I slipped into my coat but slipped out of my too-tight shoes, grateful for the soothing, biting cold of the pavement as I walked outside with him. This was the part of the night that I was sort of dreading. So far, Clay had been sort of perfect. And if he was a dud in the kissing department, I was going to be right back to fantasizing about blue eyes and dusky Viking lips. I couldn't have that.

"Thanks for putting up with all this," I said, jerking my head toward the disheveled bar and what I'm sure was my brother's face pressed against the picture window like one of those suction-cup Garfield dolls. "I know I sort of put you through the wringer."

He grinned. "It's all right. It was kind of nice to see you out of your element. I had a good time with you tonight, Maggie," he said, leaning toward me so I had the choice to close the remaining space.

I took a little nerve-bolstering breath and kissed him, nipping at his bottom lip with my teeth. He moaned a little and worked his fingers into my hair, pulling me closer. He tasted like whiskey and cinnamon. It was nice, warm, and sweet and stoked a pleasant little fire in my belly. It wasn't fireworks and snowflakes, but it was a cozy burn. He leaned back, keeping his arms laced around my waist.

"So," he said, smiling and tilting his head, "I was thinking we might go to Burney to see a movie this week? It's a drive, but there's a new action movie opening up. Bomb squads and terrorists."

"Well, you know how much I love bomb squads and terrorists," I said with a little laugh. "How could a girl resist?"

"What if I throw an extra-large bag of Twizzlers into the deal?"

"No, no, no," I told him. "Twizzlers are fifth- or sixth-date material. You have to start out slowly, with Goobers or Sour Patch Kids."

Clay chuckled. "I thought presenting a girl with Goobers was tantamount to a proposal."

"Well, I guess movie candy is governed differently in Canada. Your country's all peculiar," I said as he climbed into his truck.

He shrugged. "Yeah, I know, funny bacon, inability to pronounce all the 'o' sounds."

I waved as he started the truck and pulled away. I was still sort of smiling as I came back through the saloon door. And my sister-in-law was making her "trying not to comment" face. She was trying hard to cover it up, fussing with Tupperware containers of leftovers and wiping down the already-clean bar.

"What?" I asked Cooper.

"Damned if I know," he said, watching her bustle back and forth. "I'm still working on the whole 'my sister's a grown-up, and it's normal for her to date' thing. Why do you think I'm still drinking?"

I snorted. "Nice."

"Just to be clear, I don't like either one of them. It's in the guy code. 'Thou shalt despise any man who wants to nail your sister.'"

"You're coping well," I noted.

His lips twitched as he raised the beer bottle to his mouth. "I'm seething on the inside."

I placed a hand over Mo's as she swept by with a damp rag. "What is going on, Mo? What's got you all OCD?"

"Nick," she said, wincing a little.

I looked around. Nick had disappeared like Wet Wipes on a porn set. "What about him?"

"He left," she said hesitantly, which was a weird look for Little Miss Resolute Face. "While you were outside. With Clay."

"Oh," I said. I realized that meant he probably saw me kissing Clay, all snuggly against the side of Clay's truck. My stomach felt sort of ripply and cold. "Oh."

"Sorry!" she exclaimed. "We couldn't keep him from leaving. I was afraid he would interrupt whatever you had going out there with Clay, but I couldn't figure out how to keep him away from the door. I thought throwing myself at him and dragging him back inside would send an upsetting mixed message."

"I think I would be upset by that," Cooper deadpanned. "The only person I want you throwing yourself at is me." Mo smiled at him in that gross, lovey-dovey, cartoon-eyes way that didn't exactly help my icky stomach.

I shuddered. "Look, it's no big deal. Nick and I, we're trying to be friends. He knew I was here with a date. It's not like I got all wound up when he was dancing with Saint Darby, the Animal Rescue Princess."

"So, you're OK with this?" Mo asked.

"Why wouldn't I be?"

"Because you called her Saint Darby, the Animal Rescue Princess," Mo said. "It expresses a certain amount of latent hostility."

"Don't try to shrink my head, hippie spawn," I snapped at her.

"Well, now you're expressing direct hostility," she said. "Which is more your speed, anyway."

"Shut it, Moonflower," I shot back, using the super-secret, never-to-be-spoken-in-public legal name bestowed on her by her hippie parents.

"That was too far," she growled. "See if I ever help you again."

"Hey!" I shouted as she stormed toward the coat rack. "If you consider pulling my eyelashes out by the root help, you can keep it!"

10

I Need to Find New Places to Hide Pepper Spray

I HUFFED OUT A BREATH through my muzzle as my paws hit the ground. I turned to see that Clay had cleared the fallen fir tree right after me.

He gave me a triumphant little wolfy grin and leaped ahead of me. I barked and chased, falling into step with him. Clay had insisted on taking me running after another grueling pack meeting, and I couldn't help but be grateful that he knew exactly what I needed. The pack structure had been somewhat unsettled over the past week.

Somehow, my abandoning Lee in the middle of a patrol to chase after Nick's scent was some sort of final straw for Uncle Frank. He went from quietly grumbling about how I wasn't doing what he would do in this situation to straight-out questioning my ability to lead. Frank told the uncles that maybe he voted for the wrong alpha candidate. Maybe having a woman for an alpha wasn't such a good idea. Maybe they should consider my first year on the job a "probationary period," during which I was failing miserably. After all, there had been attempts on my life and destruction of pack property in my first few months on the job. It had taken Cooper years to get into that much trouble.

Still, I'd stayed true to my word and let Nick study the valley. We started out with short visits, introducing him to my aunts as a cultural anthropologist studying communities in remote rural areas. It raised a few eyebrows, but with Cooper's endorsement and my own, Nick was soon charming his way into kitchens. He was stuffed with cookies and roast hare, while he asked innocuous questions about how the ladies of the pack spent their days. What were their favorite recipes? How often did they get to visit friends outside the valley? How did they meet their husbands? He never mentioned werewolves or packs or mates, but I gathered that he was picking up information about our other nature, here and there. He could see things that the average human couldn't, just because he was open to it.

Nick had this engaging way about him when he was interviewing that kept people talking. He asked questions, kept a funny running commentary. It was subtle without being sneaky or manipulative. Hell, he found out things about my relatives that even I didn't know. For instance, I had no idea my uncle Louis once ran away to Canada to try to join a carnival . . . although when I thought about it, it made a certain amount of sense.

I found myself accompanying Nick on these visits, telling myself that I was just keeping an eye on the outsider and learning more about my own pack history. But more than anything, I just wanted to watch him work.

Of course, Nick's presence in the valley was another bone for Uncle Frank to pick. I was playing too fast and loose with the pack's secret, he said. I was wasting time that should be spent looking for a mate. I thought about storming into his toolshed and giving him the verbal ass-whipping of a lifetime, maybe in front of a few of the uncles if I could manage it. But then I realized that probably wouldn't serve much purpose, other than making Frank madder and ramping up his screwball campaign to undermine my authority.

Instead, I took a page from my mother's book. When we were kids, Mom didn't punish us often. If she had, I would have been grounded from birth to, well, pretty much now. But when she did lower the hammer, the dread of waiting while she considered our "sentence" was almost worse than the punishment. So, I asked one of the kids to drop by Uncle Frank's on their way to school and ask him to come by my office around noon, giving him a good, solid, four-hour window in which to soil himself.

Uncle Frank had built up a healthy reserve of bluster when he came through my office door that afternoon. But I could smell the sweat on his palms and hear the little hitch in his pulse. I didn't bother looking up from the ledgers I was scribbling until he was standing right in front of my recently replaced desk, like a kid being called to the principal's office.

I finally leaned back and gave him a thin smile, gesturing for him to sit down.

"Uncle Frank," I said, "I'm told you have some concerns about how I'm running the pack."

"Hell, yes, I have 'concerns.' I have a heap of concerns. It's like the whole family's gone loco. First, your brother runs off and marries God knows who. You let him live a full hour's run away from the valley. Now you're letting some human waltz around the valley like he's one of us, asking questions he doesn't have any business asking, while you make calf eyes with Billie's nephew. And let's not even talk about what a bad alpha candidate he is. You keep tarting around like you are, and we're ripe for another takeover. Other packs will perceive us as weak. Bad enough that we have a female alpha, but—"

"I'm going to ask you not to finish that sentence. Know your place."

"I know my place," he shot back. "I'm your elder."

"I'm your alpha." I gave him a hard stare, which he returned . . . for about a second.

He snorted dismissively and shifted his eyes down, a reluctant act of submission. "Well, you aren't acting like any alpha I've ever seen. I don't understand why you're running around with these no-accounts when my nephew is just waiting for Cooper to finish negotiating for your paw. Lee is a leader. He can make this pack strong again. Our alpha is being attacked on our own territory, for pity's sake. We need his pack's protection if we're going to survive. It's the only choice that makes sense. And if you weren't so pigheaded and prideful, you'd agree to mate with him. We don't know anything about this Clay or his pack. Hell, we already know Billie's gene pool carries some crazy. Why take the risk of passing it along?"

"Watch your mouth, Uncle Frank," I growled. "Billie's pack. Just like you and me."

Frank snorted again. "Maybe she was."

"Is," I said. "As long as I'm alpha, I decide who's pack and who's not, something you need to keep in mind. I'm going to say this once. Whoever I date, whoever I mate with, is none of your business. And you will not sit around gossiping about my love life like some little old woman. I don't care if you have a dozen nephews you think would be a good match for me. Keep your opinions to yourself. All of your opinions."

He shot up, placing both hands on my desk in an attempt to loom over me. "And if I said I don't want to live in a pack where my opinion's not welcome?"

I did my best to look bored, picking up my pen and scribbling a note on my ledger. "I would remind you that you're free to leave the pack anytime. And if you push me much farther, I'll give you an extra nudge out the door."

A boot up the ass could be considered a "nudge," right?

He stood, his nose in the air. "I know where I'm not wanted. I'll just go stay with Lee's pack."

"I think that would be for the best."

Fortunately, Uncle Frank had enough sense to act as if it was his idea to move. He wanted to save face, so he told everybody how much better life was over in Lee's pack. Better housing, better hunting, more wolves. He made it sound like some swanky were-wolf retirement resort, but I don't think many of my relatives bought it.

And after a nearly appropriate cushion of time passed, we could laugh about Uncle Frank's defection. I happened to pass by as Pops and Uncle Jay were playing checkers at the community center one afternoon and heard Jay say, "Frank's mouth has been writing checks his butt couldn't cash for years. Glad somebody finally called him on it. If I had to hear one more story about his idiot nephew, I was going to bite him myself."

A bit later, someone hung a bottomless "suggestion box" in my office, situated so the suggestion slip would fall through the slot, right into a wastebasket. Such was life in the pack. If something good happened, we were smart-asses. If something bad happened, we were smart-asses. If we weren't all that emotionally healthy, at least we were consistent.

Behind me, Clay caught the scent of rabbit on the trail. He yipped to let me know he was going to chase it north. I barked back, wishing him luck. Heading in the opposite direction, I ducked under the brush, venturing to the very edge of the valley's boundaries.

I sat at the end of the crescent, watching the wind play over the fir trees, like an annoying uncle's hand ruffling the valley's hair. I phased, eager to feel the weak rays of sunshine on my bare human skin. The breeze had a bite to it, although it wasn't cold enough to make a werewolf shiver. We tend to be a bit impervious to the cold.

It was so blessedly quiet up there, more peace than I'd enjoyed in weeks. Sometimes I forgot what my life was like before potholes and cranky seniors took up all of my time. The days when I could run whenever and wherever I wanted. If I wanted, I could sleep until three in the afternoon, and nobody would blink an eye. I loved my pack. And I was happy that I could provide some stability after so many years of turmoil. But every once in a while, I missed my downtime.

I closed my eyes, inhaling the scent of pine and smoke curling from the pack's chimneys. And slithering under the current of the breeze, I smelled the floral, obnoxiously clean scent of fabric softener.

Someone was there. And I was naked.

Hearing the softest of footfalls behind me, I turned. But the dark shape was on me before I could see. A black nylon bag was wrapped around my head and knotted behind my neck as I kicked and struggled. The smell of fabric softener was overwhelming, clogging my nostrils with the burning chemical scent of false flowers. I couldn't breathe. I tried to focus on the man behind me. I stomped on his bare foot, making him grunt. I could feel jeans rubbing against my bare legs, but he wasn't wearing a shirt. He stretched at least a foot taller than me, pressing me against his solid body as he dragged me back from the rock outcropping.

The guy's hand was pressed over my mouth,

through the material, and the other hand wandered to my chest. His fingers skittered greedily across my breast, pinching the nipple. I bit down on his hand, hard. He yowled, wrenching his hand away. I bucked my head back. I hoped to catch his face, but I guess I just hit his collarbone. The impact against his chest loosened his arms. I slung an elbow back, catching his face this time, cracking the bridge of his nose. "Oof!" He huffed out a harsh breath and dropped me.

"Fucker!" I shouted, my voice muffled by the material as I kicked out toward the noise. I think I must have clipped his knee, because his weight shifted toward the ground. I tugged at the bag, but he'd managed a pretty decent knot at the base of my neck, and the material was too slick to get a grip on. Struggling and ripping at it would only disorient me and possibly send me stumbling off the rock face. I stayed still, listening for any noise that could tell me where he was. But I heard nothing. He knew what I was doing, tracking him, and he was staying as still as the stone under our feet. Why? Why not just push me off? Why—

Oh, screw this. I phased, but my neck was actually thicker in wolf form. With the bag knotted so tight, I couldn't wriggle out of it, no matter how I scraped my head against the ground. Plus, the material was so tight at my throat I could barely breathe. I'd pass out after a few minutes, and the last thing I needed was to be unconscious around this dirtbag. Growling in frustration, I phased back to human. From nowhere, a fist slammed into the side of my face. I was knocked to my knees but swung wide at my eye level. I'm guessing I nailed the guy right in the crotch, given the way he yelled.

Gently tugging at the bag to loosen the knot, I nudged my foot left, feeling sharply ridged pebbles prickling at my skin. I kicked them soundly, listening as they tumbling over the edge into the air. I kicked some right and then behind me, and each time, I heard the same descending noise. The cliff face was behind me. I advanced forward and was rewarded with another punch to the eye. His breath hot and moist against the skin of my shoulders, he wrapped his arms around my waist and dragged me away from the cliff. I didn't struggle; no use in throwing him off balance and over the edge.

When his body relaxed, I assumed we were safely away from the cliff. I pushed my feet from the ground, throwing my weight back against him. He stumbled and fell. I threw my elbow hard into his ribs. His hands wrapped around my neck, twisting the material, tightening it. I kicked wildly, catching his knees and not much else. I coughed, my head pounding as the bag constricted around my throat.

"Maggie?" He froze, the tension in his hands bleeding away as the voice echoed across the trees. I gasped, drawing huge lungfuls of air through the material.

"Maggie, where are you?"

Without warning, the weight of my attacker's body disappeared. There was a beat of silence, the hiss of a zipper, and then a growl.

He'd phased. I could hear his footfalls as he ran away on four paws.

"Maggie?" It was Nick's voice, getting closer. I sat up, my fingers plucking frantically at the knotted hood. It loosened, but I couldn't get it untied. I tore at it now, desperate to breathe clean, unscented oxygen.

"Maggie, what happened?"

With a few quick pulls, the hood was untied and yanked from my head. I blinked, blinded by the light as I sucked in air. Nick's hands were on my face, his eyes wild with worry. I didn't realize I'd been crying until he swiped his thumbs across my wet cheeks. Exhaling a ragged breath, he brushed kisses along my brow, my cheekbones, my eyelids. My hands clutched at his jacket, pulling him to me as I tucked my face into his neck.

"Tell me you're not hurt," he demanded, stroking my tangled hair. "Please tell me you're OK."

I nodded. I was afraid to speak, afraid my voice would crack and I would start sobbing like a little girl. He held me in his lap, close against his chest. I decided to overlook this blatant violation of the "just friends" agreement and laid my head there, listening to his heartbeat and waiting for my own to slow. I needed him, much more than I cared to admit. I needed Nick Thatcher, fancy degrees, geek obsessions, and all.

This was a problem.

"What happened? Who did this to you?" he asked, his voice softer now. "I thought I saw a wolf running away, a big gray one."

"I don't know. I was running. Clay took off north, after a rabbit. I was just sitting there, and the next thing I know, there's a bag over my head and some guy's feeling me up."

"Feeling you up?" His eyebrows rose, and I saw cold fury seep into those blue eyes. For the first time, I was a little afraid of what he could be capable of. He was just smart enough to murder someone and get away with it. I pressed a hand to his cheek.

"Just enough to piss me off and get bitten for his troubles. Then I pissed him off, fighting back, and he was trying to strangle me with what looks like a cheap garment bag," I said, tossing the overscented bag aside, next to a discarded pair of torn, muddied jeans. "I don't think he wanted to hurt me seriously. Otherwise, he would have just tossed me off the cliff. I think he wanted to . . . take me? Or maybe just scare me. He kept trying to choke me, to drag me away. He only ran off when you yelled out for me. What are you doing up here, anyway?"

"I was in town, trying to talk to your Pops—who does not like me, by the way—and I heard you'd been up here with Clay since lunch. You were gone so long, I thought maybe someone should check on you."

I would have teased him about being worried, but it seemed cruel, given the way he was holding me— as if I would break or float away at any moment. Instead, I eased away from him, putting an invisible wall of space between us. He recognized the gesture for what it was, and the tenderness leeched out of his voice.

"You said Clay ran north?" he asked quietly.

"Yeah, about twenty minutes ago. He's probably miles away by now."

"You think so?" Nick asked.

"What? You think he doubled back so he could wrap a bag over my head?" I laughed.

"Why would that be such a crazy idea? You haven't known him for very long. He has mechanical experience and would probably know how to fix someone's brakes so they'd fail at the right time."

"For one thing, Clay wasn't carrying jeans or a bag while we were running. And second, why would he want to hurt me? What would be his end game? Clay's a part of my pack. He and his sister are taking care of my aunt Billie. He's practically family. And besides, we're dating." I paused, shuddering. "That came out wrong. He's been living with us for the better part of a year. If he was going to try something, he's had dozens of opportunities to hurt me while we were alone. Movie dates, long runs, drives to Grundy—"

"OK, I get it," he snapped irritably. "You spend a lot of time together."

"My point is, why wait so long to pull some clumsy, half-assed attempt? Besides, he wouldn't want to hurt me, unless he's some sort of date-'em-and-murder-'em werewolf serial killer."

Nick frowned as if he were considering it as a theory.

"Are you sure this isn't coming from a jealous place?"

"Of course, it's coming from a jealous place!" he

exclaimed. "That doesn't mean it's not true. Look, just talk to someone you trust about what happened today. Tell your pack members and see whether they think Clay could have been involved."

"Oh, that's a great idea. I'll tell the pack I was caught off-guard and nearly choked to death by a strange werewolf. That will really inspire some confidence in my ability to lead. Uncle Frank was already calling for some sort of alpha recall. Do you really think I should tell them that I can't defend myself, much less them? For all we know, this guy could be some weirdo rogue male looking to claim a mate caveman-style. He's probably run off to look for the next pack."

Nick clearly didn't follow this line of logic, which was unsurprising, since even I was having a hard time with it. "Or he could come back and catch one of the other females by surprise. You've got to tell somebody, Maggie. Cooper, Samson, somebody."

"No." I pushed to my feet, trying to brazen my way through the fact that I was bare-ass naked. "I'll take care of this myself. And if anyone finds out, I'll know it was you who told them. And then—"

"Yeah, yeah, no one will be able to find my body, yadda, yadda."

"I need to come up with new threats," I muttered, picking up the jeans. Like the bag, it reeked of fabric softener. I could probably track him, but at the moment, I didn't feel quite strong enough to confront the guy who tried to choke me with cheap luggage. Plus, Nick would probably follow me, and that could get ugly. I grunted, tossing them off the cliff. "If he comes back, he's not going to be able to find his pants." Nick gave me a questioning look. I shrugged. "It's about the small victories."

"I'm walking back with you," he insisted.

"What about Clay?"

"I really don't give a shit about Clay."

"Fine," I sighed as he wrapped his jacket around my shoulders and we started back to the valley. "So Pops doesn't like you, huh?"

"No, he does not," he said, shaking his head. "I asked him if I could keep him company while he worked in the shop, and he shut the door in my face. Actually, he shut the door on my face."

"But he likes everybody. Even Mo."

"Well, apparently, he draws the line at humans who are 'sniffin' after' his granddaughter," Nick said, in a spot-on impersonation of Pops. "His exact words."

I laughed weakly. "I'm sure he didn't mean anything by it."

"Says the person who didn't have a door shut on her face."

11

Karma Is One Organized Wench

I GOT MY FIRST GLIMPSE of Nick's spider-monkey powers about a week later, when I found him gallivanting through the freaking treetops without so much as a harness, clinging to the branches by the goodwill of gravity.

I thought I was imagining that flash of red jacket a good thirty feet off the ground from a distance, a sort of signal flare against the patches of white and green. Pops had told me that Nick and Samson were headed in this direction with a bunch of Nick's high-tech gear earlier in the day. While he didn't seem thrilled to see Nick in the valley again, he seemed to approve of whatever Nick was planning to do . . . which he said I would have to see for myself.

I hadn't been able to see much of Nick or Samson lately. I spent every spare minute patrolling the perimeters, since I couldn't explain why my packmates would suddenly need to step up patrols. I did ask Clay to join me most of the time, mostly to see if he would try to come after me while we were alone. He was fun and easy to talk to, and he did not, in fact, try to kill me. I like that in a man. And since he didn't try to murder me, I let him take me to that bomb-squad movie. A box of Sour Patch Kids and a few interesting pecks on the lips had the aunts scheduling a spring wedding for us.

Despite Nick hinting, nudging, and downright pleading, I'd yet to tell anyone about the "bagging" incident. I occasionally woke up from nightmares, clawing at the nonexistent bag over my face, but I hadn't told anyone about that, either.

Instead, I was devoting a lot of energy to ensuring the pack's safety. I checked the brakes on every vehicle in the valley. Hell, I checked the village's cistern to make sure there was no tampering with the water supply. But nothing. Every once in a while, one of us would catch the scent of a strange wolf near the border of our territory but never close to any of the buildings. And I never caught another whiff of fabric softener outside the laundry room.

Every day that passed without incident put me more on edge, waiting for the other shoe to drop. And now I was waiting for my favorite paranormal investigator to drop.

I thought that surely someone with multiple graduate degrees would know not to put that much distance between himself and terra firma. Particularly when the wind chill was somewhere near "guaranteed frostbite" and the branches were slick with snow and ice. But as I drew closer, I found him propped against an alarmingly thin pine branch, wiring a black plastic box against an even less stable-looking branch at least three stories up. My idiot cousin was napping in a little burrow he'd hollowed out in the snow at the tree's base.

Nick had a black cannonball-shaped helmet on and weird metal cleats clamped over his boots. They seemed to be shoved into the bark of the tree, giving him a toehold. But the idea that a flimsy piece of metal was the only thing holding him up there was making my stomach pitch to my knees.

"Nicholas Thatcher, what in the hell do you think you're doing up there?"

He chuckled. "I'm almost done, Mags. I'll be down in a minute."

"That doesn't answer the question!" I yelled, finally waking Samson.

"What's going on?" Samson mumbled.

"Some spotter you are," I grumbled, kicking at Samson's shins. Samson made a halfhearted attempt at an obscene gesture and seemed to be considering continuing his nap.

"Look out below!" Nick yelled, depositing his tool belt near my feet. He yanked his cleats out of the bark and turned, facing the tree trunk. He dropped suddenly, and I let out a scream, before realizing that he was just hopping down to the next branch. He carefully and methodically chose each movement, mapping a route toward the ground. In my head, his descent was on fast-forward, and every branch looked as if it was ready to snap. Frankly, I was ready to snap.

"Hi!" Nick's cheeks were flushed pink with excitement and the cold wind. He looked so happy and sweet . . . and the moment his feet touched the ground, I smacked his shoulders until my hands hurt.

"What in the hell were you thinking, Nick Thatcher?" I growled as he dodged my fists of fury. "Are you trying to kill yourself?"

"Suddenly, I'm glad I have the helmet on." He grunted as he put his hand on my forehead and held me a safe swinging distance away. Samson snickered and scratched his belly, stretching his arms lazily over his head. "Maggie, stop!"

"Total overreaction, Midget," Samson told me. "I watched him like a hawk the whole time."

"You watched your eyelids the whole time," I shot back as Nick rifled through the duffel bag at the base of the tree. "And you, I count on you to be the adult in this weird-ass buddy comedy, Nick! How could you trust your 'not dying in a plummet from a tree' to Samson? What were you even doing up there?"

"This," Nick said, clicking a little black remote that looked like a garage-door opener. A little red light on the remote switched on . . . and I was left considerably unimpressed. Then Nick brought out a little portable TV and showed me a video feed that focused on my mother's front door. He toggled a switch on the TV, and the screen showed the front of my office, then the school, the north perimeter, the east and south boundaries of the packlands.

"This one will show the western view of the valley," he said, pointing up at what I now realized was a security camera. He pulled out a map of the valley, with orange circles marking where he'd placed the cameras. "They're on full power right now, but I'm switching them over to thermal-sensor mode. They'll only pick up a feed when a warm body passes. So we don't end up with two hours' worth of windy tree-branch footage."

"Unless it was a tree branch that cut the brakes on your truck," Samson said, tenting his fingers and arching his brow at the wavering tree limbs supervillain-style.

Nick chuckled. "I can't cover the whole valley. And it might take a few weeks to work out all of the kinks, but I thought it could help, right?"

Suddenly, I felt really bad about hitting him.

"Someone owes someone an apology," Samson sang under his breath.

"I do. I'm sorry," I said. Nick beamed at me. "This is great."

"I think I hear Mom calling me!" Samson announced, scrambling to his feet.

"Did that seem sort of abrupt to you?" Nick asked, staring after Samson as he ran toward home.

Without Samson there as a buffer, Nick suddenly seemed too close. What little emotional space I'd been able to put between us had sort of been shredded by the whole naked-assault-victim vulnerability thing. I stepped away and took the portable monitor. "So, show me how to work this."

Nick was in full professor mode, taking fifteen

minutes to explain how the little monitor could bounce among the various feeds and wirelessly upload clips to my office computer. I thought I was going to have to start fanning my face to keep from bursting into flames. Curse his sexy brains!

Using the toggle thing, he scanned past the signal coming from my mom's front door and did a cartoonish double-take. "What the?"

Nick squinted at the screen, aghast at the image of what appeared to be a dozen or so of my male cousins, lined up in front of my house with their pants around their ankles and their bare asses aimed directly at the camera. There were enough full moons to orbit Jupiter.

"You really shouldn't have shown Samson where the cameras are," I muttered.

"How did he organize that so quickly?" Nick asked, nodding toward Samson's naked rear at the end of the butt-cheek chorus line.

"Well, when properly motivated, Samson can do just about anything. We're fortunate that his main interests are food and pranks."

"I mean, I can see grabbing one or two guys, but so many? He could take over the world," Nick marveled.

I snorted. "As long as the world's governments could be cowed into submission by a bottomless army, yes."

He shuddered. "Well, there's an image that will never leave my head. Thanks for that."

"I do what I can."

*   *   *

FULL-BLOWN WINTER CLOSED in on the valley like a fist. The temperatures dive-bombed below freezing, putting us all in instinctual panic mode. And even though we spent the better part of the year preparing our houses, putting up food, winterizing our vehicles, I still ended up scrambling around, helping my aunt Doris patch a weak spot on her roof, helping Samson with last-minute runs to the bulk warehouse store in Burney for toilet paper and batteries. Clay and I took a day trip to a big pharmacy in Burney, where we could stock up on Billie's meds. When the snow blew in and covered the valley in a fluffy white blanket and I finally had a chance to stop and breathe, I sort of collapsed and slept for two days.

Weeks passed, the holidays came and went, and even with the relative quiet, I was scared to relax into the season, to give myself downtime. I used pack morale as an excuse. Werewolves tend to get sort of restless when we're boxed in. Little disagreements over a poker game or the last buffalo wing can turn into full-on duels to the death if you're not careful. So, I spent a good portion of my day sending my family members on random errands, finding some weird chores that needed to be done, or sending them on extra patrols around the perimeter. I organized checkers tournaments, darning bees, Scrabble nights. I basically became the pack's cruise director.

The pathways between Grundy and the valley were kept warm. Mom worried too much for Mo to drive the baby from Grundy, so she phased every few days so she could run over and visit Eva. Neither snow nor sleet nor an act of God would keep my mother from snuggling that fuzzy-headed baby.

Eva seemed to be on some sort of mission to work her evil/cute baby magic on me. Ever since she'd started toddling around on those chubby little legs, she'd been targeting me, the least enthusiastic baby person in the room. I think she enjoyed the challenge, which proved that we were related.

Eva would tug on my pants leg until I picked her up. And then she'd basically stare me down with those big blue-gray eyes of hers, daring me not to snuggle her. It was like facing down a tiny, diapered mastermind.

And of course, I caved. I snuggled her. I babbled. I read her *Where the Wild Things Are* until I was hoarse. I actually found myself watching my language. *Shudder.*

Every once in a while, I'd bury my face in the talcum-powder-scented fluff on her head and have a little "maybe I am ready for a baby" twinge. And then I would slap myself. Because my smart-ass karma combined with my genes might create some sort of evil superbaby. I just wasn't ready. Imagine baby-proofing for that.

Being around Nick so much wasn't exactly helping my hormone surges. He'd bought a snowmobile, so he could visit every other day. He'd stopped the interviews, but he still liked hanging out with Samson and Pops, whom he was determined to win over. I wasn't sure what he was doing with his research, but Nick told me he was working on something that wouldn't result in me kicking his ass, so I was happy.

Mom was already a fan, but he met some resistance from some very unfriendly uncles. But I think that was more traditional "we don't want you sullying our little girl" hazing than anything else. Clay usually made some excuse to get out of their card games, but I think that was mostly because of the "I want your woman" vibe Nick was still giving off.

Nick stayed in Samson's guest room most nights, which had me worried. Samson seemed to think of him as some sort of human chew toy. For instance, just the other night, I'd come home to find Samson in my mother's living room, holding Nick upside-down in some half-nelson wrestling hold.

"Hey, Midget, Nick won't tell me whether he has sisters. I figure, he's pretty, he would have to have pretty sisters."

"You're a sick man, Samson," Nick said, his face reddened by the sudden flow of blood to his head.

"But you laughed, so what does that make you?"

Nick deadpanned, "Humoring you."

"Samson, put him down!" I cried.

"But he's so light and portable," he said, jiggling a bemused Nick.

"When you wonder why we don't introduce humans to our pack's secrets, this is why," I told Nick.

Samson jostled Nick again to get his attention. "OK, Dr. Werewolf Whisperer, you told me you could get out this. Now, the rules are: One, no punching me in the junk. And two, see rule one. Let's go."

"This is not healthy." I sighed, shaking my head. "Even for werewolves, this is messed up."

Nick grinned at me, bent at his waist, and did some weird finger-strike thing against the back of Samson's kneecaps. Samson yowled and dropped to his knees, bringing Nick's head precariously close to the floor. Nick stopped short of cracking his skull by catching himself with his hands. He sprang to his feet and put Samson in a headlock.

I think Samson was more shocked than strong-armed.

"Never fuck with a guy who worships at the altar of Vulcan martial arts," Nick told my cousin as he administered a merciless noogie.

"Seriously, you Vulcan-nerve-pinched him?" I barely suppressed the grin that threatened to split my cheeks.

"Awesome!" Samson exclaimed, shaking Nick off like a troublesome Pomeranian. Nick was flung ass-over-teakettle onto the couch. "You'll have to show me how to do that sometime," Samson said before he wandered into the kitchen looking for food.

Nick hopped up from the couch. He was warm and slightly sweaty. I could feel the happy thrum of his heartbeat under his skin. I cleared my throat and stepped back from him before I did anything drastic. "You in one piece?"

"It's kind of fun. I never had a big brother growing up. I always wanted to be hung upside-down by my ankles."

"I worry about you," I told him.

"Guess who's been invited to guest-lecture at University of Alaska's Anchorage campus?" he asked, grinning.

"Mo?" I suggested. "They have a great culinary department there."

He frowned. "Me. They've asked me to lecture on shape-shifting creatures and their prevalence in northwestern American tribal culture."

"In academic terms, I'm pretty sure that was supposed to get me all hot and bothered."

He grinned and wiggled his eyebrows. "Well, I want you to come with me. We can snowmobile as far as the highway and then drive in. We can go to a movie or some of the bookstores. There's a restaurant I wanted to try. I just think it would be sort of cool to get you all to myself for a little while." Then he added hastily, "As a friend. We can spend time together without things getting all naked and confusing."

"When have we ever been able to spend time together without one of us getting naked or confused?" I asked.

"There's always hope, Maggie."

It sounded awesome. Seeing Nick in his element. Going somewhere where I wasn't known, so I could relax a little. Soft hotel sheets and a certain bespectacled hottie . . . enjoyed separately, of course. And I was on the verge of saying "Yes, yes, take me now, yes," when "I can't" came out of my mouth instead.

"I'd like to, but I can't leave right now. I know nothing has happened in a while, but I don't think it's OK for the alpha to go waltzing off on what will be seen as a sexy weekend with someone who is not her boyfriend, when there are maddeningly vague threats on the horizon."

He groaned. "Why'd you have to say 'sexy weekend'? I was going to be all noble and selfless and un-derstanding until you said 'sexy weekend.'"

I snickered at him.

He sighed. "You're right," he said. "You're abso-lutely right. You have to take care of your respon-sibilities. I respect that. I just got excited about it, that's all."

"And I want to go. I just wouldn't feel right about it," I said. "Maybe Samson would go with you."

He nodded, sort of glum, and pushed my hair behind my ears. Samson yelled at him from the next room, threatening to kick his ass at Halo. "Big Brother is waiting for you," I told him.

"You think I could get him to go after some kids from my high school?" Nick asked as he led me to video-game Valhalla. "I wasn't bullied, really, but I'd just like to see the looks on some of the obnoxious jocks' faces when a ten-foot-tall werewolf came bar-reling at them."

"You've got some unresolved issues, don't you, Nick?"

I tried not to mope in general, but the days lead-ing up to Nick's departure were a little gloomy. Even Clay noticed that something was a little off with me, suggesting that we sneak away to try to find the parts to salvage my old truck. I agreed and tried to force myself into a brighter frame of mind. No one likes a sulky alpha wolf. I'd chosen this job. I'd campaigned for it. I wasn't going to get all whiny now that there were certain sacrifices involved, such as not getting to go on a road trip with my cute "platonic" friend.

It wasn't even the distance or losing a few days with Nick. I just hated the idea that I was going to miss something important to him. I mean, friends cared about that sort of thing, right?

I think I'd scared him with my drive-time estimations, because he was leaving a few days before his lecture. The day before he was due to leave, I got a little anxious. What if he didn't come back? What if he got into an accident on the long drive? What if he met someone in Anchorage who didn't scoff at *Doctor Who* or occasionally leave him with bite wounds?

And so I was piling through the waist-deep snow on four paws.

"Hello?" I called as I came through the kitchen door. I shrugged into an oversized flannel shirt he kept hanging by the door.

"I'm still packing!" he called from his room. "There's sodas and sandwich stuff in the fridge. Help yourself."

"OK!" On my way past his kitchen table, my elbow caught on a stack of books and knocked them onto Nick's open laptop. I chuckled at his screensaver, a picture of evil bearded Kirk and Spock, smirking at each other. I bumped the keyboard as I was gathering them up, and a Word document popped up on the screen.

It was a title page for something called "The Werewolves of Crescent Valley." I arched an eyebrow and sat at the table with a thump. The document was more than a hundred pages long, and it wasn't just notes. Nick was writing a freaking book about us! There were pages and pages about our origins, our social structure, how the pack broke tradition by installing me as alpha.

Hurt, hot and acidic, burned through my chest. He'd promised. He'd promised me that he understood, that he couldn't tell anyone about us. And here he was writing a frigging book? Who had he shown this to? Did he plan to publish it? The whole damn thing was dedicated to me, by the way. "To Maggie, without whom this wouldn't be possible."

Unfortunately for Nick, I read that just as he came through the kitchen door. And he was met by a very large book thrown at his head. "What the hell is this?" I yelled.

"What the?"

He ducked and, with impressive speed, dodged several flying objects as he crossed the room and grabbed my arms.

"I trusted you!" I yelled, fighting my way out of his grasp and slapping his chest. "What the hell were you planning on doing with this?"

"What is wrong with you?"

"Your book, you asshole! The freaking book that meant more to you than keeping your word to me."

"What—the only thing I'm writing now is a history of your pack."

"Are we not having the same conversation?" I growled. "That's what I'm talking about."

"I'm writing that for your grandfather."

"What?"

"I'm putting a book together for Pops. I was going to bind it myself, so no one would even see it. I was hoping it would, you know, soften Pops toward me. And if he hated me a little less, you might stop fighting me so hard on the 'being crazy in love with you' thing."

"What?" I huffed out a breath.

Nick's cheeks flushed. "I haven't told anyone about you. I've barely been in contact with the outside world since I got up here. If you don't believe me, you can check my e-mail accounts, my phone records, anything you want. Your family, they were exactly what I was hoping for, Maggie. Yeah, you're the academic find of a lifetime. You could make my career, after I proved to the world that I wasn't nuts. But your family, for the most part, has been kinder to me than the people who raised me. I can't expose them. I can't put them in harm's way. You don't do that to people who have been good to you."

"Then why do this?"

"I don't have a lot of measurable skills, as far as your grandfather's concerned. I figured this would be the one thing I could do for him that no one else could. I wanted to show him that I'm serious about you. I wanted to show you how much I love you. And I do love you," he said. "Even if you don't know whether you love me yet. I don't care whether you're human or a werewolf or a yeti, I love you."

The overwhelming rush of warmth and love through my chest nearly knocked me to my knees. That was it. I had this strange moment of crystal clarity in which I knew I loved him right back. Everything outside our circle of two was sort of blurry and inconsequential. I'd never be happy without him. I'd never want anyone else. My hands slipped up to his chest to steady myself as I spluttered, "W-well, that's just—"

I grabbed his lapels and crushed my mouth to his. He hummed against my lips, slipping his hands into my hair and pulling me closer. I pushed him toward the bedroom door. He turned his head, seeing where I was heading, and raised his eyebrows.

I pushed the jacket back from his shoulders and untucked his shirt while he struggled with my buttons. I shrugged out of the shirt and tossed his belt over my shoulder, slipping my hand under his waistband. Nick lifted me and carried me to the bedroom, to his bed.

"Are you sure?" he asked, cupping his hand around my jaw as he settled his weight over me. I quirked my eyebrows, peering down at the grip I had on his manly bits. He laughed. "OK, then."

I didn't have time to be nervous. I didn't know how this would feel, but it couldn't be bad. Werewolves had very healthy attitudes toward sex. Hell, sex was one of the primary winter activities in the valley. Which was why we had so many babies every spring.

Babies.

I arched off of him long enough to dangle off the bed and grab for his nightstand. Nick nibbled along the curve of my spine, biting at my hip as I rooted around for the long string of condoms I found there. I turned back to him, giving him a speculative look. He smiled sheepishly. "I had high hopes."

I laughed and helped him ease out of his pants. He guided my hands as we slipped on the condom. I expected him to, well, get right to it. But he pushed me back onto the mattress, kissing down my bottom, hitting all of the places I loved best, the valley between my breasts, the hollow of my belly button. His fingers were already deep inside me, stretching and teasing me, while his thumb worked little circles around my clit. His lips closed around my nipple, flicking and teasing it with his tongue.

He rolled onto his back, pulling me with him. "This might hurt a little," he said, smiling up at me, concern reflecting back at me in those blue eyes. "It might be better if you were running things."

He helped me position him near my entrance, and I sank down over him, hissing as I stretched. It was more pressure than pain, a strange alien sensation that disturbed more than it hurt. I stayed still for a second, waiting for my body to adjust around him. I tried not to overthink, but damn, it was a lot of stuff to process. The stretching and pulling sensations deep inside. The way his hands wrapped around my waist. Nick looking up at me, his expression so happy, so adoring, that I couldn't help but smile at him. I moved just a little bit and gasped at the friction it produced.

"Slow," he whispered, kissing my neck. "Go slow."

My first couple of movements were awkward as I searched for the right angle. He lifted my hips and thrust up gently, helping me find a rhythm. His hand slid up my neck, rubbing his thumb along my jaw. I leaned into his touch, and he pulled me down to kiss him. He nibbled along the line of my chin,

my throat. He pressed his teeth against my collarbone and nipped a little harder.

I rose on my knees and slid down just a little
harder, huffing out a little moan. I rose a little
higher and did it again. I paused to absorb the
strange, hot lightning sensation that shot through
my stomach. That was nice. I pushed up with my
feet, riding so high that Nick almost slipped out of
me. He groaned in protest until I slammed my hips
down on his.

"You're a natural." He sighed, sitting up and
wrapping his arms around me as I rode him. He slid
his hand between us and stroked my clit.

I giggled again until I felt my inner muscles
tighten, clenching around him. I shrieked at the first
pulse, clutching at his shoulders. Nick lay back, pulling me down and rolling over. He hitched my legs
over his hips, pulling me up so my ass rested on his
thighs. He gave one good, hard thrust, spreading
me wide for him, and I yelled out. He was thrusting
upward, hitting some wonderful place that made me
want to squeeze my thighs together and lock him
there. I tensed again, and the wave was longer, better. A rush of heat seemed to radiate up through my
chest, making the blood roar in my ears. The pulses
were coming quicker, more intense. Everything
seemed to seize up at once, and I was screaming his
name.

I must have yelled some other, dirtier stuff, because Nick answered with a yell of his own and was
coming with me. He laid his head against my heart,
panting against my skin and listening to its beat. I

threaded my fingers through his hair and pulled him closer.

I tried to find some tiny bit of regret inside myself but couldn't. I'd done it. I'd chosen Nick. There was no going back now. I stroked my fingers along his cheek. "This might hurt a little," I whispered.

He blinked dreamily at me. "Hmm?"

I closed my eyes and prayed that I was making the right choice. I sank my teeth into his shoulder as gently as possible, just breaking the skin. He yelped but gritted his teeth and took it like a man. I licked the wound and nuzzled his jaw.

"You couldn't have warned me?" he asked, frowning down at the thin trail of blood dripping down his chest.

"Sorry. You would have tensed up. It would have hurt more," I told him, handing him a tissue. "But we're mated now. There's no escape for you."

"Not looking for one," he said, dabbing at the wound. "You OK?"

I nodded. Physically, I was great. Relaxed and dandy. But I was a little worried. While I'd refused any detailed descriptions during Mama's birds-and-the-beasts talk, the one thing I did ask was how she was sure she and Dad were mated. She said she "just knew," and when I gave her an irritated look, she added that she felt complete, whole, happy with her choice. But frankly, I'd felt that way for a while, so how could I tell if there was a difference?

"Is something supposed to happen?" he asked.

I propped myself up on my elbow. "I don't know."

"Maybe you should bite me again?"

I gently touched my fingertips to the edge of the wound on his neck, which was raw and red. "I think I got you pretty good the first time."

"Don't worry, we'll figure it out," he said, kissing me. "Personally, I am willing to do that over and over until we come to some conclusion."

"There's that confidence again."

He climbed out of bed, muttering about finding his drawers, and I noticed the faint white scar on his butt.

"Oh, no," I moaned.

Nick was back on the bed in a flash. "What? Are you hurt?"

"I claimed my mate with a bite to the ass!" I cried, pressing my face to the pillow.

"I'm sorry, what?"

"Your ass. I bit it, months ago!" I moaned as he pried my hands and the pillow off my face and made me look at him. "And ever since then, I've felt this weird protectiveness . . . and possessiveness toward you. And I've been calmer, with the exception of the whole possible werewolf intruder thing. I've been happy, content. I've been *mated*."

"But, but, but—"

"Exactly!" I exclaimed, gesturing at his matrimonially marked ass.

"But if that were true, if all it took was a bite, werewolves would find themselves accidentally mated to random people all the time."

"It's not about the bite, it's about the intention," I said. "The werewolf magic sort of does the rest." I thought back to the day I bit him. I'd been angry because he thought I was Mo. I wanted to show him that I was the woman, the animal, he was looking for. And I was staking my claim, marking my territory. Permanently. My stupid instincts made my decision for me. I could have spared myself all that angst over Clay versus Nick. "Oh, this is bad . . ."

"Why is it so bad?" he asked. "It just means we arrived at our destination a little early. I think it's kind of cool."

"We can never tell Samson, do you understand? If he knows I accidentally claimed your glutes, I will never live it down."

"Maggie, it will be OK. This is a good thing. You chose me. And I love you for it."

"I'm serious. We can't tell Samson or Cooper or Mo. Or my mom."

His tone was exasperated as he kissed my forehead. "Maggie."

"Shutting up."

He nuzzled my throat and traced the curves of my collarbone with his fingertips. "So, I love you."

"Uh . . . thanks?"

"Do you have anything you might want to express to me in return?"

"You are . . . awesome?" I suggested. He leveled me with eyes that contained no amusement whatsoever. "I'm sorry! I've never said it before. OK, if feeling like your heart's been ripped through your chest, jammed back, and scrambled around means you're in love, it's possible that one day I could be in love with you. "

He quirked his lips. "Well, that was . . . descriptive, while still remaining vague."

"I will say that I don't want to be without you. The idea of you leaving makes me want to throw up. When you're not around, I feel empty and nauseated."

"Aha!" he crowed. "So you admit it! I have a profound effect on your stomach . . . Speaking of which, I've been thinking."

"That was a terrible segue."

He ignored me pointedly. "I was thinking, what if you went and found some werewolf who didn't gross you out entirely and you mated with him? You could have as many babies with him as you wanted. As long you came home to me every day, I think I could live with that."

I kissed him long and hard. "Just the fact that you're willing even to consider that means I couldn't possibly go through with it. First of all, it wouldn't exactly be fair to the random werewolf I picked. He wouldn't be able to have babies with the female of his choice."

"You could pick a gay werewolf who wouldn't want a female—"

"You came up with this scenario pretty quickly," I muttered.

"I'm a creative thinker."

"Oh, my God," I groaned, burying my face in my hands. I laughed and shook my head. "OK, second, it wouldn't work anyway, because I chose you, I marked you. Remember? No substitutions, no takebacks. My body won't accept, uh, contributions from anyone else. You're my mate, for better, for worse. Human or werewolf. You're mine, and I'm yours."

"Good," he said, wrapping his arms around me. " 'Cause I'm going to ask you to marry me, sometime soon. I know this is sort of a good moment, what with the successful deflowering and biting and all. But I didn't want to do it when you were expecting it. And I didn't know whether you wanted an engagement ring or not. I didn't see any of the women in the pack wearing them."

I smiled and was amazed at how easily I accepted the idea after a lifetime of sneering at happy married couples Then again, engagement is sort of a bump in the road, compared with lifelong bonding through a bite on the ass.

"Rings slip off too easily when we change," I told him. "Most of us have our bands tattooed on our fingers. But if that's too much for you, some of the women accept necklaces as a sign of betrothal. The chain has to be sturdy and long enough to wrap around our necks in either form."

He grinned. "Is that what you want?"

"I'm not much on needles." I wiggled my eyebrows. "I like stones with some color to them. Don't get me a door-knocker-sized diamond. Just a little stone."

"What color?"

I grinned up at him, pushing the blond strands of hair out of his eyes. "Blue. I'm awfully partial to blue."

12

Some Orphans Have All the Luck

I WOKE UP, THANKFUL TO be in my human form.

I was in Nick's bed, snuggled up on his blankets. I could smell him all over me, as if I'd been rolling around on him all night. I smiled, stretching across the bed and its cozy, nestlike arrangement of pillows. I don't think I'd ever been more comfortable.

I sat up, propping myself on my elbows, listening for sounds of him moving around the house. Through the bedroom door, I felt a weird tension coming from the living room. I threw on one of his T-shirts and padded toward the sound of his voice.

"You know exactly why not!" Nick was in a shirt and tie, complete with a tweed jacket, pacing back and forth with the cell phone clutched against his face. He noticed me standing there and froze as the person on the other end of the line seemed to be whining at him. He gave me an embarrassed shake of the head and then shouted, "I don't care! I don't care if you end up 'evicted,' which we both know is code for 'dealer is going to beat me up.' I don't owe you a fucking dime. If we're going into debts, let's talk about the money Dad sent over and over to help you 'move home' that never seemed to get your ass on the bus. Or how about the shit you took from my apartment when you just had to sleep on my couch for a week? Trust me, I've paid back whatever you spent on my miserable childhood twice over."

With my supersensitive hearing, I could hear the tenor of the caller's voice change from helpless sobs to a vicious stream of curses.

"You know what, go ahead and call the press. Tell your fake fucking sob story to whoever will listen. I don't give a shit. Hell, people will probably feel sorry for me. Game subscriptions will go up by the thousands."

He clipped the phone shut and roared, tossing it across the room, where it bounced off a steer skull and landed on the counter with a clatter.

"You're right, it was a bad phone," I said, lifting an eyebrow. "Look at it, lying there, all superior. The phone had it coming."

He swooped in on me, claiming my mouth with a ferocity that took my breath. "Your family," he said, his hands trembling at my cheeks. "Do you know how lucky you are to have that?"

I nodded. "Yes. Now, what's wrong?"

"My mother." He sat down and sighed, his head slumping forward. I straddled his lap, pushing his hair out of his face. "Same old song and dance. She's living in Nashville. When she's sober, she wants to be the next big country star. She's behind on her rent. She just needs a measly thousand to make it until the end of the month. Doesn't see why I'm being so unreasonable and stingy when I have so much. She had to chase her dreams, and she did me a favor, leaving me with my dad. She couldn't help it if he turned out to be a drunk. And she did send me a birthday card that once. And she would hate to have to resort to selling her story of an impoverished mother of a gaming magnate to survive. To tell about how she bought me my first computer secondhand at a yard sale, sob sob. I don't even write the code for the damn game. But she doesn't realize that. She doesn't take enough of an interest in what I did, just how much money I made."

I couldn't fathom that. Until Eli's betrayal, I'd never experienced family members turning on each other. It was a foreign concept to want to suck resources away from a pack member. Of course, in the pack, if you needed money, it was practically in your pocket before you could even ask. We took care of our own. And if some people tended to mooch more than others, we just accepted it as part of their personality and teased them about it.

I stroked my hand down his cheek. And he looked up at me with his baby blues, begging for some sort of acceptance, comfort. I kissed his forehead. "Don't worry about her. People like that, you can't make them go away by giving them what they want. They'll only come back for more," I told him. "Besides, you don't need her. You have a new family. We're not exactly normal, but once you're ours, you're ours for life."

I tipped my forehead so it was touching his. "I love you," he said in a voice that had my heart breaking.

I covered it by stroking his arms, gently rotating my hips over his. "I love you."

"And it's very naughty of you to dress this way right before you leave town," I purred as his pulse quickened and his breath grew ragged. His hands slipped under my shirt and traced frantic little patterns on my back. "You did this on purpose to provoke me," I murmured against his mouth as I unzipped his pants, sliding my hand under his waistband and wrapping my fingers around his hard, hot length. "This is like the nerd version of answering the door in Saran Wrap."

He gently eased me back onto the couch, settling his weight over me as I pushed his jacket from his shoulders. "I've been thinking—"

"I love it when you're thinking."

"I know you don't want to have a baby right away. And I'm fine with that. I don't think we should stop using birth control anytime soon. But we can, say, lessen our chances by participating in activities that aren't as chancy but just as satisfying."

I laughed as he eased out of his jeans and kicked them off. "Why do I have the feeling that you have charts showing the fertilization risks of various sex acts hidden behind the couch?"

"I'm just saying we should test a few theories," he said, rolling off the couch and settling in front of me on the floor, stroking his fingers along my instep.

I raised my eyebrows.

"Well, I mean, touching you with my hands doesn't count as sex, so there's no danger there," he said. He wiggled his eyebrows, ghosting his fingertips along my shoulder, up my chin, and over my lips. "It doesn't count as sex."

"So we're going with Clinton's rules?" I asked, just before catching his thumb with the edge of my blunt front teeth and biting down gently. He trailed his fingertips between my breasts, over my belly, and through the wisps of dark hair between my legs. He traced the outlines of my sex, dipping the very tip of his finger just inside me, barely brushing his thumb across my clit. My head thumped back against the table behind the couch as my hips shot up off the couch.

"That's so mean," I moaned.

Chuckling, he kissed across my hips, biting gently on the little bumps of my hipbones, before nibbling his way down my thighs, to my knees.

"There's no danger in kissing you," he said, running his lips along the little bone in my ankle, brushing them lightly over my shin, tickling my knee with his beard. He grinned at me, balancing his chin on my kneecap. "No matter where I do it."

"Hmm." I arched my eyebrow skeptically.

"No, really," he insisted, kissing my kneecap again and pushing me back against the cushions. He spread my thighs, settling between them. He pressed soft, hot little kisses along the smooth skin, his beard leaving a little ticklish trail in its wake.

"Even if I kissed you, say, here." He kissed the juncture of my leg and thigh, nibbling the sensitive skin that stretched as I held this weird yoga pose. "Technically, that's not sex."

His breath puffed hot and moist over me, and I bucked up toward his mouth. Seriously, he wasn't going to . . . yes, he was.

He smirked up at me and slid his tongue from the very lowest point to the top, dipping and twirling his tongue across my clit. My head dropped back, thwacking against the table behind the couch. I knew I should be seeing stars, but I didn't care. All that mattered were the shapes he was drawing against me with the tip of his tongue. As soon as I thought I found the pattern, I lost it to the spiraling pressure coiling in my belly like a snake.

I closed my eyes and melted into him. Hearing those words and feeling his teeth pinch lightly over my clit sent me reeling right over the edge into a dark tunnel of screaming, pulsing sensation. My eyelids snapped shut as I howled out my release and fell into soft, sweet oblivion.

I felt Nick slide up onto the couch and pull me against him. I pressed my face into his chest and hummed happily. "You're wrong, that was dangerous. I think I've gone blind. Which is too bad, because I was planning on reciprocating." Nick gently nudged my eyelids with his fingertips. I popped them open. "Oh, there we go."

"I'm a problem solver," he said as I kissed my way down his chest. I stopped, my ears perking at a soft noise outside. I cocked my head toward the door. "Hey, is your door unlock—"

Cooper stuck his head in through the front door and called, "Hey, Nick, you ready to go?"

His jaw dropped at the sight of me lying at eye level with Nick's navel, both of us buck naked. He clapped his hand over his eyes.

"Ack!"

"Cooper!" I yelled.

"Sorry!" he exclaimed, stumbling into the door frame and smacking his head into the wall. "So sorry! I'm just going to go . . . gouge out my eyes now."

"I forgot he was coming over," Nick groaned as Cooper turned a corner and continued whacking his forehead against the wall. "You were naked, and I lost track of time."

"Why is he here?"

"The whole leaving early thing was sort of a smokescreen. I've been talking to Cooper whenever I go into the saloon. He was worried about you not having a truck. And since I sort of played a role in its destruction, I wanted to help you replace it. We were going to go look at dealerships in Burney before I drove up to Anchorage. Surprise . . ." he finished weakly.

"You were going to buy me a truck, just like that?" I asked, my heart doing that weird fluttering thing again. "And you were wearing your professor duds to cover your trail?"

"No, I wanted to look respectable at the dealership," Nick said, all defeated and puppylike. "I was going to make it look like Cooper found some older model for a song."

"Aw!" I rose on the balls of my feet and kissed the tip of his nose. "That's incredibly sweet but unnecessary. I have money of my own saved up. It's not like I pay Mom rent or anything. And Clay thinks he might be able to save my old truck."

"I hate to be the one to break up this little love fest, but could you two go put on some clothes, please?" Cooper demanded.

I rolled my eyes. Nick threw me some sweats and a T-shirt.

Cooper finally uncovered his eyes. "Look, I like you, Nick. I've seen the way you are with my sister, and I approve. The love of my life is a human and an outsider . . . and an incredible smart-ass. So, who the hell am I to judge who Maggie chooses? And considering the fresh bite I see on your neck, I know you're mated and not doing anything wrong. But right now, I'm trying to control my brotherly instincts to kill you . . . just give me a minute, OK?"

"Yep," Nick said, wisely stepping away from my brother and bracing himself behind the breakfast bar.

"So, um, Mags, would you mind telling me why

you're here at this hour? Without going into specif-
ics, please?"

"Nick and I are putting on a puppet show, Coop,"
I responded dryly.

"Please, Lord, don't let that be a position I
haven't heard of," Cooper said, shuddering.

13

Damn You, Milton Bradley

Nɪᴄᴋ ʜᴀᴅ ᴛᴏ ʟᴇᴀᴠᴇ for his lecture, though I managed to talk him out of the truck purchase so we could spend the extra day . . . um, talking. Cooper was happy to leave us alone before we could start another conversation.

And because my brother is basically a gossiping old woman, nobody was surprised when I returned to the valley and announced that Nick and I were mated. In fact, the aunties had already arranged a potluck supper in our honor when Nick returned a week later, which was a little embarrassing. Nothing says family closeness like a "Congratulations on Doing It" dinner.

I can't say every member of the pack was thrilled with my choice. An aunt or two sniffed at another Graham taking a chance with the family wolf genes. And a few of my cousins took bets on how long it would last before Nick's body turned up in a gulley somewhere, which was sort of mean.

Pops's contribution was to shake Nick's hand, level him with that inscrutable gaze, and say, "You're not good enough for her."

It was times like this that I wished I wasn't Pops's favorite granddaughter. But Nick, who was managing not to fold like a cheap card table under Pops's unrelenting grip, simply smiled and said, "I know that, sir, but no one is."

Pops sniffed and sauntered toward the beer weenies. I gave Nick a wink to let him know he'd handled that very well.

And at the end of the night, as much as it pained me, Nick went to sleep at Samson's house. Because as evolved and open as my family was, the idea of having sex under my mother's roof really creeped me out. It was bad enough having the first "post-game" conversation with my mom. After I made the mating announcement, she took me aside and asked me if I "wanted to talk about it."

I sprang up from my chair, suddenly very keen to know whether the top drawer of my filing cabinet was locked. "God, no!"

Mom seemed perplexed. "I don't know why not. It's nothing to be afraid of. My first time with your father was fantastic."

"Mom, I don't want to hear about your honeymoon hijinks, OK?"

"Oh, honey, it wasn't on our wedding night. We took care of that a long time before we got married."

"Ohmygod!" I howled. "Why would you tell me that?"

"Well, we were already mated. Your dad had claimed me. Why wait until the wedding when we wanted to have kids right away? Honey, what are you doing?" she said as I rifled through my desk drawers.

"Looking for something to gouge out my eardrums."

It was obvious that Nick and I were going to have to make some sort of separate living arrangement soon. Obviously, I couldn't move too far away. There was no way we could stay at his place in Grundy. Sure, I'd been relieved that despite my dire sense of foreboding, I came home to find nothing had happened while I was gone. Still, I needed to be among my packmates, to help with the everyday management of the valley. And it helped to have some semblance of authority in their midst. I'd worked too hard for their respect and trust to walk away now.

But the idea of a separate address, where we could be alone at the end of the day, was definitely appealing. I mulled it over for a few days, trying to find a way to fit it into the conversation that wouldn't make me sound like a demanding potential wife. Mom saw this as some sort of sign of maturity, that I was actually taking his feelings into account.

The problem was that there were a limited number of houses in the valley, and all of them were occupied at the moment. Houses were passed through family lines, like everything else in the pack. And there hadn't been a new house built since the early 1980s. Then again, we didn't get a lot of new arrivals here in town. Alicia and Clay were the last people to move to the valley since my mother had arrived.

Speaking of Clay, he seemed to be spending less and less time in the valley. I wasn't sure if that was because of my choosing Nick or because the garage was keeping him that busy. When I realized how little consideration I'd given him during the whole mate-choosing thing, I felt a pulse of guilt constrict my chest. Even if we weren't committed or exclusive, he deserved more than that. I kicked myself for not ending things with him before taking any sort of step with Nick. But sometimes life is messy and complicated, and you just don't have time to pencil things into your schedule, such as "Dump perfectly nice werewolf suitor before getting naked with human sweetie." Clay skipped the pack dinner, and he didn't seem to want to talk to me or Samson, and I couldn't blame him. And because I didn't want it to fester, I ended up cornering him down in the work shed one afternoon as he tinkered with a chain saw.

Overall, it might not have been my *brightest* idea.

After I stepped into the shed, Clay gave me the silent treatment I so richly deserved for a few moments. But before long, his lips were twitching, and he gave me crooked little grin. "So . . . Nick, huh?"

I grimaced and gave him a sheepish little smile. "I should have talked to you about it first. It just sort of happened. If you want to kick my ass over it, I'd understand."

He shook his head. "Nah. Don't get me wrong.

I'm disappointed. But sometimes the heart just wants what it wants, right? Who am I to get in the way of my alpha's true love?" His voice was tight, but he covered by looking over the chain saw parts and selecting a few gears for cleaning.

I asked, "Need some help?"

He tossed me a rag and some mineral oil. "Sure."

And that was pretty much it. We basically broke up without really hashing it out. And considering how guilty I felt *without* talking it to death, I can only imagine how bad a prolonged discussion would have made me feel. So, silence is a method I whole-heartedly endorse. It left things sort of unsettled, but Cousin Teresa suddenly seemed much happier.

To top the guilt sundae off, Clay's occasional absences meant that Alicia was more frazzled than usual, and Billie seemed to be getting worse. The doc had to prescribe stronger sedatives for her, as her once occasional "episodes" were becoming an almost-daily event. The day I came home, Billie had wandered out onto Main Street in her housecoat, screaming that there was a "redheaded bitch" trying to run her house.

While the high school kids got a kick out of the sweet, level-headed auntie who used to knit them Christmas stockings cursing like a sailor in the middle of the street, this latest bout made me wonder whether we needed to find a better situation for Billie. There was no such thing as a werewolf nursing home, but there must be some way to make her more comfortable.

I was sitting on my front porch, mulling over calling Billie's great-nephew Matthew, the alpha of her home pack in Canada. I rarely spoke to Matthew, who was sort of hyper and always seemed to have some huge project going that inhibited his ability to return phone calls. And he still didn't know how to work his voice mail. It was sort of an ADHD werewolf's double whammy. He still hadn't responded to several messages I had left months before, thanking him for sending Clay and Alicia. But his pack was bigger than mine and located closer to urban areas. Maybe he had a suggestion (or twenty) on how to help his auntie.

I closed my eyes and tilted my head back against the sturdy pine rocking chair. It was late February, and the weather would be cold for another few months, but the sun was setting, and it was comfortable to sit outside for a while. I closed my eyes and lifted my face to the dying rays of sunlight, stretching and yawning.

Somehow, in the midst of all this, I was pretty damned content. Probably the happiest I had been in my short, surly life. I'd claimed a mate. I felt the same need for Nick, for the comfort of his presence, than I did before. Nick and I were still working on the whole "exploring" issue. It helped that we were basically chaperoned by my entire family and couldn't get away with much. I think I was learning far more about what I liked than what Nick liked. Because it turns out guys like everything. Orgasms are like pizza or a Dolph Lundgren movie; even when they're not great, you still enjoy yourself.

I was perfecting my oral skills, although I think

the whole "my girlfriend has wolf teeth" thing made him a little nervous. And my man could play "Stairway to Heaven" guitar riffs with his tongue if he wanted to, so overall, we were both pretty happy.

Of course, given all that happiness, I really should have seen this next thing coming.

My ears perked up at the sound of shuffling footsteps moving toward me. My eyes snapped open, and I saw Samson stumbling toward the porch. He was naked, which meant he'd just come in from a run. His expression was pinched, as if every step hurt him. He missed a step and stumbled onto the porch, clutching his side.

"Maggie?" he whispered, gripping his side.

I yawned again. "Ha ha, Samson, I'm not falling for that again. It was a sick joke when you pretended to be chain-saw-massacred on Halloween, and it's a sick joke now."

He didn't get up.

"Sam . . . Sam?" The wind changed directions, and the smell of his blood finally made it to my nostrils. "Mom!" I yelled, scrambling next to him. My knees hit the boards with a thud. I rolled him over and found a quarter-sized hole just under his ribs. My hands were red and wet as the blood welled over the fingers pressing against his wound.

Mom came out onto the porch. She gasped, falling to her knees beside me.

"Call Dr. Moder!" I yelled. "Now! Better yet, just run down the street to the clinic. Now, Mom, please!"

I tore off my jacket and threw it over him. I

pressed my shirt to his side to stanch the bleeding. There was so much of it, and the slick coppery smell was starting to turn my stomach. If the bullet hit something vital, something Dr. Moder couldn't handle, we were going to have to get him to a real hospital. There would be questions I couldn't answer, reports that wouldn't be safe for us to file. And what if we couldn't get him there in time? He'd lost so much blood. How much more could he have?

"Sam, please hold on, OK? Just keep breathing. I'm sorry. I'm so sorry. I thought you were kidding."

"Woods," Samson whispered. "Shot me. No smell."

I shushed him. "OK, OK, just save your breath."

I kept watching the wound, hoping that the bullet would be pushed out by his natural healing ability. The wound was growing smaller, but the little lead round seemed lodged inside. I heard Mama's footsteps thumping up the street as she practically carried Dr. Moder to us. Sensing Mom's growing panic, the doctor told her to fetch a blanket and towels from inside the house.

"What do we have here?" Dr. Moder asked, dropping her massive medical bag next to me as she kneeled down. She sounded a lot calmer than I felt. I guess she'd seen a lot worse from us over the years. I just don't remember feeling this frantic when Cooper got his head stuck in a stair railing.

Up and down the street, I could hear doors opening, my family coming out of their houses to see what the ruckus was. For a second, I considered sending them into the woods to look for the shooter.

But that could result in more werewolves with gunshot wounds. Or a hunter with wet pants.

"Does anyone know who was running with Samson today?" I yelled. A few of my relatives shook their heads. "Everybody go inside!" I barked. "Do a head count. Figure out who's not here. Don't come out until I come to you."

Immediately, doors snapped shut, although I could still see a few of my aunts silhouetted against their windows.

After slipping on a latex glove, Dr. Moder probed the wound with her fingertip while I cringed. She pulled out a huge bottle of hydrogen peroxide and poured it into the wound. She pulled out a plastic-wrapped scalpel and forceps.

"I think the bullet probably missed his organs, but I need to open him up to make sure."

I made an embarrassing squeaking noise. "You're going to do this right here? On my front porch?"

Dr. Moder's teeth were on edge as she said, "The bullet's pretty deep. If I wait any longer, to give him anesthesia or get him to a sterile room, the wound will heal over, and I'll have to open him up again to get it out. He stands less chance of infection and will heal faster if I get it now. Trust me, your cousin Wayne's been shot by enough grumpy locals that I would know. Just try not to breathe too much on him."

I gritted my teeth, blowing a breath out through my nostrils. I handed her the scalpel, which she used to widen the wound, dipping the forceps past the bloody ring of tissue and rooting around.

OK, I could handle a lot, but this was pretty gross. I tried to think of it as a game of Operation. And the only consequence of Dr. Moder screwing up would be a buzzing sound and Samson's nose lighting up red.

Samson's hand twitched as Dr. Moder's instrument gripped the bullet. I threaded my fingers through his, willing the tears gathering at the corners of my eyes not to fall. How could this have happened? Other than my dad and Cousin Wayne, no one in the pack had been shot in years. We'd learned to shy away from any signs of hunters.

At this point, I didn't care if it was just some dumb-ass tourist who wanted a scary trophy for his den. I wanted to rip him limb from limb. But Samson needed me here now. And I was doing well not to phase on the spot and start howling like a lunatic.

Dr. Moder pulled the bullet free, and I blew out a breath. The little hole in his skin was closing, pink and healthy and shiny, as Dr. Moder poured more antiseptic over it. Samson groaned.

"Let's get him to the clinic," Dr. Moder said. "Maybe call a few of the bigger cousins, 'cause it will take all of them to cart his heavy butt. And we're going to need anyone with his blood type to come down to the clinic and donate. He's lost a lot of blood. Come on, Maggie, let go of him and get moving."

I shot an incredulous look at her. She put a light hand on my shoulder and shook me gently. "It's OK, Mags. He's going to be fine. You can let go of his hand."

I looked down at our joined, stained hands, and gripped tighter.

Dr. Moder frowned. "Or . . . maybe not."

THE NEXT FEW hours were among the longest of my life. I did a head count and was ridiculously grateful to find everyone accounted for, except for Clay, who had stayed late at the garage where he worked. I questioned my relatives. I called Nick, who didn't understand my sudden need to check up on him while he was working from his place in Grundy. And even more confused when I told him to stay there until I came for him.

As I walked into the clinic, I felt as if I was moving through molasses. I felt helpless. I didn't know what to do. And I hated it. No wonder Cooper ran from the responsibilities of running the pack. This feeling sucked.

"Sam?" I called softly. I poked my head into the sole treatment room at the clinic. Shirtless and swathed in gauze, Samson was propped against a pile of pillows, with a full gallon of Mom's chicken noodle soup and a full pan of Mo's triple chocolate brownies in front of him.

"I think you scared everybody pretty good," I said.

"I'll say," he said, chewing happily. "There's two more batches of brownies in the office. Mo was panic-baking. She and Cooper are going to stay the night. Cooper was, er, a little nervous."

Some small voice in the back of my head balked at the idea of having Cooper and his family here.

He'd brought them right into our mess. If there was still someone out there with their sights trained on the pack, Mo and the baby were in the crosshairs now. But of course, if I tried to send them away, Mo would just swing at me with some heavy piece of kitchen equipment. I made a mental note to search the clinic for tranquilizer darts.

"I'm really glad you're OK," I told him, pinning his eyes with my own. I wanted him to understand that I was having a rare moment of absolute seriousness. And of course, he responded by grinning at me through the chocolate like a toddler.

"That said." I paused and then smacked the back of his head.

"Ow!" he yelped.

"What the hell were you thinking running alone? After I specifically told every member of the pack to use the buddy system," I demanded. "No one had any idea you were out or where you were. What if you hadn't made it back home? You could have bled out, in the woods, alone. Leaving behind the biggest fucking corpse the bears had ever seen. It took pints from me, Cooper, and Mom to get you up and going again. Pops tried to donate, and it took four of the uncles to keep him from sticking the needle in his own arm."

"Maggie—" Samson started, before I smacked him again. "Ow!"

I crossed my arms over my chest to prevent further smacking. "Sorry, go ahead."

"I got restless," he admitted. "Clay is my running partner. And he said he couldn't make it out today

because he was working late. Sometimes you just
have to phase and go, you know? I was just running
along the edge of the valley. I heard a weird popping
noise, then another, and *wham*, I felt like I'd been hit
by a truck."

"Do you think it was a hunter?"

"No, a hunter probably would have collected my
carcass as I lay bleeding on the ground."

"Good point. An accident, maybe?" I suggested,
knowing I was grasping at straws at this point.

"You mean, oops, I took my high-powered rifle,
looked through the scope, and happened to fire at
the bear-sized wolf in my crosshairs?" he suggested.
"'And then I fired again, because I missed the first
time?'"

"I didn't say it was a *good* theory," I snarled at
him. "Forgive me for trying to grasp at any possibility besides members of my pack being picked off by
an unseen but well-armed menace."

"Look, Midget, I will admit, there is a pattern
of shit that's happened in the last few months. Your
truck brakes. Your office. Strange wolves sniffing
around the borders. Hunters getting all trigger-
happy . . . though who could blame them for wanting such a fine trophy as yours truly. But there's no
reason to circle the wagons and get all paranoid."

"If you call me a hysterical female, I am not above
pulling the plug," I deadpanned, reminding myself
that it was a good thing Samson didn't know about
the bag incident.

He yawned. "We'll just do what we always do.
We'll keep an eye out. We'll keep the youngsters

close to home. No one goes out alone, using my little incident as a painful example. But until some rogue werewolf trots down Main Street and declares war, I say we relax."

"That's your solution to everything."

He shrugged. "And so far, it's worked out great for me. Up until getting shot."

There was a light knock at the door. Alicia stuck her head in and gave me a sheepish little smile. I glanced from her to Samson, who was staring at her with a completely smitten, stupid expression, and back again.

My lips twitched, but I maintained my neutral face.

"I hope I'm not interrupting," she said.

"Uh, no," I said, hopping up from the bed. "Did you hear from Clay?"

"Yeah, he'll be home as soon as he can," she said, her gaze never leaving Samson. "Your mom came over to watch the boys and Billie. She knew I wanted to stop by and bring this, uh, Jell-O." She put a very full Tupperware container on the little roll-away table.

I eased toward the door. "Yeah, she knows how much Samson loves Jell-O."

Truth be told, Samson hated Jell-O. He said food should only twitch if it's recently deceased. And maybe covered in barbecue sauce. But he really liked Alicia, that much was clear.

I wandered out of the clinic, pondering this new development. Alicia was a good match for Samson. I mean, she was used to wrangling dangerous preschoolers. Although Alicia's previous mating meant that Samson would never have children of his own, he was good with Paul and Ronnie, who seemed to view him as sort of a man-sized jungle gym. And he would get all of the benefits of having sons without the cranky pregnant wife, two A.M. feedings, and diapers.

I jogged to my office, sat at my desk, and fired up my computer. When he installed the cameras around the valley, Nick had hooked a wireless transmitter into my modem to record anything the cameras picked up to my hard drive. I'd expected the activity to escalate after the incident on the cliff. But so far, we'd mostly gotten footage of elk prancing around the tree line as if they owned the place. But when I opened up the video cache folder on my desktop for that night's feed, I found . . . nothing.

There was a clip of a young bear cub wandering on the southern ridge the day before, which I'd found on my daily check of the folder. That was it.

"Damn it." I sighed.

I don't know what I'd expected. A clip of some Elmer Fudd lookalike waving at the camera and showing ID?

I sat back in my office chair, chewing up my lip. My mom was probably wondering where I was. And Nick had already texted me five times, demanding a less cryptic phone call. I couldn't seem to bring myself to face either of them.

I sprang up from the chair. What if the cameras weren't working? Some of the units on the south side of the valley hadn't deposited a video in the cache folder. It couldn't hurt to go check, right? It was something to do, and I was itching for something to do that didn't involve talking or emotions.

I dashed out of my office and jogged up the slope behind the clinic, shrugging out of my jacket and boots. My feet slipped through the patches of tough dead grass, the edges of each blade pricking my ankles. I closed my eyes and breathed deep, searching for a trace of Samson's blood on the breeze. My face naturally inclined north, to one of Samson's favorite napping spots in the valley. A patch of dirt he'd dug out on the north lip of the crescent. Nothing. I faced south and caught the faintest scent of rust. I followed it on human feet, silent and swift, my braid bouncing against my back as the scent grew stronger. There was a trail there, worn through the trees by generations of paws.

I skidded to a stop when I recognized the shiny black patch of blood on the ground. Samson's pawprints hadn't gone any farther, as if he'd come running along and stopped suddenly before he was hit. Had he heard a noise? I couldn't smell any sign of a human or a wolf nearby. I looked up at the bare, imposing limbs overhead. There was nowhere to hide. And there was no camera in sight. Was that blind luck on the shooter's part? Or did he know where the cameras were?

Samson would have seen a human standing close. The shot must have come from a distance, which could have meant a skewed shot from the game preserve. But there were so many trees. What was the probability of a hunter shooting wild and then the bullet making it all the way through the forest without hitting anything but Samson? I'd say it ranged from no freaking way to none. This was the work of our fabric-softener-loving friend.

I sat on the ground and considered the possibilities. And then I realized that I was just a few yards from the spot where I'd claimed Nick with that ill-conceived bite. He'd been sitting a short distance from where Samson had been shot.

There was a crushing tightness in my chest, leaving me unable to draw in air. I could see Nick in my head, sitting alone on that ridge, scribbling in his little notebook. The wind was playing with his gold hair, and he was pausing every few minutes to shove his glasses back up on his nose. Suddenly, there was the loud crack of a rifle shot, and Nick slumped to the ground, a patch of red blooming on the chest pocket of his shirt. The notebook fluttered out of his hand as blood trickled over his lips. He was unable to move, unable to call for help, unable to do anything but stay there and die. Because of me, because he was too close to me.

Unlike Samson, my mate would not be capable of transforming into a giant wolf and defending himself. I would spend the rest of my life worrying about Nick. I mean, the man had wandered into the path of rogue werewolves and been involved in a serious motor-vehicle incident just since meeting me. I would worry about him getting sick, getting shot, getting caught in the crossfire of whatever weird pattern of phenomena was circling around the valley. Mo had barely survived her ordeal, and that was with just one crazed werewolf after her. What if a whole pack came after us?

As long as Nick was close to me, he'd be in some form of danger.

I thought I could regulate that paranoia. I thought I could handle the constant anxiety. Hell, when I found out that my brother had abandoned Mo in an effort to protect her, I tracked him down, called him a lot of anatomically detailed names, and threatened to rip his head off. But now, the idea of Nick loving me somehow getting him killed had me throwing up in a mossy bank near the tree line. This was definitely a case of "it's different because it's me."

I couldn't wait and think this through. I had to stop it now. I had to get Nick to leave now. If I let it go on any longer, it would hurt that much worse. Sure, I was basically kissing my life good-bye. No babies. No Nick. No sex. But at least he would be alive. I stumbled toward the woods, toward Grundy, not bothering to tear off my clothes so I could transform. I burst into my wolf state, leaving a trail of scraps in my wake. I ran faster than my four paws had ever carried me, following Nick's scent across the miles that protected him from my crazy-ass life. I found him on his couch, typing on his laptop.

He grinned at me as I came through the door, and I felt as if I was going to throw up again. He set aside his work and opened his arms to me. "Hey, are you OK? No more shorthand messages without follow-up; they make me nervous." When I didn't dive into his embrace as usual, his brow furrowed. "What's wrong?"

"Look, Nick," I said, smiling at him and giving my best "bad news" face. "This whole thing has been a lot of fun. But I think you're taking all this way too seriously. It's time for you to move on."

Nick's face flushed, then went bone white. "What?"

I sighed, trying to seem exasperated. "It's time for you to find some other pack to pester. I mean, we had some good times, but I think we both knew this wouldn't work out in the long run."

"But we're mated now, you said—"

"I made it up!" I said, adding a sarcastic little laugh for good measure. "Like human girls who tell the guys who take them home from bars that they 'never do this sort of thing.' Weres feed that whole 'mated for life' line to humans all the time. It makes you feel special."

He was staring me down, searching my face for some sign of the lie. And I was *this* close to folding. Fortunately, Friday-night card games with Pops and Samson had given me a pretty steady poker face. I gritted my teeth and stared right back. Nick's eyes narrowed. My lips tightened into a thin little line. And suddenly, he was grinning like a loon.

That I had not expected.

"You're pulling a *Lassie* on me, aren't you?" he crowed, laughing.

Now my exasperation was genuine. "What?"

"You're pulling a *Lassie* on me," he said again. "It's like some old episode of *Lassie* when Timmy thinks Lassie's about to be taken away and shot by some old mean farmer for eating chickens. Timmy tells Lassie he hates her and throws rocks at her so she'll run away."

"Are you high right now?" I demanded.

"You're trying to hurt me so I'll leave. You want to get me out of the way so . . . what, so I won't get hurt? What's going on, Maggie? Why are you scared?"

"I'm not scared. I want you to leave because I want you out of my face," I shot back.

"Not true. You love me."

"No, I don't."

I scowled as his little dimples winked at me, and he said, "Can't live without me."

"I don't like to harp on this, but you do know I'm capable of killing you, right?"

"I think I should move in with you."

"Oh, my God, you're such a pain in the ass," I grumbled.

"A pain in the ass that you're madly in love with," he said.

I gave him my best death glare. He gave me that damn smile again, and I folded like a frigging accordion. I groaned as he wrapped his arm around me.

"Come on, baby, tell me what has you so wound up," he whispered. "You're Maggie Fucking Graham. You're not afraid of anything."

"Not true," I admitted, tapping my forehead against his collarbone. "Losing you scares the crap out of me."

"Not going to happen."

"Samson was shot today," I murmured into his shirt. "He's going to be OK, but we couldn't find who did it. And of course, Cooper came running, bringing Mo and the baby with him. And I started thinking about how stupid that was, because he could be bringing his family right into the whirlwind. I'm not any better than he is. I'm worse, because I want you close to me. And I can't protect you. I can try, but nothing I do can guarantee that you'll be safe. I can't keep anything from happening to you. It would be so much better for you to get as far away from me as you can. "

"Not going to happen," he said.

"I know," I grumbled. "Damn it. It was worth a shot." I looked up at him, my eyes pricking hotly. "I don't want anybody else. I can't be with anyone else." He pulled me close, and I murmured into his neck, "I love you."

"Who was wrong?" he asked.

"I was wrong." I sighed.

He poked my shoulder. "Who was right?"

"Don't push it."

"I'm not leaving you," he told me. "I don't care what you try to do to push me away. I don't care what comes along. I'm here. If you think I'm going to back down now, you're crazy."

"So, you're going to love me out of spite?"

"Yes."

I sighed. "Ah, spite, the stuff of fairy tales."

14

Wedding Belled

Instead of me driving Nick away, he ended up driving me back home, with a truckload of his stuff. He was moving in with Samson, he said, until Samson was back on his feet and we could build a house between Pops's place and Mom's. I didn't even have to ask; he just knew that was what he needed to do. He said he would start calling construction companies as soon as possible, so we could break ground when it thawed.

Oh, and apparently, we were getting married that summer.

Nick didn't get down on one knee, but he pulled me into his lap and looped a little sapphire pendant around my neck. He reiterated his whole "not going anywhere" plan and told me that if I ever tried to protect him by sending him away again, I would have two fights on my hands—from the perceived danger and from Nick.

"I can't say we're always going to be deliriously happy," he said as his fingers worked the chain's catch at the nape of my neck. "But we'll be together, and that's a lot more than some people have. So, Margaret Faith Graham"—he stopped when I growled at the mention of my middle name—"cut it out, your mom told me—would you please stop being so stubborn and agree to marry the man who will love you until the day he dies?"

"Yes," I mumbled, fingering the pretty blue stone. I liked the way it sparkled, a quiet sort of shine that seemed to give off deeper flashes of cobalt within. He could have given me the Hope Diamond, and I wouldn't have been happier. "I will stop jerking you around. It's not fair to you."

"And?" he prompted, cupping his hand to his ear.

"Yes, I will marry you." I sighed, slipping my arms around his neck. Suddenly, I shifted back and poked him in the chest. "But I'm not wearing a froufrou princess dress."

His eyebrows quirked, and he tilted his head. "I'd be fine with what you're wearing right now."

I glanced down at my naked body. "Nice."

When we got home and told my family our somewhat bizarre proposal tale—minus the nudity—Mo suggested listening to my grand plans in my head to make sure they make sense before I act. I suggested she take a long walk off the nearest cliff. Then, of course, when she and Mom realized we had about five months to plan a wedding, the squealing began.

Oh, my God, the squealing.

Mo got on the phone with Kara, and there was more squealing, in stereo. Kara said she would come over with an armload of bridal planners the next day.

"Wait, wait, we can't plan a wedding now," I said, grasping at any straws that kept me away from the words "manipedi." "Samson just got shot. We have a problem with intruders. Nick and I can just go off to Anchorage one weekend and have a courthouse thing."

Mo and Mom looked at me as if I'd just suggested shaving baby Eva's head and piercing her eyebrow.

"I'm happy either way," Nick said.

"Oh, that's sweet." Cooper chuckled. "You think you have a vote."

"I don't have a vote?" Nick asked. Cooper handed him a beer, clapped his hand down on Nick's, and shook his head.

"Your best bet is just to sit back, relax, and wait for the cake."

Nick frowned. "Do I at least get a vote on the flavor of the cake?"

"No."

Do you know how annoying it is to suspect something but not be able to do anything about it? I didn't know if these "happenings" were a focused effort to harass my pack or someone with a really lame sense of humor. I didn't have a suspect. I couldn't even give a description beyond "smells like flowers." There was no interpack police agency. There was nothing to do, other than contacting Alan to complain about hunters getting too close to the border between the nature preserve and the valley.

Oh, and I finally told the pack about the "bagging" incident, which, along with Samson's shooting, helped them realize exactly how serious the problem was. Cooper and Samson had the decency to wait until the rest of the pack was gone before lighting into me for not telling anyone. Mom was so angry I thought she was going to try to take me over her knee. Instead, she hugged Nick and thanked him for helping her idiot daughter.

Signs were posted. We expanded the perimeter into the preserve. We patrolled in threes. No one left the confines of town by themselves. Whenever possible, the kids were kept inside, which was driving the parents and Teresa insane.

I was running myself into the ground. I was coming to depend on Nick more and more, which scared the hell out of me. When I came home and collapsed after all-night patrols, he was the one who dragged me into my room and tucked me in. He made sure there was food nearby when I woke up. On more than one occasion, he bathed me, but that was more recreational than anything else.

My deranged sister-in-law, she kept plying me with wedding magazines and books on how to be a beautifulhappyfluffyprincessbride. I think she saw it as some helpful way to take my mind off the pack's troubles, which was woefully inaccurate. I wanted to elope. In fact, I spent several days campaigning diligently for a chapel in Vegas. But Mom and Mo convinced me that it would be a shabby move for the alpha to run off and get married without the pack being able to see it. Plus, it would be a nice gesture to invite other packs to the wedding. Mo actually used the words "political maneuver." Sometimes that woman scared me.

I'd never been one for change. I liked my routine. I liked knowing what to expect. But now, I'd changed my plans, my expectations, by choosing someone completely outside the realm of what I expected, and I had change coming out the ying-yang. It was as if I'd opened a little door and the whole world was opening up.

I was still on the fence about to whether that was a good thing.

So, I did what I could to maintain normalcy and escape the house, which included regular visits to see Billie. Alicia was also looking a little the worse for wear lately, and she appreciated it when she could step out of the house to take a walk or do . . . whatever it was that she did with Samson. I tried not to think about it.

"Alicia!" I called as I came through Billie's door. "My mom made a blueberry pie. It's Billie's favorite."

My ears pricked up as I closed the door behind me. There was an odd stillness to the house. No TV blaring cartoon songs from the next room. No thunder of little running feet. The only sound was the dryer running in the utility room. The rusty scent of dried blood spiraled out of the kitchen, raising the hairs on my arms. The instinct to change, to defend, was overwhelming. I had to force myself to stay in my human shape.

I dropped the pie, breaking china and splattering purple goo over my boots. I inhaled deeply, searching for some sign of an intruder.

I crept on silent feet toward the table where I used to sit and eat Lucky Charms on the mornings after Eli slept over at our house. Mom would send me to Aunt Billie's for sleepovers, so Billie wouldn't get lonely. I wanted to be that little girl again, in the Smurf nightshirt, with nothing to worry about but which cartoon to fit into her Saturday-morning schedule. Time seemed to stop in my head, and I couldn't force myself to approach the source of that rust smell.

Well, screw that, I was Maggie Graham. I wasn't scared of anything.

Squaring my shoulders, I strode through the front room to the kitchen. Flour was spilled across the counter. A jar of peanut butter and a loaf of bread sat open near the stove, with sticky slices strewn on the floor. I stepped around the corner and saw faded pink slippers on still, splayed feet. Billie was on her side, wearing her favorite blue plaid housecoat. There was a kitchen knife just out of her reach, by her right hand. Her hair was matted with red. The corner of the counter near the fridge was crusted with dried, brick-colored blood.

"Oh, no," I murmured. "Oh, no. Aunt Billie, no."

I dropped to my knees. I clasped her wrist in my fingers but found no pulse. The body was still warm, but her eyes were open, fixed on the ceiling. There was no spark. There was nothing to be done for her.

I laid gentle fingers on her eyelids and closed them. I leaned over, my forehead almost touching her hands. "I'm so sorry," I whispered.

She'd hit her head. That much was clear. Had she passed out? Tripped? Pushed? Where was Alicia? Why wasn't someone with her?

I kneeled there for what felt like hours. I heard chatter from just outside the back door. Alicia was leading the boys up the stairs. I ran for the door. "Keep the boys outside," I told her.

Alicia blanched at my tone. "What's going on?"

"It's Billie . . ." I said, glancing down at the boys, who were clamoring for juice and SpongeBob.

The color drained from Alicia's face. "No. I just left for a few minutes. I took the boys out to play. The weather was so nice for once. And she was taking a nap. I thought it would be OK."

I put my hand on her shoulder and offered her a reassuring squeeze. "She must have gotten up. She was in the kitchen."

Alicia seemed to be gasping for air as tears welled in her eyes. "I'm so sorry. I didn't—"

"Don't." I squeezed her shoulder and shook it gently. "You took good care of her, Alicia. Why don't you take the boys to my mom's? I'll stay here. You call Dr. Moder."

"I think I should stay—"

"Alicia, you did everything you could for her. Let me take it from here. That's my job. Get the kids away from here. You don't want them to see this."

Alicia nodded, robotically leading the boys down

the front steps. Dropping to my knees, I sat next to Billie and waited.

I SAT AT my desk, staring into space. I kept waiting for tears or sweet, clarifying anger. But I was numb. My brain had shut down all emotional responses in some sort of survival mode. All I could do was list the dozens of things I needed to do.

I needed to call Matthew, Billie's great-nephew. I needed to go through Billie's papers and try to figure out what accounts needed to be closed, whether she had a will. We needed to plan the service. Mom had stepped in to pick the music and the flowers. Samson and Clay had volunteered to make the casket, which was a pack tradition. We used a were-owned funeral home to sign off on the arrangements, so we didn't have to worry about the state looking too closely at death certificates.

Dr. Moder had taken the body to the clinic. She said Billie had hit her head against the corner of the counter with enough force to break her neck. As if that wasn't enough, the fall also cracked Billie's skull, causing a hemorrhage that would have been fatal. The only good news was that the broken neck most likely prevented any suffering. The doc couldn't tell me how Billie had fallen, but given the state of the kitchen, she'd probably been in the middle of an episode and either lost her balance or passed out. As much as I wanted to blame Billie's death on some unseen intruder, Dr. Moder said it was more likely that she'd simply fallen hard enough to do that sort of damage. As strong as we are, our bones can only stand up to so much as we age.

I made a mental note to pick up some calcium supplements for Pops.

Suddenly, all of the weird occurrences seemed silly by comparison. I felt indulgent and paranoid for trying to find hidden dangers while missing out on the real threat Billie posed to herself.

For the fourth time in an hour, I picked up the phone to call Matthew. As alpha, it fell to me to inform Billie's kin of her passing. These were the rare times when my job sucked ass. I'd left three voice-mail messages, but by now, I knew the best method was to keep calling until he picked up. This time, in a near-miraculous show of cell-phone mastery, Matt managed to pick up before it went to voice mail. He chattered from the other end of the line about births and matings in his own pack, physically incapable of letting someone else enter the conversation until he had to take a breath.

"Look, Matt, I'm sorry to have to tell you this, but Billie is gone." Blunt, yes, but necessary if I wanted to shut him up for a minute. "We're not sure what happened, but it looks like she fell and hit her head in the kitchen."

There was a long pause on the other end of the line, the longest pause I could remember while talking to Matt. He sighed and gave the expected platitudes about long life and Billie being in a better place. We talked about the funeral, made arrangements for a contingent from Matt's pack to stay in houses around the valley. Matt had clearly been expecting this call for a while, because he seemed to have the end planned out. He loved logistics, which was part of why he was a pretty effective pack leader. Handling the mundane details seemed to help. I could handle busy work.

As the call was winding down, Matt said, "Maggie, I hope you know how much I appreciate you taking care of Billie in her last months. I know it was difficult, but deep down, I'm sure she really appreciated being able to stay in her own home."

I smiled and felt just a tiny bit of the weight on my chest wiggle loose. "Oh, I can't take all the credit. Clay and Alicia did most of the work."

Another long pause from Matt. Two in one phone call, which was unprecedented. "Who?"

"Clay and Alicia," I repeated. "Renard. Your cousins? Billie's nephew and niece?"

"Mags, I have fifty-six first cousins alone, and none of them is named Clay or Alicia. And Billie was an only child. Where did these people say they were from?"

The office door opened, and Clay stepped inside, an amiable grin stretched across his face. All of the blood in my veins seemed to flutter and freeze.

The phone was hanging heavily against the side of my face. I took in a breath, jittery from shock and rage and the knowledge that I had actually kissed this guy. I'd given him the benefit of the doubt when Nick suggested that he could have been the one on the cliff, when I considered the damage to my brakes and his mechanical know-how. I believed he wasn't capable of it because of the way he took care of Billie.

I steadied my voice and tried to loosen up enough to smile back at the son of a bitch. "OK, that's great news. I'll talk to you later."

Matt noted the suspicious lift in my tone. "Maggie, are you OK?" he demanded.

"Sure, I'll tell Mom you called. Dinner on Thursday," I said. " 'Bye, Coop."

"Maggie—" Matt's voice was cut off with a click as I dropped the receiver onto the cradle.

Clay gave me a subdued little half-smile. "Dinner on Thursday? Is it wrong to hope for a doggie bag? Because Mo can make a mean . . . well, pretty much anything."

I looked up at him. The relaxed expression on his face was what killed me. He'd been lying to us for months, and it didn't seem to bother him in the slightest. He'd lived with my aunt, in her house, living off the pack's goodwill, for months and seemed to have every intention of continuing. And he wasn't even nervous.

I sprang over the desk. Clay's eyes widened briefly before I gripped his collar and slammed him into the wall. But as I snapped and growled, he just looked amused.

"I knew we should have left when Billie died." He sighed, shoving back at me but not moving me. He didn't seem perturbed by this, as if I wasn't *this* close to ripping his throat out. "Alicia said it would look suspicious if we just ran off now. I think maybe she got too used to living in one place. And she liked the old lady. She wanted to stick around for the service. My sister's a sentimental girl, never could cure her of it."

"Who the hell are you?" I demanded.

"Oh, Maggie," Clay said, tilting his head and grinning nastily. "I know we're not dating anymore, but I hoped we could still be friends." I sneered at him and swiped my fingernails down his cheek. He didn't even register the welts of blood I left on his face. "No? Well, that's a shame."

He shoved me again, sending me flying over my desk this time, tumbling into the far wall. He'd phased and lunged for me. I shot up to my feet and ran at him again, phasing on the fly. Our wolfen bodies collided, and his teeth scraped my throat. I turned, yanking my exposed fur out of his mouth, and landed on two human feet. He phased to human again, and I head-butted him, the thickest part of my forehead cracking his nose. He grinned. And punched me right in the mouth.

"You know, I was sort of hoping we could avoid all this cloak-and-dagger shit. You're a pretty girl, and you can be downright tolerable sometimes. I thought maybe you and I could get married, you could make me the alpha male, and I could bring my family in, no questions asked. But you're just so damned stubborn, aren't you, Maggie? You have to do things the hard way."

Papers and books scattered around the room as we pounded on each other in wolf and human forms. But despite several opportunities, he didn't strike any serious blows. He just kept slapping me around and phasing, wolf to man and back again, and honor sort of dictated that I phase, too, to keep us on the same footing. The exhaustion of the constant shifting combined with being smacked around was draining and demoralizing.

"You still haven't figured it out, have you?" He sneered, standing over me. "Well, that's disappointing. You know, you're not a very smart girl."

I picked up my desk chair and threw it at him, catching his shoulders and knocking him to the ground. I lunged, kicking him in the ribs and knocking him onto his back. "Who are you?"

"I'm a little hurt that you didn't notice the resemblance," he spat, dribbling blood onto the tile floor of the office. "Everybody in my pack told me I looked just like my dad. Of course, you and your brother killed those people."

I stared down at him, analyzing the sandy hair, the light brown eyes. When I'd seen that mouth, it had been twisted into a feral snarl. The eyes had been sharp and too bright, burning with hate and desperation. I felt my arms drop to my sides, the shock leeching all of the energy out of my limbs.

I was a dumb-ass.

"You're Jonas's son?"

"His one and only heir," Clay said, pushing to his feet. "Your time here is over. I've seen enough to know that you're not strong enough to hold on to the valley. It's time for a new pack, a stronger pack, to take over. You have three days to clear your ragged excuse for a family out of *our* new home. Otherwise, people will start getting hurt."

"People are already getting hurt." I grunted.

He smiled, his teeth tinged an awful red. "No, this is minor damage. I mean, really, truly hurt.

Throats ripped out. Paws missing. How'd you like to walk out of your cozy little house to find your mother, your grandfather, one of those little brats, dead and cold on your doorstep?"

"Why are you trying to provoke me?" I demanded, shoving at his shoulders. "You are not this guy."

"You don't know what I am!" he shouted, shoving me back.

"Look, I can't change what happened—" When he looked vaguely bored, I slammed his head against the wall. He snarled, and I grabbed his chin, forcing him to look me in the eye. "Listen to me. I am sorry for what was done to your pack, but you will *not* threaten my fucking family and make it sound like a Sunday picnic, do you hear?"

He leered at me and threw one last upper cut to my chin. I stumbled over the wreckage of my office furniture and nearly landed on my ass. Fine, I landed on my ass, but after that whooping, I needed a rest.

"Three days, Maggie. And then I bring the rest of my pack home, whether you're here or not. It's Old Home Week, and we plan on throwing a hell of a party."

Clay disappeared, so quickly I didn't even have time to reply, and Samson came running. I assumed that Matt had managed to call him as soon as I hung up on him. It was nice to know Matt could operate his phone when he was in a jam . . . or that someone else had dialed for him.

"Where is he? What hurts?" Samson demanded. "Do we need Doc Moder?"

"Clay's gone." I sighed, sitting up slowly. "I don't want anyone chasing after him. Who knows how many he's got in his 'pack'?" My ears rang as Samson helped me into a sitting position. He kept checking me over for wounds until I had to slap his hands away. "I'm fine, I'm fine!" I moaned, clutching my head in my hands. "Though I wouldn't say no to a new skull. Look, I don't want to explain this more than once, so could you round everybody up and bring them to Mom's? I'll meet you there."

"Sure," he said, gently pulling me to my feet. "Are you sure you're OK to walk?"

I nodded, and he sprinted for the door. "Hey, Samson?" He stopped and poked his head back through the doorway. "You're an awesome second. I don't care what anybody says."

He winked at me. "Try not to get your ass kicked on the walk home."

He ducked out the door before he could see the rude gesture I was making.

15

Homecoming

I CHOSE TO LIMP HOME quietly, using buildings and vehicles as cover. Not to protect my dignity but to keep the pack from suffering another blow. OK, it was to protect my dignity.

How could this have happened? How could I have been so blind? They knew so much about Billie, about our pack. I kept calling Matt to check them out, but he never returned my calls, and after a certain amount of time, when Alicia and Clay hadn't killed us all in our sleep, I just sort of took for granted that they were legit. And sure, maybe I trusted them a little more because they had the boys with them, and I like to think that a mother to two toddlers couldn't be completely evil. I was new to being alpha. I was kind of overwhelmed. I appreciated all the help I could get.

Ugh, that was a bunch of rationalization crap.

I'd dropped my guard, and now I was paying for it.

Billie had tried to tell me that she didn't know them, that I'd let strangers into her house. But I'd chalked it up to her illness. Had she had moments of lucidity? Had she woken up in her own home, frightened, surrounded by strangers? I didn't think I'd ever forgive myself for that.

Mom found me lying on the couch in one of Nick's old *Star Wars* sweatshirts with a steak pressed to my face. She hadn't seen me this bloody for a couple of years, so it sent her into a bit of a panic. I closed my eyes for a couple of seconds, and the next thing I knew, Nick was there, looking stricken and pushing my hair away from my battered, healing face.

"Maggie, baby, you're scaring me. Please, wake up, talk to me," he begged. His shirt was smeared with my blood, as if he'd gathered me to his chest while I was out. "Just let me know you're OK."

I nodded, wincing when the action made my head spin. I closed my eyes again and awoke to more people, simultaneously trying to hug me and demand answers from me. Who hurt me? Where were they now? And on and on and on until—

"*Quiet!*" I bellowed, just so they would shut up enough to let me sit up and get a word in. My ears rang with the volume of my own voice, and I had to close my eyes to keep from throwing up. Nick pulled me up, gingerly pressing my back against his side. I winced, knowing that even with werewolf healing abilities, I was going to be bruised all to hell. Mo brought me a mug of Mom's special herbal tea, which I accepted with no intention of actually drinking it.

"Clay did this," I said, using the towel Mom handed me to dab at my healing lip. "He's long gone by now. And so, I would imagine, are Alicia and the boys."

"Why in the hell would Clay do this?" Cooper demanded.

"I'm still confused about that myself. I thought he was OK with you mating with Nick," Samson said, his lips pressed into a tight little grimace.

"I'd say my not dating him probably ranks lower on my list of offenses than, say, Cooper and I killing his whole damned family. Clay is Jonas's son, all grown up."

Cooper sat down heavily on the couch, looking stunned.

"Wait, so that means Alicia . . ." I heard Samson curse and throw a chair across the room, apparently just now realizing that the girl he considered a possible mate was also a possible homicidal maniac. I made a mental note to feel bad for him as soon as my brain unscrambled.

"All this time, I knew there was something familiar about him, something that made me uneasy," Cooper said, his face paper-white. "I just thought it was the typical big-brother reaction to your first boyfriend. I can't believe I let that psycho get so close and not even recognize him for what he was."

"Well, he's a well-informed psycho," I muttered. "I don't know how he got his background information on the pack, but he knew just enough about us to make his story plausible. I'm assuming that he's behind the truck brakes and my office and shooting Samson. Because when I think back on those days, I don't ever remember seeing Clay near the valley, which seems odd."

Cooper wondered, "If he was going to try to stage a coup, why would he wait such a long time? None of this makes any sense."

"Because all coups follow a rigid code of conduct." I snorted, groaning when that made my skin, lip, and nose burn. "I think at first, Clay just wanted to gather information on us. And then, after sticking around for a while, I don't know, maybe they started to like us. Alicia became fond of Billie, and Clay said he hoped that I'd choose him as a mate, and we could skip the whole dramatic-takeover thing. And when it became clear that I was becoming interested in Nick, I think Clay started playing all those tricks to make me think I needed someone like him around, someone like me. Instead, I just leaned on Nick. Now that they've been discovered, they have no choice but to go on the offensive." I pressed the compress to my face and moaned. "I should have seen this. I feel so stupid."

Cooper shrugged but didn't disagree.

Nick glared at him. "Like you handled your first attempted coup any better."

"I handled it OK," Cooper mumbled defensively. "It was the aftermath that sucked."

"Territorial disputes are not all that uncommon in the animal kingdom," Nick told me, in that "hot for teacher" tone I knew was supposed to make me feel better. "All life is basically a competition for re-sources. A cuckoo instinctually knows to lay eggs in other birds' nests, so their eggs can hatch faster than the host birds'. The cuckoo chick grows faster. In most cases, the chick evicts the eggs of the host spe-cies, and the baby cuckoos suck up all the food and nurturing. Cicada-killer wasps sting and paralyze in-sects twice their size and weight, drag them back to their dens, and lay their eggs in the cicadas' heads so the newborn wasps can eat them."

"So, this is Alicia and Clay's version of paralyz-ing me and laying eggs in my head?" I asked, dumb-founded. Nick rolled his eyes at me. "I'm not good with metaphors!"

"OK, let me get this straight," Mo said, holding up her hands. "Alicia and Clay are Jonas's kids." She continued, "Clay's the alpha of whatever half-grown pack was left behind when Cooper killed all of the adults. Sorry, babe, but it's the truth. And Alicia is his slightly-scary-in-a-quiet-way second in com-mand?" Mo shuddered. "It's like they're the bizarro version of Cooper and Maggie."

When we glared at her, she rolled her eyes and huffed. "I said 'bizarro.' It means the opposite. It's not an insult!"

"I got your back," Nick assured her, giving her the nerd fist-bump. Mo preened. Cooper and I shared a commiserating "we chose them, we did this to ourselves" look.

"So, they've been waiting all this time, for what, to do what their parents couldn't? To move into the valley, like it was some sort of Promised Land? Were they just gathering information this whole time?" Mo asked. "How could they do that? I mean, if they hated you that much, how could they live with you for almost a year? How could they stand it?"

"If you've got enough patience, enough will, you can stand just about anything," Mom suggested thoughtfully.

"Is it wrong that I feel a little sorry for them?" Mo asked, cringing. "I mean, yes, their tactics are obviously questionable, but to be fair—"

"We killed everyone they loved," I said, nodding. "Even if they started it, we finished it in a really bloody way. And I get it. If somebody killed members of my family, nothing would stop me from ripping them apart. I'm not going to say I feel sorry for them, given what they've done. But I get it."

"What now?" Samson asked.

"Clay said he's bringing his pack here in three days to 'evict' us. We either stand and fight, or everybody moves to Cousin Lee's packlands, which I really don't consider an option."

"I vote 'stand and fight,'" Samson declared.

"There's a shocker," Mo muttered.

"This isn't a democracy, Samson," I reminded him. "But you're right. It's the only way."

"No, Maggie, you can stop this," Nick told me. "Break the cycle. Try to talk to them, figure out a peaceable solution. Otherwise, in ten years, Paul and Ronnie are going to come looking for Eva and our kids."

"So, I'm supposed to what? Go to a mediator?

Family therapy? Wolves don't do that. We don't talk things through. We don't share our feelings."

"Look, you don't think I understand the kind of pressure you're under," Nick told me. "And you're right, I'll never understand what it's like to have a whole extended family depending on me, to be responsible for all those people. But I do know what it's like to have a family that either can't take care of you or doesn't care to. I know what it's like to have a family that's more interested in taking from you. Your pack, they're good people. They didn't know who I was and, after a few rough patches, took me in. Stop underestimating their capacity for kindness."

"Our capacity for kindness is what got us into this," I shot back, regretting again the ease with which Clay and Alicia had been accepted.

"You think we should let them move in?" Cooper said incredulously. "Tell me, Doc, in all your years of studying animals, have you ever seen two herds or whatever able to merge and share living space peaceably?"

"Well, I guess you're going to have to appeal to their more human sides," Nick retorted.

"Open our hearts and our homes to the children of a bunch of psychos who tried to murder us?" Cooper scoffed. "This is the dumbest idea I've ever heard."

"Do you think maybe Alicia would still want to date me?" Samson wondered.

Cooper pointed a finger at Samson. "I stand corrected."

"Never underestimate the excitement of sex with the crazy," Samson said, wincing when Mo smacked the back of his head. "It's like a Tilt-A-Whirl and a scary movie all in one."

Mom covered her face with her hands and sighed. "It's like I'm not even in the room."

"OK, everyone stop picturing Samson's upsetting sex life," I told them. "I need some time to think. Samson, I would really appreciate it if you stepped up patrols, starting now. Keep it quiet; just gradually increase the number of runners and the frequency. Nobody goes out without at least two partners."

Samson phased on his way out the door and set up a summoning howl.

"I could swear I asked him to keep it quiet," I grumbled, leaning back against Nick.

"Samson was never one for subtlety," Mo said, bringing me a bowl of my mom's chicken noodle soup. "How can I help?"

"The soup's a good start," I told her.

Mo leveled that bizarrely calm gaze at me. "You know what I mean."

As Cooper warned her that any violent acts on her part would be over his cold, dead body, I wondered whether Mo had always been so cool under pressure or if living through so much of our pack drama had given her such strong nerves. Still, I told her, "This isn't your fight."

She huffed, "Oh, right, Cooper and I will just trot on home and let you handle this. Because if Clay's pack runs you off, they'll just stop at the valley, right? They won't come after me or my family because we're connected to you. They won't be threatened by the presence of a strong male wolf in their territory. The same wolf who, you know, killed their *dad*. They'll just ignore my family, my baby, except for the obligatory 'new neighbor' Bundt cake they'll be bringing over."

"Damn it, Mo, stop making sense." I muttered around a mouthful of soup. "No, no, I can't let you get involved. The best thing for you to do would be to take the baby to Grundy and stay there until the coast is clear. Or better yet, go to Washington. Go visit your parents."

Cooper snorted.

Mo was aghast. "First of all, Samson's wanting to date Alicia makes more sense than me going to visit my parents. Second, this is it for you, Mags. This is the defining moment in your leadership of the pack. And it's your chance to change things. You can't keep the dead-liners out of pack business anymore. Or us humans, for that matter. You're our family. This is our home, too. What are we supposed to do? Send you off into a fight with this bunch of wackos, sit on our hands, and wonder whether you're coming home or not? It's not fair, Maggie. I can help. Nick can, too. You can't exclude us anymore."

"So, what, you're going to stand on the battlefield with a fire extinguisher?"

"Helped me kick your ass," she retorted.

"You didn't kick my ass, you just bruised it a little."

Mo smirked, winked at Nick, and dragged Cooper into the kitchen with Mom. I leaned my aching temple against Nick's shoulder and rolled my options over in my head. I'd charged into fights before, but I'd never led. And I'd never been so frightened—but not for myself. Every face in the pack hovered at the edge of my brain, the feeling of responsibility, of obligation, dragging me under rushing black water. I would never be strong enough. I would never be fast enough to protect all of them. Some of us probably wouldn't survive this, and knowing that made me want to throw up.

Sometimes being a leader really sucked.

16

Leave the Gun, Take the Cannoli

ONCE MY FACE HEALED up to something that didn't resemble a recalled eggplant, I called a pack meeting and instructed members to bring all of their family members—even the dead-liners. After I convinced them that I was not kidding and they went back home to retrieve said dead-liners, I laid everything on the line for those who hadn't been invited to pack meetings until now, every weird coincidence and hinky feeling I'd had since Clay had moved into the valley. And when I dropped the bomb about Clay and Alicia's dubious family connections, two of my uncles literally wolfed out and chose to destroy a couch to express their anger.

The reaction was a sort of venting by proxy for the other pack members, and by the time Uncle Jay and Uncle Rob were trying to digest spring coils, my relatives looked a little bored.

"Does this happen at every pack meeting?" Mo asked Evie. Having never attended a pack meeting before, Evie shrugged.

Nick was grinning like an idiot. "This is the coolest thing I have ever seen!"

I buried my face in my hands for a second and contemplated chlorinating my gene pool before wedging myself between the furry idiots and shaking them by the napes of their necks until they phased back to human.

"Sit," I told them both as they shuffled back to their seats and looked as sheepish as two wolves could. "So, do we have that out of our systems?"

Rob and Jay refused to meet my gaze. I outlined what I considered to be a pretty damn reasonable plan. Able-bodied adults, wolf and dead-liner alike, would stay in the valley. My mom and the older aunties would take the kids, even self-proclaimed bad-ass teenagers, and split them between Cooper's and Nick's places for the next few days.

"And then we go to the mattresses, right?" Jay said, his white teeth gleaming. Evie rolled her eyes. For Jay, all situations related somehow to *The Godfather*.

"And then we try to talk to them," I countered.

Jay's face fell into a contemplative frown. "I did not expect that."

"But they killed Billie!" Uncle Rob protested.

"We don't know that," I snapped. "It's a possibility. But from what Dr. Moder said, Billie could have tripped and hit her head. Which is sort of my point. If we rush into this, rush into judgment, rush into action, we're going to find ourselves even more vulnerable and screwed up than we were after Cooper left, and we all know how that turned out. Sorry, Cooper."

Cooper shrugged.

I added, "What if we say, 'Fuck it, we're going to kill them all'? Say we chase them down, and we find that their pack is twice the size of ours. Or that they've set some trap that we've walked right into? What happens then? We're dead."

"Never took you for a coward, Maggie." Jay snorted and then turned white after the look I gave him.

"OK, fine, we go after them with both barrels. We'll lose a couple of our pack and take down a few of theirs. And in a few years, their kids are going to show up and what? Fight our kids for what we did? We're going to leave our kids to make this same choice? What would you want them to do?"

Rob, whose little girl was two and as wolfen as kids could be at that age, shrank down in his seat at the thought.

"I'm not saying we won't end up fighting them anyway, but we at least have to try to figure out what's going on in their heads."

"So, we talk to them?" Rob said, as if it was the first time he was hearing the concept.

"Yes."

"And if that doesn't work?" Jay prompted.

"Then we go to the mattresses." I sighed.

ONE OF THE uncles must have tipped Uncle Frank off about the coming "invasion." Lee called to volunteer his packmates, but I told him to stay home and keep safe. Sure, the extra bodies would have been handy, but we were less likely to get Clay's pack's respect if we ran tattling to another pack for backup. Plus, the situation was likely to escalate too quickly if Lee was around, posturing and growling.

Lee was pretty smug about the whole "Clay's a traitor" thing. He went on and on about how you "just didn't know who you could trust these days" and how Uncle Frank had never liked Clay anyway.

But we actually had a conversation that didn't end in my threatening him, which I took as progress. Until a few seconds later, when he started making noises about taking me out for a movie as soon as the snow cleared, you know, if we survived the inter-pack war thing. And then he followed that charming invitation up with "Who knows what could happen when you and I are in a dark room?" And I threw up in my mouth a little bit.

"Lee, I'm mated now," I said in a clipped, busi-nesslike tone, remembering that Uncle Frank hadn't been around for the "big announcement" about Nick. And I doubted that any of my packmates wanted to call Uncle Frank and listen to the bitch-storm that would follow if they told him about my formal mating to a human. "I would appreciate it if you didn't make comments like that. And by ap-preciate, I mean I will restrain myself from shoving your head up your own ass."

"What do you mean, mated?" Lee shouted. "But Clay—why wasn't I told?"

"You weren't told because it was none of your business."

"But if it's not Clay, who is it?" he demanded. "It's not that human, is it?"

"I'm hanging up now, Lee."

"With the human!" Lee shrieked petulantly as I set the phone down on the cradle.

"And this is why I haven't let Mom send out the wedding invitations yet," I grumbled.

THE NIGHT BEFORE Clay's "deadline" was hectic. I'd underestimated the amount of persuasion, strong-arming, and, finally, begging it would take to get the aunties out of the valley. None of them wanted to miss the fight. None of them wanted to be left, as Mo said, sitting on her hands, wondering if we would come home. And my mom was the ringleader of the rebellion.

"I don't understand why you're asking this of me," Mom growled as I shoved her inside Mo's truck, where Eva was blowing bubbles in her own spit.

"Mom, look at Mo." I nodded. "You think it's easy for her to pack her daughter into her car seat and watch Eva blow bye-bye bubbles, not knowing how this is all going to turn out? But at least she's handling it with some dignity."

"That's because you didn't hear the argument she and Cooper had earlier. I've never heard Mo cuss that way before. I thought she'd blister paint. I think you're a bad influence on her."

I was really sorry I'd missed that. Cooper and Mo

had several blow-ups over Mo's decision to stay at his side. Cooper tried to appeal to her motherly instinct and the possibility that Eva could be left without either parent. Mo countered that that was far less likely to happen if she was covering Cooper's back. And around and around they went, until Cooper was blue in the face and Mo was threatening him with a large frying pan if he tried to force her into the truck. It didn't stop him from trying. And now he had a pan-shaped bruise on his back. We considered it a draw.

I sighed. "Mom, if you get into the truck right now and we all survive this thing, I will let you plan the wedding, from bottom to top, without any arguments."

"That's not funny."

"I'll even let you do that stupid white-dove-release thing."

Her eyes narrowed at me. "Well played, Margaret."

After a little more prodding, Mom finally got into the truck and led the caravan of kids and aunts out of the valley. I looked around at the clenched, determined expressions on the parents' faces as they waved good-bye to their departing children. And I felt a little twinge of emptiness.

Mo snickered and slipped her arm around my shoulders. "You know, for the alpha—"

"Don't say it," I warned her.

"Not that many people listen to you."

"You can be such a bitch sometimes," I told her.

She smiled sweetly at me. "I'm becoming more and more like you every day."

Behind her, Cooper shuddered.

*   *   *

I MANAGED TO talk everyone into a sundown curfew. The larger, younger of us were running alternating patrols along the border to watch for an early ambush. I did a door-to-door check to make sure everyone was tucked away safely for now. As I slumped toward Mom's house, exhausted to my bones, Rob and Jay kept yelling lines from *300* at my back, which made me think they weren't taking the whole Gandhi approach very seriously. It felt like lights-out at a particularly violent summer camp.

Mo and Cooper had agreed to stay at Samson's for the night. It struck me as sort of crappily ironic that our first night alone in the valley was so dark.

Nick had cooked, or at least warmed up something Mom left behind. Without speaking, we settled on the couch. I took his face between my palms and kissed him.

"Is this the part where you tell me it's my duty to sleep with you because you're going off to war and you could be killed?" Nick asked.

"That is so wrong," I told him. "But yes, it would be a nice gesture."

He pulled me into his lap, sliding his hands along my ribs

"Are you scared?" he asked. "About tomorrow?"

"I'd be stupid not to be," I said. "I'm not thrilled that you're going to be there, but given the *Lassie* conversation and Mo's cast-iron-pan antics, I know it's a waste of breath to try to push you out of harm's way."

"Damn straight."

"I love you. I'm not trying to make this some dramatic good-bye moment. I just want to tell you now, while it's quiet and we're not facing certain ass-whooping, that I love you. I've never loved anyone the way I love you. I'm going to love you until the day I die."

He pursed his lips. "Wow, you will do anything to get laid, won't you?"

I laughed. "Thanks, I needed that."

"I love you, too," he told me, kissing me.

He pushed my shirt over my head, pulling my hair from its ponytail and letting it fall around us in a dark, shiny curtain. He took his time, touching me with an aching slowness that built a searing heat in my belly. His kisses consumed my breath, my fear, my worry. I eased his zipper down, and he moaned as my hand slipped around him. He pushed up from the couch, with my legs still wrapped around his waist, and carried me down the hall.

We'd never managed to make it to my room, in a bed, with the lights off before. It was sort of decadent and naughty, getting naked in the room where I used to have Smurf curtains. He trailed kisses from my neck to my belly button, taking the time to nip lightly here and there, leaving little marks behind. I tugged at his shoulders, bringing him back to eye level, so I could thread my fingers through his hair while he settled between my thighs.

When he reached for the condoms in my nightstand, I stopped his hand. His eyebrows arched. I'd told myself that I would know when I was ready, and I did. I wanted a baby with Nick. There were things in life I still wanted to do—school, travel, leading my pack. But I didn't think Nick would let me get out of doing them. In fact, he'd probably drag me to whatever pipe dream I was shying away from if he spotted any backtracking on my part.

"I consider it a hopeful gesture," I told him. "We might get pregnant, we might not. We might get through tomorrow only to get smooshed by a semi next Tuesday."

"This is the worst declaration of hope ever," he told me. "What's next, detailed forecasts of my possible male-pattern baldness?"

I snickered. "The point is, I love you, and I don't want to put any more restrictions on however much time we have left together, whether it's hours or decades. I don't care what tomorrow brings, as long as I have you."

He smiled and kissed me, then slipped inside me without a barrier between us, skin on skin. I sighed at the warm intrusion as his fingertips traced the lines of my face. He rocked into me, and we settled into a soothing, gentle rhythm. This was different, quiet, better. And when we both were sated, he pulled my back against his chest and held me without speaking. And somehow I managed to fall asleep.

THE MORNING ROLLED in quietly, leaving us restless and edgy. I didn't know what I expected—Clay and Alicia leading a parade of tanks down Main Street, maybe. And when the strange pack seemed to coil out of the trees like mist, I thought I was seeing things.

There were thirty or so of them, fewer than half of what we had gathered against them. They were so young, a handful of them as old as me, with the rest in their late teens. They all had that lean, ragged, wary look of someone who's had to survive. I wondered where they'd been while Clay and Alicia spied on us. How close had they been all this time?

The kids were trailing behind, holding on to the hands of a few older ladies, including Ronnie and Paul, who were waving at us. I realized then that Jonas had probably done the exact thing we'd done, all those years ago. He'd left the kids with the older women, while he marched off to conquer their "new home." And he'd never come back. I thought of my mom, taking care of dozens of kids, waiting for news. And my throat grew a little tight.

I felt the pack align behind me, watched as my packmates guarding the borders paced them on four paws as they entered our territory. A chorus of growls sounded behind me, and I felt several of my packmates phase as Clay sauntered toward me. I held up my hand, and the sounds faded to a dull, constant grumble. The light glinted off his light brown hair, and he grinned that same crooked smile at me, but it was hollow, a stupid boy's ploy to try to cover the fact that he was scared shitless.

When Jay and Ron, who were part of the escort, sniffed a little too close, I made a little warning growl, and they backed off immediately. Yes, they were excited and twitching for a fight, but these were the situations where you had to listen to your alpha if you wanted to get out unscathed. I felt my fear and my anger subside a little. This wasn't the snarling, hate-filled foe I was expecting. They were a bunch of scared kids.

Clay stopped just a few feet in front of me, and I was struck by a sense of déjà vu. He looked so much like his father now, minus the crazy eyes. Clay gave me a hard stare, and I returned it.

"What now?" I asked him, my head tilting.

Clay looked a little startled at my light and conversational tone. Not at all like my more recent threats to "end him." "You know why we're here, I just can't believe you were dumb enough to stick around."

My voice so low only he could hear me, I said, "Clay, I think we both know what's going to happen if I give an order for my pack to take yours. Please don't make me do it."

"You're not giving me a choice," he whispered, glancing over his shoulder. His jaw was so tense I could hear his teeth grinding.

"Do you want to talk privately?" I asked.

"What, so you can drag me off to the woods and let one of your uncles rip my throat out?" he said loudly enough so the rest of his pack could hear.

I growled. "Clay, stop being a jackass," I snarled. "You bring your second, I'll bring mine." Samson stepped forward and gazed longingly at Alicia, which was not appreciated by one of the younger males in Clay's pack. I added loudly, "And everyone here will behave themselves like good boys and girls!"

Uncle Jay, wolfed out and ready to go, huffed and rolled his canine eyes.

I led Clay to a little clearing behind the clinic, with Samson and Alicia trailing on our heels. The farther we got away from Main Street, the more Clay's shoulders seemed to sag. By the time we reached our destination, he looked liked a haggard old man.

"OK, this is just us here, and when we leave, no one's going to know what was said, right Samson?" Samson was busy giving Alicia moon eyes. "Samson?"

"Huh?"

I looked across the clearing to see Alicia giving him the same stupid look. I rolled my eyes. "Never mind."

"Before we go any further, I have to ask, did you hurt Billie?" I asked. "And I'm not just talking about at the end. Did you ever lay a hand on my aunt?"

"We wouldn't have hurt Billie," Alicia insisted, her eyes welling up with unexpected tears. "We actually liked the old lady, no matter how many butter knives she threw at me. She reminded us of our own aunties. And she had these moments, I think, when she knew we weren't who we said we were, but she knew that we were taking care of her. I always thought of those as her good days."

Clay shook his head. "I'm a lot of things, but I wouldn't hurt a defenseless old woman."

"What happened the day she died?" I asked.

Alicia wrung her hands a little bit, looking more at Samson than at me. "When I left, she was napping, I just wanted to take the kids out for a breath of fresh air. I just wanted to get out of the house for a few minutes. I wasn't even gone that long, just long enough for Paul to need a fresh pull-up. I came back, and you were there, and she was dead."

I looked to Samson, who seemed relieved. And although I didn't quite trust his skewed judgment on the subject, I found I believed her. Why would they lie at this point? They didn't have much to lose. If anything, Clay would have used killing Billie to provoke me into a fight when he was outed.

"OK, and I want honesty here, what about the brakes on my truck? Or the break-in at my office? Or me getting my head bagged that day we went for a run together? Or Samson getting shot?"

Alicia shook her head. "Honestly, no. We were just as surprised by all that as you were. The sneakiest thing we did was tell our packmates where the video cameras were planted, so they could sniff around without being seen."

"We came here to watch you, to try to find a way in," Clay said. "That was all."

"Considering your dad tried to kill my whole family, I have a hard time believing that."

He shot back, "Well, your brother did kill my entire family."

"He was provoked!" I yelled.

"Don't you think I've considered that?" Clay yelled back. He took a steadying breath. Several inquiring howls drifted up from the valley. "Look, I see my Dad's mistakes. What he did was wrong. But he was still my dad. Do you know what happened after your precious brother killed my father? We'd been drifting around for months, nomads, before

Dad finally decided to make a move on your valley.
There were only three old women left to take care
of us. Our parents were supposed to come back, take
us to our new home. We went to bed, feeling like
it was Christmas Eve. When we woke up, everything was going to be different. No more sleeping
in the woods. No more bathing at campgrounds,
when we were lucky. No more shifting around without a home. And it was different, all right. We woke
up, and my aunt Sarah was crying. She didn't know
what had happened. She and Aunt Linda waited and
waited for my parents, for the other adults to come
back. But they never did. I was too young to join
the fight but old enough to know that we'd been
screwed out of what was ours. That my mom and
dad were dead, and I couldn't let that go unpun-
ished. Aunt Linda tried to convince me that it was
time to forget, to move on. When she died, I found
letters from my dad to Eli, plans for the new pack
they were setting up.

"So I contacted our good friend Eli. I told him
I was going to blow his whole 'man of the people'
thing wide open. I wanted to meet him, but he kept
putting me off, said he had an ailing mother to
care for. It made it hard for him to find time. Your
brother killed him off before we could meet up, so
he wasn't of much use. But thanks to his letters, it
was easy to tell you some nice story about being Billie's long-lost relatives. You were so willing to let
us step in, to let us take care of Billie. It was disappointing, really. I thought you'd put up more of a
fight. I thought you'd be less trusting. But we moved

right in. Hell, you practically rolled out a red carpet. And we stayed, and we stayed, and hell, I even started to like it here a little bit. And the whole time, I kept going back to my pack and telling them to be patient; just a little longer, and we'll have the home we always deserved. And then Billie died, and it all went to hell."

"But why did you come back now?" I asked him, scanning his pack. "You knew how many of us would be here. Why would you come back, knowing that we could destroy you?"

Clay threaded a handed through his hair, leaving it disheveled. He looked tired and scared and much younger than he was. "I'd spent so much time talking it up, I couldn't *not* bring them here. I already have a couple of cousins who think that I shouldn't be alpha, considering the fuck-up my Dad made of the position. If I backed out, I would lose any authority I had. There was no way out of it. And now I don't know what to do. I can't go back to them now and tell them that the story we've been surviving on for years was a load of crap. That we're not even going to try to fight for this place."

"But you don't have to fight. You could have a home here."

Clay stared at me as if I'd grown a second head. He scoffed. "What, you're just going to let us waltz in and join you? Sure."

"We would. Don't make the same mistake Jonas made, Clay. Take the offer," Samson said, his gaze never leaving Alicia.

Clay's brow furrowed. "What do you mean?"

"Cooper offered Jonas a place in the valley. He offered your pack a home, and Jonas refused," I said.

"That's a lie."

"It's not," Samson insisted. "And you can ask any member of the pack who was there. Cooper only acted when Jonas threatened to kill Maggie right in front of him."

"He threatened to kill you as leverage?" Clay's face paled. "But you were just a kid, just a few years older than me."

"He must have been desperate, to do something like that," Alicia said, her lip trembling. "He wouldn't have accepted an offer to share, Clay. You know that. He was a proud man, too proud. He wouldn't have accepted help. He wouldn't have accepted letting his packmates see him as weak."

"And I'm supposed to let my packmates see me as weak?" he demanded.

"I'm just saying maybe we should think about it," she said.

"There's a way out of this, Clay," I said. "We can avoid another bloody scene if you would just—"

"Like you would trust me enough to let us live here," he spat. "You'd watch me like a hawk every minute. No pack can work with two alphas."

"Well, I'd kick your ass at the first sign of you trying to take over, true. But who says it couldn't work? Most packs have an alpha couple. We'll still have an alpha male and an alpha female. We just won't be, you know, together."

"But—"

"Stop giving me reasons why this wouldn't work!"

I cried. "The way we live is changing; we have to change with it. I'm not saying it's the ideal situation or that there's not going to be a lot of resentment and hurt feelings we're going to have to get over, but what other choice do you have? Both packs need fresh genes. You need a place to call home. We can make it work."

"How are we going to explain this to them?" Clay said, nodding toward the packs.

"It will be our first official joint alpha duty," I told him.

Clay gnawed on his lip and looked at my out-stretched hand as if it was a coiled snake.

"Clay, stop being an ass and say yes, already," Alicia said, giving Samson a long, meaningful look.

"Please, make the better choice," I said. "Be a better leader, a better man, than our predecessors."

Clay huffed a breath and put his hand in mine. "On a trial basis. That's all I'm willing to promise."

All of the tension drained from my body as if a plug had been pulled. I smiled. "That's all I ask. It's going to take some work, but we can do this, Clay."

"Can we at least tell my pack that I beat you bloody and then we arrived at a compromise?" he grumbled.

"No."

17

The Monkey Man Swingeth

I WALKED INTO NICK'S KITCHEN, exhausted and drained by yet another conversation with Clay about how we could merge the two packs. I closed my eyes and took a moment to appreciate the blessed silence of the house.

It took a while to sort out the whole "sorry my brother killed your dad" mess, but I felt I could trust Clay. He wasn't a terribly aggressive guy. He didn't want attention or recognition. He just wanted what was best for everybody in his family, which I considered the mark of a good leader. Being able to respect him made working with him a lot easier.

It might have been more awkward if Cooper was still living in the valley. Cooper and Clay were cutting each other a pretty wide berth. As open-minded as Clay seemed, I doubted that patricide was a basis for the two of them to be BFFs. We were fortunate that so little time had passed. Blood feuds could take generations to take root in a pack. With so few of our kind remaining, we couldn't afford that sort of pride and vengeance. Clay understood that, where Jonas had not.

As happy as I was that we were working toward tentative peace, I still had a pit of nagging worry that would surface when I least expected it. Something felt unsettled. To help build the trust between us, Clay had accounted for every member of his pack and their whereabouts surrounding the dates when my truck crashed, my office was trashed, Samson was shot, and Billie died. Dr. Moder had ruled the death accidental on Billie's death certificate, but she couldn't make a determination one way or the other. It's not as if we could send the remains to a medical examiner.

The loose threads were still worrying me. I was missing something, and I hated that. But between the chaos of discovering who Clay and Alicia were and trying to keep our two packs from brawling, I was too exhausted to try to figure it out. I needed quiet. And a house that sheltered fewer than a dozen people. Samson had agreed to keep an eye on things for me long enough for a surprise visit to Nick's place.

Nick was in the final phases of packing up to make room for the next renter. There were boxes strewn all over the living room. The wires for Nick's DVD player were hanging forlornly from the entertainment center. Several taped cartons near the door were marked "Books that should not be thrown away upon penalty of junk-punching."

I sincerely hoped Samson was the one who wrote that.

I shut the door, closed my eyes, and reveled in being able to hear myself think.

"Hey!" I called when I was centered, stripping out of my jacket. "You would not believe my day. I was actually glad to get away from the valley for a while."

I kicked off my boots, which were caked with mud from the recent thaw. "Mo would probably say that's a sign of personal growth or some shit. But I think it just proves how sexy you are—"

The silence of the house hit me full-force. The rooms were empty. It wasn't just that Nick wasn't responding. He wasn't there. I couldn't hear him breathing. I smelled blood, just the faintest trace of it. It was Billie all over again.

I looked back at the kitchen door, which had been unlocked. The front door was unlocked, too. There were no signs of a struggle, no forks and knives thrown on the floor, no torn pillows. I stumbled into the living room, the bedroom, terrified of what I might find. "Nick!" I yelled.

I forced myself to still, to focus on deep breaths, to pull the scents around me into my head and process. Some instinct was pulling me outside, toward the mountains behind the house. I ran out, following the faint scent of blood, trying to gauge how fresh it was, how much there was.

When the trail disappeared into the woods, I phased without bothering with my clothes, leaving a cloud of scraps in my wake. He'd been dragged. I could see the gouges his feet had made in the softening dirt. But who was doing the dragging? There was no other scent, just . . . dryer sheets.

For years to come, the smell of April Fresh was going to make me gag.

I followed the trail up the north face of the ridge, toward the outcropping of rocks that overlooked the town. Nick had talked about rappelling there a few times but had never made the trip.

Please, please, please, I begged. *I can't lose him now. Not now. Please.*

The scent was getting stronger, the higher I climbed the trail. And the trees were getting thinner, meaning that I was getting closer and closer to the rock face. I could hear Nick's heartbeat, strong and steady, through the trees.

He wasn't scared. This was a good thing. Nick was calm. And if he was calm, the situation might not be as bad as I thought.

I burst through the tree line to see Nick lying on the muddy ground. He wasn't calm; he was unconscious.

"Stop!" I yelled as I phased to my feet. "Lee, what are you doing?"

Lee had dropped Nick's limp body dangerously close to the edge of the cliff. He had a rappelling harness strapped on Nick's body. The harness was tethered to a tree a few feet away. Lee was rubbing the belay rope back and forth over a sharp rock, fraying it, so that when he tossed Nick over the side, the stress on the damaged fiber would snap.

"It has to look like a climbing accident," Lee told

me, his tone like that of someone explaining how to tie a fishing lure. "We don't want anybody connecting his death with you."

"Lee, just step away from Nick," I said, trying to keep my voice calm. Cautiously, I stepped toward Nick, but Lee's head snapped up. I froze.

Even in my gut-churning panic over Nick's proximity to the cliff, I couldn't process what Lee was doing. Why? He'd always seemed so puffed up and harmless. I hadn't seen. I didn't want to see. How could someone betray me like this again? It almost hurt worse than Eli's betrayal, because it was so random and needless.

Lee looked up at me, confused, and frowned. "This has to stop, Maggie. I'm going to help you tidy this one last mess up, but then I expect you to clean up your act."

"What are you talking about, Lee?" I tried stepping closer, my palms upraised in a submissive gesture, but he stepped in front of Nick, cutting me off. He was so close to the edge. All it would take was the slightest push or movement, and he'd plummet off the rocks. I whimpered a little, shaking away the image of Nick's body broken on the ground. I had to focus on Lee, make him move away, use some sign of dominance to remind him who the fuck he was dealing with.

But at the moment, my hands were shaking so badly I didn't feel like Maggie Fucking Graham. I felt like throwing up.

"Overall, I think I've been pretty understanding about your little quirks," Lee said, snapping me back to reality. "But really, a human?" His face flushed, darkened; his eyes narrowed. "Did you think I was going to sit by and let you humiliate me like that? Do you know what it was like for me, when members started whispering and snickering about my girl—*my future mate*—carrying on with a human?"

"Lee—"

"Stop saying my name like that!" Lee hissed. "Like I'm crazy! Like you're trying to talk me down from a ledge. You don't even know what I've done for you. You never appreciate how hard I've tried. You never see me. It's always about you."

"Just explain it to me," I said. "Baby, please, I'm sorry. Just explain what I did, and I'll apologize." My voice shook as I called him "baby," probably because it made me gag. But it seemed to calm him, to make him a preen a little, as if this was how he wanted the conversation to go. "What did I do wrong?"

"You never turned to me," Lee said, exasperated.

"What do you mean?" I asked, stepping back, leading him away from the cliff.

"I wanted you to turn to me!" Lee yelled, pounding his chest with his fist. "I thought that if you could get off your damn high horse long enough to ask me for help, we might finally connect. But you always ran to Cooper or Samson. You never had time for me. And I thought maybe if Samson wasn't there, in the way . . ."

"Did you take a shot at Samson?" I asked. He nodded. I groaned. "And the brakes on my truck?"

"I thought if I came along and helped you, it would be a good ice breaker. But the lines failed before I expected them to. I was waiting at the halfway point, waiting for you to pass by so I could follow. But you never showed. I doubled back, and I found your truck. I found you with him—"

He turned on Nick. "What else?" I barked, demanding his attention. His head swung toward me, his eyes sharp and indignant. I softened my voice. "What else don't I know about? I just—I need to know what I owe you, Lee. Please. I just want to make it up to you. Every single thing you did. I owe you. Did you set fire to my office?"

He sneered, nudging Nick hard with his foot. "Yeah, I thought it would be a good chance for us to spend time together. I called you up, offered my pack as backup for patrols. I wanted to show you how helpful I could be, how considerate. I made sure I was partnered up with you. But no, you took off, the first chance you got. You ran to him! I followed your scent to his house. I saw the two of you on his couch—"

I stepped closer, and Lee tensed. I moved sideways, drawing Lee a step away from Nick. I forced the corners of my mouth up. "What about the cliff? Please explain to me what you were trying to do."

"I wanted to show you how much you needed me. I figured I'd scare you, show you how easily you could get hurt. I'd rough you up a little and pretend to chase off the guy who was hurting you. That's why I put the bag over your head. To keep you from seeing me. And then *he* came running after you and ruined everything *again*."

"You rubbed yourself with dryer sheets to try

to cover up your scent, right?" I interjected as he turned his gaze on Nick. "So I wouldn't recognize it? That was pretty smart. Tell me how you came up with that idea."

Lee must have picked up on the undercurrent of tension in my voice, because he shook his head and returned his attention to the rope. "No. You're just trying to find something wrong with me. Like you always do, you're trying to find some reason not to be with me. You drive me crazy, don't you see that? If you'd just settled down with me, I wouldn't have done all these crazy things. I never would hurt Samson or you or Billie—" He bit down on the last word, as if he could keep it from escaping.

My mouth wouldn't seem to work right. "Billie?" tumbled from my lips in a mangled gasp.

"It was an accident!" Lee cried. "I didn't mean to hurt her. Uncle Frank told me how you thought so much of Clay, like you were ready to make him your second. I went into the house to try to get some dirt on him, something to get you to stay away from him. Billie came downstairs and freaked out. She said I didn't belong in her house, and she came after me with a kitchen knife! The crazy old bat almost nicked me. I pushed her back, and she fell and hit her head on the counter. It was an accident."

"She was a sick old woman."

"It wasn't my fault!" Lee yelled. He glared at Nick. "None of this would have happened if he'd just stayed away!"

"No!" I cried, putting myself between them. Lee

grabbed at my arms, shaking me. "This is my fault, not Nick's. Don't punish him for something I did."

"This *is* your fault. You messed everything up," he told me. "You're my mate, mine! I'm supposed to be the one who helps you lead. I'm supposed to be the one you have babies with. This is all your fault!"

I shoved Lee away, putting some ground between him and Nick. "According to who? When have I ever even implied I feel anything for you?"

The sudden change in attitude seemed to shock him. He sneered. "You think you're too good for me? You let *him* touch you. You'd be lucky to have me."

"I didn't just let him touch me," I said, licking my lips. "He had every little piece of me. I chose him. I mated with him. I could be carrying his pup for all you know."

"No!" he screamed. "You selfish whore!"

He phased on the fly and leaped at me. I jumped, blocking his body from colliding with Nick.

I thought of all the times I let my own fears, my stupid insecurities, my dumb-ass pride push me away from the only person I'd truly loved. And I pushed back. I pushed and I shoved, digging my paws into the dirt, scrambling for purchase.

Lee huffed, battering his head against my flank, trying to throw me off balance. He seemed to give up, turning on his heel and cowering away into the trees. I didn't drop my guard. I'd seen Lee do this any number of times when he was roughhousing with my brothers. He'd act hurt or submissive and pretend to slink away, only to turn and suckerpunch his opponent. I braced myself for his coming strike.

He didn't disappoint, turning suddenly and lunging, springing at me full-force. I pushed up, phasing to my feet and shoving my hands against Lee's belly. I pivoted, throwing his weight over my shoulder. He yelped as his rear paws slid over the edge of the cliff, his front paws scrabbling over the dirt, catching Nick's legs. He dug, trying to pull himself up, but all he was doing was dragging Nick over with him. I grabbed Nick's arms, digging my heels into the ground. Between Lee's weight and Nick's, I could hardly hold them. Seeing that I held on to Nick, Lee bit down on the leg of Nick's jeans. His eyes were defiant, daring me to let him die, knowing that it would mean losing Nick, too.

I snarled at him, grunting as I threaded my arms under Nick's and yanked with all my strength. I'd managed to pull Nick's knees up onto solid ground when I heard the sound of fabric tearing. Lee's wolfen eyes widened as the waistband separated from the pockets of Nick's jeans, and the denim lifeline he was counting on started sliding down Nick's leg. Lee scratched and scrambled, but he was fighting a losing battle with gravity. His paws were still frantically clawing for a grip as he slipped over the rock face. He howled as his body hurtled toward the ground. I shuddered when the howl abruptly ended.

I gave in to the need to relax my arms for just a second, to ease the screaming muscles. It took that brief instant to realize what a huge mistake it was, as Nick's weight shifted, and his legs slipped over the

edge. "No, no, no!" I grunted, desperately scrabbling my left hand over the dirt to grip the end of
the fraying climbing rope. As the dead weight of
Nick's torso pulled him away from me, I wound the
rope around his wrist.

The rope slipped through my hand, burning and
biting into the flesh of my palms as Nick free-fell.
The elastic rope stretched under Nick's weight as he
dropped. The loop closed around Nick's wrist and
held him suspended as he flopped against the rock
face. "Ow!" I heard him yelp. "What the hell?"

"Nick!" I yelled, leaning over the edge. The loose
knot Lee had tied around the tree slipped open and
let Nick drop again. He was now a good fifteen feet
below me, hanging over the open maw of the mountain.

"Oh, come on!" I shrieked as the looped cord
tightened around my hands again, tearing my skin.
The bleeding wounds on my palms made the rope
slippery. I couldn't keep a good grip on Nick's lifeline.

He squinted up at me, confused, angry . . . well,
mostly confused. "Maggie, what the hell is going
on?"

"I need you to calm down, OK?" I shouted.
"That rope is frayed, and I don't think I can hold
you. I need you to find a good grip and climb up."

"Using what?" he yelled.

"Your monkey-man skills!" I yelled. "Just shut up
and climb, damn it! I'm losing my grip!"

I felt the tension on the rope slack slowly. I
peered over the edge to see Nick curling his fingers

around a rough knob of rock. He let go of the rope entirely, digging his fingers into a divot. He found a foothold and pulled up. His eyes locked with mine as his hand stretched toward another hold. His grip faltered, and his right hand slipped.

"Don't look at me! Look at the rocks! If you fall to your death because you were being all moony and sentimental, I'm going to kick your ass!"

"Which will be a bit of a moot point, since I'll be dead!" he shouted back.

"Don't say that!"

Ignoring me, he focused on finding the right place, the right hold. Again and again, until he was within an arm's reach. I tucked my arms under his shoulders, yanking him up as his legs gave one last push.

I buried my face in Nick's neck as he landed on top of me. He huffed, "How do you find time to yell at me, even when I'm dangling over my certain death?"

I clutched his face in my hands, looking him over for signs of permanent damage. I kissed his cheeks, his nose, his mouth, and clutched him close to the point where he had difficulty breathing.

If I hadn't just inadvertently killed a distant cousin, I would have found Nick's nearly bare ass and lost boots sort of funny. He'd been pantsed by a falling werewolf.

OK, that was sort of funny.

I started giggling, recognizing even as the laughter bubbled from my lips that it was a hysterical response. But damn it, I'd nearly lost my fiancé to a secret stalker, whom I'd been too blind to recognize, and the only thing that had saved said fiancé was really old jeans and his ability to channel Spider-Man.

Nick groaned.

"Nick?" I sniffed, pushing his bloodied hair away from the gash in his forehead.

He looked down and saw the frayed belt loops ringing his waist, belt buckle still intact. "I'm not wearing any pants."

"I know," I said, laughing as tears streamed down my cheeks, splattering onto his face.

He winced as he tried to sit up. He thought better of it and lay back down. "I love you."

"I love you, too. So much. I just want to spend the rest of my life with you, loving you and doing stupid, girlie romantic crap until the day I die."

He grinned, patting my head. "That's nice of you."

I laughed, pressing my lips to his forehead.

He closed his eyes and rested his chin on top of my head. "So . . . what happened to my pants?"

18

Going to the Chapel, 'Cause I'm Obviously Crazy

I HAD TO LOVE THIS guy.

Otherwise, I would not be standing here in this stupid clearing, wearing this stupid, foofy white dress, waiting for my brother to walk me down a makeshift aisle.

There was a light dusting of snow on the ground, which Mo assured me gave everything a sort of "fairy-tale quality." I'll be honest. I didn't care much. I just wanted to be married.

I walked down the aisle. Clay, who was standing awfully close to Teresa, waggled his eyebrows at me. I waggled mine right back.

Clay and I were a lot more comfortable as co-pack leaders than we ever were dating. And it was a damn good thing, because between the online college classes I was taking and the honeymoon Nick had planned, I was going to need him to keep an eye

on things for a while. I'd never been farther than Seattle, and now I was going on a honeymoon. I had
no idea where we were going. All Nick would tell
me was that we would start with a ferry ride to Bellingham.

A few of Clay's younger packmates snickered at
my Cinderella getup, earning them a smack on the
back of their heads from Alicia. I winked at her.
Blending the two packs hadn't been easy. For one
thing, we didn't have room for everybody. We had
to bring in a bunch of trailers for temporary housing, which were hideously expensive thanks to the
difficulty involved in moving them to the middle of
nowhere. Thank you very much, fiancé with unlim-
ited financial resources.

Nick was also paying a huge crew of construction
workers secret double overtime to finish the dozen
or so new houses we needed for the new-arrival
families. And then, of course, there was the jealousy
over the newbies getting brand-new houses while
some of our people had been living in the same
cramped places for more than forty years. So when
the crew wasn't completing new construction, they
were doing renovations.

Nick said he didn't mind footing the bill, that
the money was going to make us a lot happier than
it could make him alone. And since we were getting
married, it was going to be half mine anyway. Besides, he said, it wasn't as if he was getting nothing
out of the deal. With the presentation of the newly
bound pack history to Pops, my grandfather had finally, grudgingly accepted Nick as my mate. And

he'd agreed to share as much of the area's folklore as he could remember. Nick's entire career could be spent in the valley, taking down the folk tales and lore as told by my grandfather and publishing them as just that, folklore and wild tales.

While the big issues of housing, hunting, and pack structure were sort of easy to work out, it was the little things that caught us off guard, like what to serve at the village's Christmas dinner (ham versus turkey) or whether to watch the American Hockey League or the NHL on the community center TV. There were a few false starts and more than one dispute that ended in the two packs fighting it out in the middle of Main Street. But fortunately, the newcomers were younger and looking for the kind of guidance from the elder generation that they'd been lacking for so long. They tended to revere and dote on the older members of the pack, which was kind of nice.

Alicia and Clay were going to move out of Billie's place, but by the time they'd decided to pack up, it just made more sense for them to stay there. Plus, it seemed that Alicia and Samson might be heading up the aisle themselves pretty soon. And Teresa and Clay had already declared their mating. They were just nice enough to wait another month to have their own ceremony. We were all about compromise.

Still, I didn't want to test Alicia's patience or generosity of spirit by making her a bridesmaid. Instead, I inflicted that on Mo and Kara . . . because it amused me to see them in matching baby-pink dresses with huge bows on their asses.

I stumbled a little over my hem, snapping me out of my musings and back to the present as Cooper caught my elbow and subtly righted me. Even though Mo and Mom had let me keep the dress pretty simple, I was having a hard time maneuvering in the full-length skirt. I had, however, let Mo strap me into some of that fancy miracle lingerie she loved so much, because I wanted to see Nick's eyelids flap like window shades later. I only hoped that shimmery lip goop Kara had smeared on me an hour before would last long enough to make Nick's face all sparkly for the photos. I had to find the bright spots somewhere.

Nick had been worried about the ceremony. His buddy Dane, the best man, had posted our engagement announcement on the video game's Web site. I assumed it was to prove to the fan boys that one could have both games and a sex life. The announcement got a lot of traction on the Internet. Nick was convinced that his mom would show up to cause trouble. He, Cooper, and Clay were discussing increasing security around the valley for the wedding, until I pulled him aside and asked, "Have I ever mentioned that we have very, very distant cousins in Kentucky?"

"No."

"Well, we do. And I asked them to drop by and visit your mother in Nashville. Just to talk to her, convince her that the loving, selfless thing to do would be to stop harassing you and let you move on with your life. I just wanted her to know that you're part of a family now and have people watching out for you. I don't think she'll be calling again anytime soon."

Other than subtly threatening my future mother-in-law, I was far more interested in planning our life after the wedding than in the actual wedding, which, according to the one bridal Web site I was willing to admit to looking at, was a good sign. I was enrolling in a few online classes at U of Alaska Anchorage. I hadn't mentioned it to Nick yet, but I was sure he'd be thrilled and would probably help me if I had any problems. I foresaw a lot of study sessions that ended up with us being naked.

And then, of course, Mom found my brochures, which I'd stashed under my mattress like dirty magazines. When I confessed my interest in taking a few classes, she burst into tears. I immediately said that I was just holding the brochures for a friend. Then Mom sniffled and said she was so proud, which I have to admit was a new thing for me. I swore her to secrecy, because given the level of crap I gave Cooper over wanting me to go to college, I didn't think I could live through the epic "I told you so."

"I can't believe you're making me do this," I whispered after Cooper had handed me off to Nick. "We could have gone to Vegas!"

"You're beautiful," he told me.

I was probably the only bride to scowl at her husband while being led to the altar. (Well, the only non-mail-order bride, at least.) But when Nick turned with me toward Pops, who oversaw the vows as the oldest member of the pack, I was grinning like a big, happy idiot.

I tried to think of some other words to describe my state. But big, happy, and idiot seemed to sum it right up. I would probably learn fancier words when I started those college classes. Nick clasped my hand in his, and I mentally calculated exactly how many hours stood between us and boarding the ferry to Washington. Nick was finally going to visit my happy place, in the less sexual sense of the word.

Surely, normal brides did not have these thoughts as their grandfathers/officiants began reciting the wedding vows.

I grinned up at Nick, and he winked at me. We turned toward Pops with joined hands. I was going to see the world, a little bit at a time. But for right now, I was where I was needed, and loved.